PRAISE FOR EMILY SCHULTZ

Sleeping with Friends

"This propulsive thriller will have you on the edge of your seat as old friends reunite to solve a mystery that implicates them all. Schultz raises questions of art and artifice, memory and trust, all while telling a page-turning, unputdownable story."
—Anna North, *New York Times* bestselling author of *Outlawed*

"Funny, sarcastic, and unavoidably tragic . . . Schultz's handling of means, motive, and opportunity cements her, once again, as a dependable and bitingly clever writer."
—*Booklist*

"Schultz presents a haunting, grimly humorous psychological mystery . . . A fast-paced amateur-sleuth mystery full of flawed characters and their sinister secrets. Recommended for fans of Tarryn Fisher, Lisa Scottoline, and Colleen Hoover."
—*Library Journal*

"There is a wonderful caustic darkness to *Sleeping with Friends* . . . Schultz has deftly captured the tensions and resentments of longtime friendships, revealed in shifts in tone and delicately snarky dialogue. It's a subtly powerful approach, one of the highlights of a novel which questions the value of friendships and the nature of relationships."
—*Toronto Star*

T0203184

"Whether she's writing about rage zombies or afterlife office politics, Emily Schultz balances empathic characterization with incisive concepts. In her latest book, the twisty thriller *Sleeping with Friends*, Schultz introduces us to an amnesiac protagonist with a detailed knowledge of film and very little else—except a sense that someone might be trying to kill her."

—*Vol. 1 Brooklyn*

Little Threats

Apple Books Best of November 2020 Pick

"Fans of Tana French, Kimberly Belle, and *Orange Is the New Black* will fall under this book's spell . . . Terse and tense, *Little Threats* investigates righteous anger, teenage angst, and the enormity of setting the record straight."

—*Booklist*

"A taut psychological thriller . . . Schultz knows how to keep the reader engrossed."

—*Publishers Weekly*

"Brilliantly structured and gorgeously written, *Little Threats* is a captivating mystery about a young woman accused of a brutal murder—one she isn't sure she's committed. It's a story of love and loss, the power of guilt, and the savagely delicate fabric of family."

—Kimberly McCreight, *New York Times* bestselling author of *Reconstructing Amelia* and *A Good Marriage*

"Emily Schultz unfolds her story with masterful precision and restraint, delivering a novel that is pure emotional dynamite."

—Wendy Walker, bestselling author of *The Night Before*

"A pulsating mystery, where small details enlighten and illuminate."
—Lori Lansens, author of *The Girls* and *This Little Light*

"Emily Schultz's *Little Threats* is a complex, powerful, emotionally wrenching thriller with a deceptively simple premise: What if you agreed to serve fifteen years in prison for a murder you have no memory of committing? Intense, twisty, and compelling—once you begin reading, you won't be able to stop!"
—Karen Dionne, author of the #1 internationally bestselling *The Marsh King's Daughter*

"At its heart, *Little Threats* is a devastating and elegiac novel about teenage friendships, sexuality, drug use, and, ultimately, betrayal. Emily Schultz is unflinching in revealing the way prison isn't merely a place but a feeling that can haunt a girl who grew into a woman behind bars. Freedom isn't absolution, and the answers are as painful as the questions in this heart-stopping, powerful story."
—Bryn Greenwood, author of *The Reckless Oath We Made* and *All the Ugly and Wonderful Things*

"*Little Threats* hooked me from the first line. A gripping, haunting story about family, memory, and, most of all, grief—this book is difficult to put down and more difficult to stop thinking about."
—Rob Hart, author of *The Warehouse*

"Emily Schultz's *Little Threats* is an exquisitely written and thrilling novel about growing up and breaking apart, about the past refusing to loosen its grip on us, and about the impossibility of going back and righting the wrongs that send us spiraling out of control. And, of course, it's a whale of a whodunit. This is a riveting and powerful novel about friendship and fate, youth and time, and the toll these things take on all of us. Don't miss it!"
—David Bell, *USA Today* bestselling author of *The Request*

The Blondes

Best Book of 2015 by NPR, BookPage, and *Kirkus Reviews*

"*The Blondes* is scary and deeply, bitingly funny—a satire about gender that kept me reading until four in the morning—and a fine addition to the all-too-small genre of feminist horror."

—NPR (also a Great Reads 2015 selection)

"*The Blondes* is intelligent, mesmerizing, and fearless. An entirely original and beautifully twisted satire with a heart of darkness."

—Emily St. John Mandel, author of *Station Eleven*

"A nail-biter that is equal parts suspense, science fiction, and a funny, dark send-up of the stranglehold of gender."

—*Kirkus Reviews*, Best Books of 2015

"Funny, horrific, and frighteningly realistic, Schultz's second novel is a must read."

—*Library Journal* (starred)

"[A] ferociously clever, exceedingly well-written variation on the pandemic novel . . . This canny, suspenseful, acidly observant satire cradles an intimate, poignant, and hilarious story of one lonely, stoic, young mother-to-be caught up in surreal and terrifying situations."

—*Booklist* (starred)

"This frighteningly realistic nail-biter is as acidly funny as it is twisted."

—*People*

"Schultz spins an eerie tale with perspective into our cultural attitudes about beauty."

—*Entertainment Weekly*

"Skin-crawling, Cronenbergian satire."

—*Rue Morgue*

"Corrosively humorous commentary on social, sexual, and cross-border politics."

—*Toronto Star*

"Emily Schultz balances biting humor and thrilling suspense in a complex story."

—*Us Weekly*

"*The Blondes* [aims] to be both a realist narrative about loneliness, insecurities, and maternal anxieties and a fantastical, not-quite-allegorical tale of a semiapocalypse. It's a testament to author Emily Schultz's immense gifts with tone, detail, and the crafting of a compelling first-person voice that this novel is never less than engaging even when this balance begins to feel absurd."

—*National Post*

"A wild and smart look at cultural theory, gender roles, and societal expectations."

—Longreads

"A campy, King-inspired nightmare sure to satisfy the scream queens in the audience."

—*Bustle*

"*The Blondes*, by Emily Schultz, gives a twisted meaning to the phrase 'Blondes have more fun.' I giggled and shivered."

"With a lively sense of danger . . . and an absurdist but compelling feminist premise, the book has the enviable qualities of a smart page-turner."

"A hybrid novel at the crossroads of the history of zombies, a nightmare scenario, and the story of an adulterous liaison gone wrong, *Blondes* is bathed in light humor and self-mockery."

Brooklyn Kills Me

OTHER TITLES BY EMILY SCHULTZ

Friends and Enemies Series

Sleeping with Friends

Other

Little Threats

The Blondes

Brooklyn Kills Me

EMILY SCHULTZ

THOMAS & MERCER

Text copyright © 2024 by Emily Schultz
All rights reserved.

Published by Thomas & Mercer, Seattle

www.apub.com

Amazon, the Amazon logo, and Thomas & Mercer are trademarks of Amazon.com, Inc., or its affiliates.

ISBN-13: 9781662513497 (paperback)
ISBN-13: 9781662513503 (digital)

Cover design by Sarah Horgan
Cover image: © alexasokol83 / Shutterstock; © cybermagician / Shutterstock

Printed in the United States of America

For my mother, who showed me the joy of storytelling

Something more goes to the composition of a fine murder than two blockheads to kill and be killed—a knife, a purse, and a dark lane. Design, gentlemen, grouping, light and shade, poetry, sentiment, are now deemed indispensable.

—Thomas De Quincey, "On Murder Considered as One of the Fine Arts"

I'd begun to see the rich not as one evil, but evil itself.

—Pier Paolo Pasolini

Guest List

Agnes Nielsen, struggling detective
Jessica Chu, communications
Nic Kelly, musician
Madi Ricci, personal assistant
Rachel Efron, real estate agent
Sofia Stone, fashion editor
Tabitha Lane, satisfied mother
Veronica Orton, fundraiser
Whitney Astor-Barnes, author
Alexander Miroshnichenko, club promoter
Anthony Pellerito, nice lawyer
Chase Manhattan, bad artist
Cody Buckley, horny chef
Derek Anand, real estate mogul / film producer
Emmanuel Haight, playwright
Dr. Hugo Desjardins, psychiatrist
Jamie Metzger, politician
Jonathan Chapman, CFO
Lewis Grant, journalist

Bartender
Blake

Host
Charlotte Bond, art dealer

Prologue

The woman was falling. When Agnes glanced up, she saw the dark shape of her. Her silhouette seemed to arc, graceful, then dip—almost like a bird in descent. But then it changed: the face-first dive wasn't acrobatic. This was a free fall against a gray sky.

Agnes squinted; her gaze moved upward as if searching for the trick to it. A wire, the artistically hidden bungee cord. There was none.

A black shape. The woman's dress, her hair flopped over her face, obscuring her as she continued down, down, down in an imminent trajectory. Like pencil etchings, the fabric folds disturbed by wind.

The sound of her heartbeat filled Agnes's ears as if she were falling, too, and she wondered if it was one of those uncanny details that survivors relayed. *I couldn't hear the wind, just my blood pulsing.* She had an incredible urge to turn away but didn't. How could a person become an instant soft missile? In ten, maybe twenty, slowed seconds, something had indisputably shifted.

She stood, watching from an appropriate distance. Beside her, a couple who had been standing, holding their backpacks, moved away. But Agnes continued to stare. It was almost choreographed, the way she twisted. But it went from balletic to ghastly—the body settling into a stiff and vertical trajectory as it descended out of view. The outcome obvious. Agnes felt cold.

She turned, and there was Charlotte Bond, at the entrance of the darkened room lit only by the wall-size LED video screen. Everyone else had moved into different areas of the art gallery.

"That was . . ."

"Dazzling?" Charlotte offered.

"I was going to say *terrifying*."

"The texture and movement of falling is what you're responding to. The artist choreographed her performance with a dancer," Charlotte said. Her voice seemed surprisingly sunny in the dark.

The looped image, a rectangle of light, had been placed on a back wall of the high-ceilinged gallery. It was one of those impossibly detailed screens that were messing with reality everywhere from Las Vegas to Anthropologie displays. Agnes had always thought it was funny that in 1896 the first people to see the Lumière film of a train arriving ran out of the theaters, terrified of it. Now that technology had caught up to reality again, she completely understood.

"It makes you aware of your own body and gravity," Charlotte said. "Of course, it's also a tribute to Robert Longo's work *Men in the Cities*."

This was exactly why Agnes seldom went into art galleries. She enjoyed looking at paintings and photographs, but she just couldn't with the lingo and the references. Yet she'd felt pulled to come and see the work. The gallery owner, Charlotte, lived on the twentieth floor of Agnes's new condo building and had invited her.

New building. New neighbor. New dog. Maybe a new life. Agnes had met Charlotte in the building's lobby only a couple of weeks before, when she had been walking her rescue dog, Monsieur Hulot. New to the Williamsburg condo building, the Kentwood, Agnes hadn't met many of her neighbors yet.

Charlotte had noticed her, turned, and bent down to scratch Hulot's ears. The black Lab–collie mix had put his paws up onto Charlotte's white designer pants and pushed hard with all his twenty-five pounds— an instance that had occurred already with others and usually resulted in fur flying, Velcroing onto posh fabrics. Agnes, unsteady new dog owner that she was, had pulled the leash—*no, not white pants*—but Charlotte simply stood up, and the dog fell away. She'd pointed to the gray tile, and the unruly canine immediately sat and gazed up at her. She knew how to be in command.

She'd grinned down at the happy nine-month-old mutt. "What's your name?" Charlotte said softly.

"I'm Agnes."

"Hello, Agnes. I meant the dog."

"Oh, him. He's Monsieur Hulot."

The woman had laughed. "Love that name!" Her voice seemed to shimmer in the slick expanse of the lobby.

Agnes had shifted uncomfortably. She never knew how to accept compliments. "He's a rescue, so it was *Huck*—I didn't think it suited him. I do feel a little guilty about changing it, though . . ."

"Don't. I mean, it rhymes with *fuck*. He'd be so confused if he lived with me." Charlotte laughed.

She was the kind of person that Agnes was drawn to, one who didn't care that the world still thought there were things that men say and that women never should.

Now, as Agnes moved into the main room of the Chelsea gallery that Charlotte Bond owned, she noticed her new friend's large onyx necklace and sleeveless blouse. Her hair cascaded around her face like cirrus clouds. They were standing in a room with paintings hung around it, jabs of color and rips of newsprint in them, but Agnes noticed only her neighbor. Charlotte was in her midforties, maybe early fifties. It was hard to say because she was also lean and muscular. And obviously rich—*being able to afford skin care can take years off someone's age*, Agnes thought.

"Robert Longo?" Agnes repeated. "Maybe I'll google that."

Charlotte smiled kindly. "It's okay. Everything should be experienced as it is."

"Like Susan Sontag said? Against interpretation?"

Charlotte nodded, impressed. "And I'm glad you came to see this."

She touched Agnes on the shoulder as though they were good friends, and Agnes felt herself relax. She sensed Charlotte was good at this: putting people at ease in unusual situations.

Charlotte's phone chimed, and she looked at the incoming text. "My ex. Going to be that kind of day. Bit of advice—never date a journalist. They can't stop pitching themselves."

Agnes had wondered if she was also pitching herself as Charlotte's friend by showing up at the gallery on her lunch break. "How did the video artist do it, though?" Agnes said as they moved across the polished slate floor. There was a moment while watching the video where she thought she could reach out and grab the falling figure. Save her with a firm grip and good timing.

"That's the magic. I have no idea."

A text chime sounded from Charlotte's phone. Then another. Apologetically, she shook her head as she looked down at her screen. "My needy gay," she sighed with warmth. "You know how the boys can get. They want to murder you if you don't answer every text in twenty seconds."

"A little." Agnes realized Charlotte knew nothing about her. All they'd talked about in the foyer of their building were dogs, dog names, the intense heat wave they were having, or how the elevator could be coming from the North Pole it took so long.

The moment Charlotte finished typing a text reply, her phone began ringing. She looked at it. "Her? Jesus. Just ask husband three for the money." Charlotte pocketed the phone and walked briskly to the door. "Listen, I obviously need new friends, and I have this salon at my place. Next one is Thursday after Independence Day."

The word *salon* made Agnes think there would be book club–style discussion, though Charlotte didn't elaborate on homework or what the night's topic would be. This was Agnes's first invitation to anything in the building, so she agreed and thanked Charlotte as she left.

As Agnes started walking toward Midtown, she wondered who Charlotte would invite there. Bold, influential people. A party. What would she wear? She felt again, deep in her stomach, the drop of the video performer, a sudden plummet.

Even in broad daylight and the full heat of June, she felt chilled. Why did it not bother Charlotte? Or did it actually and that's why she had programmed it? *Someone happy who's drawn to danger, someone who can smile while thinking of endless falls.*

Chapter One

Agnes had lived at the Kentwood condo building only six weeks, and her unit was still scattered with moving boxes. She hopped over a cardboard crate as she tried to get ready for Charlotte's party.

Every day that she crossed the foyer of the building, she was still getting used to the vibe shift of her new home. The concierge gave her surprised looks when Agnes would walk in with a cute lamp or chair she'd obviously found on the street. And when she got to her door, 210, she always breathed again, her shoulders dropping as if they'd been carrying something bigger than she was across them. She had done the most reckless thing one could do as a New Yorker: she'd gotten herself a more expensive apartment, with more expensive problems than she'd ever had before. Never mind that it felt euphoric in the moment and Agnes finally understood the blissful equine faces on those rich girls featured in the *New York Times*' "The Hunt."

"It's okay, Monsieur Hulot," Agnes told the dog as he startled. The mini black Lab mix moved out of her way with a suspicious glance. He had a distinct stripe of white on his belly and the backs of his front legs, as if he had lain down in paint. She and Hulot had been together almost a month and were still learning each other's habits. He seemed a smart one, unlike his namesake, an oblivious character played by the French slapstick actor Jacques Tati. Like Hulot, the dog sometimes had a clumsy, lurching walk, especially when he went too quickly.

A sea of glass, the condo building was shiny, and she liked the grandness of it. She also liked the price. Agnes had never been good with money—with the exception of what was in her pocket at any given moment, money was an abstraction. Her Midwestern parents would shudder, especially her father, an accountant. But unfortunately money sense was not hereditary. Working for a book publisher, getting ahead had seemed impossible, and New York inflation had kept pushing her down. But after the Mia incident, she came away with a sense of how others lived. She had a small bundle, with the help of her friends, and after clearing down her debts, she watched her credit rating rise like a proud flag. Her inbox filled with bank offers. It felt like the right time to make a new start. The dog was part of that too.

She found the shoes she was looking for in a canvas bag instead of the cute Container Store bins she'd bought to organize. The tools she'd borrowed from her ex, Lise, lay around unused. Although Agnes was on dating apps and occasionally managed to grab a coffee or drink with a new someone, she hadn't felt this nervous in a long time. She was not going to fit with Charlotte's crowd—brilliant, sophisticated, moneyed. *Probably nice smelling too.*

As Agnes walked down the hall, she realized Charlotte lived directly above her, just many, many floors up. She could hear music through the door. She knocked, but no one answered. Had she knocked loudly enough? Glancing up, she saw a security camera with a small red light on it. She could imagine herself little, shifting from foot to foot, in the video footage.

She thought unexpectedly of the woman in the video art installation she'd watched at Charlotte's gallery, La Musa. Feeling sudden mounting anxiety, she wondered why her mind went there. She took a deep breath and banged on the door to unit 2011. It opened, Charlotte immediately grinning. She hugged Agnes close, a cumulus of Chanel emitting from her long silk dress.

"Love that color for you," Charlotte breathed into Agnes's ear, taking the bottle of wine she had brought. Her peony-painted nails wrapped around the neck of the glass.

Agnes had purchased an emerald-colored blouse, based on advice from her oldest friend, Mia. Mia had texted Yes!!! with multiple exclamation marks when Agnes had consulted via selfie. Agnes had been labeled a tomboy from an early age, and what she had once bristled at, she now embraced as a chosen identity. She owned only two pairs of heels, and one was a pair of motorcycle boots—they hardly counted. It being July, she had opted for the other pair. A pointy suede black pump. The extra boost didn't begin to bring her up to eye level with Charlotte, but looking around, she was glad she'd made the effort.

"Everyone, everyone!" Charlotte called to the room, though there were really only four people so far—Agnes was on the early side. "This is Agnes. She solves crimes! *New York Magazine* wrote about her!"

Agnes quietly gasped at the introduction and looked back at Charlotte.

Charlotte's golden arm hooked Agnes tight, as if they were the best of friends and hadn't seen each other in months. "Of course I googled you," Charlotte said into her ear.

Agnes recognized, perhaps for the first time, that she had become completely enchanted by the older woman. Her agitation wasn't just about fitting in. She was harboring a crush. Realizing it, she felt her mouth go dry. *Is this how it starts?* she wondered. *The sugar mommy phase?*

Before Agnes could interject that she was just a book editor, not a real detective, Charlotte requested in a stage voice, "Agnes, tell us one adjective that describes you. A personality trait. Something *defining*. One word." She held up a single finger.

One could never call oneself smart. Although it was true, that didn't look good. Also, presumably, everyone Charlotte would know would be smart.

"Loyal?"

"Yes! Like her adorable dog." Charlotte mock scratched her ear and released her to the room with "Now, that's a good girl. Go play." Agnes was sure everyone could see the entirety of her blood supply rush into her face.

The room was much larger than Agnes would have guessed: furnished with a terrifically long sectional that never would have fit in Agnes's place, a glass coffee table, what appeared to be an oversize painting on one wall of a woman and a man, a vintage sideboard set with numerous vases and crystal glasses, and, throughout the vast room, hues of sand, blush pink, jade. Charlotte had a corner unit, so although it was directly above Agnes's place, Charlotte's home sprawled, with one wall that looked out over Williamsburg, the rows of hipster bars and shops. Agnes could see the kitchen at the other end, outfitted with similar cabinets to her own, and in the other direction, she assumed Charlotte had her bedroom looking out at the East River—or maybe even *bedrooms*, plural. No doubt the place had cost her in the millions.

Charlotte was beckoning over a man and saying, "This is Jamie. Jamie, make sure Agnes is well taken care of. Show her the drink options, will you?"

Before the appointed chaperone, Jamie, could take Agnes across the condo to the cocktail bar in the kitchen, they were waylaid by Whitney Astor-Barnes, a sinewy woman in a linen suit, whom Agnes recognized as an author of comical books that were parodies of other bestsellers. Her book *F*ck Hard Things* played upon the bestseller *Do Hard Things*.

"The hipster detective!" Whitney said, smiling.

"Oh no, please don't call me that."

"Detective?"

"No, hipster."

Whitney laughed, and Agnes found herself feeling pleased to have made someone laugh who was known for her comedy.

Something about the man, Jamie, was familiar, but Agnes couldn't put her finger on what. Was he the ex who had texted Charlotte? He was much younger than her, but then again, Agnes guessed that would never be a problem for someone as free as Charlotte. Jamie wore a suit jacket paired with a T-shirt. He was quietly handsome, like a doomed poet. He asked her name again.

"I'm Agnes. I ruin parties." She was going for self-mockery, but the humor was lost.

"Don't worry. By the end of it, everyone will forget."

"No," Whitney interrupted. "It's her specialty."

"I don't get it," Jamie said.

"They threw a remembering party. Then everyone remembered *too* much. She solved a crime!" Whitney told him, filling him in on that intense weekend the year before with Mia, Victor, Ethan, and Zoey.

"That article," Jamie said. "It was in my feed for a minute."

Whitney wouldn't let it go. "Your friend's assault, the coma and lost memory, that crazy YouTuber. Everyone I know was sharing it!"

Agnes hadn't exactly solved it. More like helped figure a few things out—*helpful* was how she saw herself, with all her Midwestern modesty. *New York Magazine* had photographed her in the famous blue blouse for the story they called "My Friend Mia," but Agnes had not really expected to see herself in a full-body shot on a whole page of the magazine. In a large-display font over her shoulder, the deck read: **Someone tried to kill her BFF. She hosted a real-life mystery weekend to solve the crime.**

Jamie asked, "So there's a film?" He was a bit too close but looked like he didn't really care about the answer.

"Funny you should ask that. I did go to LA to sell my life rights to a producer at Margot Robbie's company," Agnes offered slyly.

It woke him up. "Wow. So Robbie is going to play you?"

"Maybe! But probably not. Turned out the producer was only her dog walker. Apparently Margot Robbie's never heard of me. So, yeah. Fingers crossed, as they say in LA. A lot." Agnes grinned after she realized how her story sounded out loud.

Jamie let the whole topic go and politely asked what drink she wanted. She asked for a sidecar because the bar looked well stocked and she wanted to seem sophisticated. He went to get it for her.

Another woman was introduced to her as Nicki Kelly. "Just Nic," she said, shaking Agnes's hand strongly. She had long straight autumn-colored hair and wore a crop top and jeans. There was a bicycle tattoo on her shoulder. Her being more casual immediately put Agnes at ease.

"Charlotte is hoping to get her salon written up too," Nic told them. "She'd love if you could put in a word."

Agnes shook her head. "A publicist might do better than me. Is there an idea behind the salons?"

"Oh, very simple," Whitney explained. "It's for singles. She started it because it's so hard for divorced people, and career people, to meet anyone. You know, too well known for Tinder, not famous enough for Raya."

"I'm almost on Raya, actually," Nic interjected. She explained she was a musician and a friend was referring her to the site. She still had to be vetted, though. "It's been four months. I heard that's average."

"Good luck," Agnes said uncertainly. Even if there was a hint of desperation in Nic's voice, she could understand where they were coming from: heart, heart, match, message, message, ghost. What did modern dating really mean? She asked if they'd come to the salons before.

"Twice." Nic swiveled a metal straw around in her glass. She nodded. "But the friend list, the guest list, it's always changing. That's the only thing you can count on."

"Not for me. It's since the beginning for me," Whitney said. "Tonight's the one-year anniversary. At first it didn't have a name, but now we've all begun calling it Charlotte's Web."

"Does it end with everyone crying?" Agnes asked, still looking around.

"Funny you should say that." Whitney snorted. "If a ten shows up, Charlotte will definitely catch and eat him." Even if the barb landed as mostly funny, a sour note had crept into Whitney's voice.

Nic, the self-described musician, rolled her eyes and moved to twist off a string of grapes from the bunch that were laid out on a platter on the coffee table.

Agnes nodded uncomfortably and changed the subject. "This is beautiful," she said, running her hand over the wallpaper. It looked like gift wrap—daubs of shiny gold everywhere.

"She told me it's screen-printed with real powdered crystal," Nic said. She nodded toward the large painting above the sideboard: a boy and girl kissing. "And that's by Elizabeth Peyton. Charlotte said eighty thousand dollars was a steal."

Agnes stared at the art. "This . . . is Robert Pattinson and Kristen Stewart in *Twilight*," she said in disbelief the moment she figured it out. She'd been inside Charlotte's space a mere ten minutes, and Charlotte was already coming into focus: a bold woman who knew what she liked and acquired what she wanted.

Agnes's gaze wandered toward the couch. Nic intuited her next question and, with a quick tilt of her head, said, "That's her ex. Lewis Grant."

"The journalist?"

"So you've heard about him already?"

Agnes had ventured a guess that made her look much more tapped into their world. She watched as Lewis bent over the cheese plate on the coffee table as though it were the most interesting thing there. He had hair that swept back from a high forehead; a strong, intelligent face; and, beneath that, a formerly nice gingham shirt that had probably lived through three major feature stories. Agnes felt sorry for him, sitting alone.

Her beverage still hadn't appeared, and Whitney said she'd go check on it.

As a few new guests arrived, Whitney and Jamie returned. Whitney handed Agnes a drink that was heavy on the brandy but didn't have either of the other ingredients in it.

Agnes took a sip and tried to hide her grimace. "A bit bitter."

Jamie apologized. "Sorry. Bartender didn't have orange liqueur."

Whitney said, "That's why I go with wine, always wine."

Jamie lifted his can of White Claw in her direction, as if to say *This is still Brooklyn, twenty stories up.*

"I got your flyer." Nic nodded to him. She had a cool way of talking: it seemed she always tilted her head back slightly, appraisingly.

Jamie's face instantly lit up. That was what Agnes had sensed: it was all about him. He wasn't creepy—just a politician. Albeit a Brooklyn version. It explained why she'd had that familiar feeling—she, too, had seen JAMIE METZGER FOR THE 18TH flyers wedged into her mailbox. In person, his grin was more subdued, and his blond hair was silvering, though he was likely only thirty-four or thirty-five.

Whitney began drilling Jamie about his issues and whether he really thought they were left enough to capture a younger vote. She went a little hard, even though she did it through a smile.

Agnes took a too-large gulp of her drink and then set it down on the sideboard.

Another small clump of people arrived together. It was to be a larger crowd than Agnes would've thought for a Thursday night. There were at least twelve in the room now. Charlotte again called out, "Everybody, everybody! Meet Cody Buckley! Chef at Tusk. Just got his first Michelin." The adjective that he chose for himself was *rare*, which got both applause and groans. Next there was Chase Manhattan, an artist who had shown his work in Charlotte's gallery. After a long pause, he chose the adjective *high*, and everyone roared. And finally, Veronica Orton, in a palm-patterned jumpsuit, ex-wife of a hedge funder and major fundraiser: *punctilious*. People were impressed by that one.

Agnes remarked to Nic that she wasn't used to parties where no one had the word *struggling* before their occupation. These people were all on the other side of success, the place where you run out of ideas of what to do with it. Nic slid a vape pen from her pocket and took a quick pull on it, then nodded and exhaled.

These people were friends, and Agnes was an outsider. She thought about how life in one's thirties was a little like the frequencies of light—magenta, yellow, and cyan—overlapping in the projection in her high school science class all those years ago. You touched circles with your friends or your boos just long enough to make a different-colored slice of pie, to see how magenta and yellow become red. Agnes looked around and felt like she could see the kaleidoscope of the room's relationships.

Forty minutes in, and Agnes abandoned her terrible half-consumed drink for another, a simpler rye and ginger. Several men were refreshing theirs as well—Lewis and a lawyer named Anthony. Her new one was still strong but less bitter. Back in the main room, there were a few more flurries of "Everyone, everyone!" and names and occupations, but now general party noise was taking over prompts and introductions. Agnes had no idea how she would keep a single name straight. Bodies swam past one another, and voices buzzed over music they'd all stopped hearing.

Someone was in finance, and another was at a real estate firm that everyone oohed and aahed over. A club promoter, a doctor of some sort, a fashion-magazine editor. Agnes couldn't keep track. She recognized Emmanuel Haight, a playwright who had won the Pulitzer the year before, sitting across the room. The central air, which had seemed quite frigid when she first arrived, had now practically vanished. Occasionally she watched Charlotte sail over and interject some piece of information into a circle to help two struggling conversationalists along, but if anything, what Whitney had said seemed true—most of the men seemed to direct their attention at Charlotte, or rather she simply beckoned it with her presence.

Across the room, she could hear Charlotte telling a story about her ex-husband, how he demanded white carpet for their newlywed house in Bedford—he was serious about his feng shui. But after one week of her dogs dirtying the carpet, he stayed up all night tearing it out himself, heaving twenty thousand dollars' worth of new carpet into the backyard. Agnes heard Charlotte laughing uproariously where she was standing, next to the artist, Chase, who was dressed in a black polo shirt and bleach-splattered selvage denim. His clothes were a bit tight for his frame, like the boy who had developed muscles over summer break. Agnes watched Charlotte swaying to the music. Her eyes crinkled in a smile when she caught Agnes's gaze.

Agnes felt warm, like when the sun hits the top of your head for a long time. She moved away from the huddle of conversation she'd been in, which she'd ceased to understand. As she extricated herself to cross the space, Agnes bumped into a shelf. A glass knickknack fell, and the playwright, Emmanuel, caught it before it could land on the floor. Even though he had only ever worked in theater, he looked like a linebacker and apparently had the fast reaction of one. Several people clapped.

She sank onto the long sectional, her body pulling her down more so than her brain. She couldn't have been that drunk. She was disassociating and decided to listen to her body's directives. *Maybe I shouldn't talk to Charlotte right now.*

It was a few minutes later, or maybe a half hour, when a curvy woman in purple named Tabitha came over to her.

"Tabitha? Like on *Bewitched*?" Agnes asked, but the woman didn't know the reference.

"You okay, hon?" The woman bent down to speak to her quietly. "You're flushed."

She started to say she was fine, but the woman insisted she go lie down in the bedroom for a few minutes.

"These after-work parties are a lot. I'll come check on you in twenty," Tabitha promised.

The rest of the evening was fragments of people coming in and out of the bedroom. Agnes recalled two women laying their work blazers and purses on her feet as if she weren't there.

"Would you ever get married again?" This came from a small woman, perhaps thirty, with very carefully parted dark hair around her lovely, worried face.

The reply came: "I don't know if it's worth the risk. You tell a guy, 'I'm only looking for a serious relationship. Something long term.' And not once. Not once does a guy answer honestly about what he wants."

Agnes sat up, leaning on an elbow, and one of the women startled.

"Do you expect they'll doff their hat and say 'I have wasted your time, madam, and shall no more. I bid you good day, my lady'?" Agnes interjected—comically, she thought. "Stop believing Jane Austen. They're dudes. That will never happen."

"Do we know you?" the dark-haired woman said. They hastily exited, and Agnes flopped back down again.

I have chosen the clown role for this party, she thought as she drifted off again.

She was vaguely aware a while later of Derek Anand, whom she often saw in the lobby, edging into the room. His family had developed the Kentwood and owned entire blocks of Manhattan. He came in with a suit jacket for the pile that had collected on top of her. He seemed to think better of adding it and left it on a chair by the long window.

Opening her eyes again, Agnes saw Emmanuel standing in front of the floor-to-ceiling windows with his phone out. She bolted upright.

"Just getting a wonderful sky," he said. The view did offer a moody blue expanse with a sunset flare of pink still hesitating to leave the skyline.

"How long was I out?" she asked.

"It's nine."

Agnes's fingers crept up to her temple. She'd arrived at six thirty. She recalled a few snatches of conversation, too many introductions, her inhibitions coming away a bit, and then darkness.

Something's wrong with me, she concluded. She felt both crystal clear and also as if she were in a dream. *Someone drugged me,* she thought, and as soon as the idea had the shape of words, an intense fear mounted. She stood up out of the bed and nearly toppled. Emmanuel dropped his phone and dashed to help her.

Chapter Two

Emmanuel steered Agnes over to the chair by the window and helped her sit. He smelled like Versace. Agnes stared down at his Ferragamo sneakers. The gym body, the Pulitzer for drama. *Gay,* she realized with relief. In her slurred thinking, she also asked herself, *But is he the needy one?*

"Did you happen to notice who I was talking to before I came in here?" Agnes asked, thinking it must have been the last person who had spiked her drink. But that might have been hours ago.

Emmanuel shook his head. "Cody might have been flirting with you. He's only ever one drink away from humping a fern."

Agnes felt sick, and it must have shown on her face, because the playwright stood up and left, promising to get her some water.

A moment later, Charlotte came in and asked how she was doing, her tone softened, almost maternal. She handed Agnes the water glass that Emmanuel had been supposed to fetch.

"I'm all right," Agnes said, suddenly embarrassed. She drank the water down.

Charlotte opened one of the long windows. It swung outward, letting in a gasp of air and the sound of laughter from the street far below. Agnes was surprised how clear the sound was, even from this height. To the west, the Williamsburg Bridge hung, its columns like black lace across the glowing sky.

"Don't worry," Charlotte said. "I drank too much at the opening of the Beatrice Inn and passed out on Devon Aoki's lap midconversation." Before Agnes could protest, something on the ottoman caught her eye. Emmanuel had left his cell phone—red on the pink fabric—and Charlotte picked it up. "I think he left already," she said. "Have you noticed women are never so careless with their things?"

"Sometimes we get careless," Agnes responded.

She was surprised Charlotte paused instead of chasing after Emmanuel. "You say whatever you think, don't you?" Charlotte leaned close to Agnes there by the window and told her she had a secret. She thought she'd met The One, but she wasn't sure what to do about it.

"Really?" Agnes said, caught off guard. "Um, who?"

"It's early days. I mean, I only date in the summer. Who wants to deal with beard trimmings on your sink in February?"

Agnes laughed nervously. Her hand crept up to massage her neck. After what she thought had happened with her drink, Agnes wouldn't trust anyone at this party, so she wasn't sure how to advise Charlotte. "How well do you know this person?"

"We've spent a bit of time. And . . . he seems special. It could be for all seasons," Charlotte said, leaning back, away from Agnes, and looking out at the sky.

"I'm sure." Agnes felt the breath go out of her. She had known Charlotte was straight but hadn't been able to keep from admiring her. The drug—Xanax or GHB—must have pulled away her inhibitions, because she thought of the faces of the men in the living room who'd been hovering near Charlotte all night. The artist had seemed glued to her side. "Is it Chase?"

"Oh no. That was a blink. Don't tell, but—" Charlotte leaned in, speaking closely to Agnes's cheek so that Agnes could almost feel skin grazing skin. "I honestly haven't sold much by Chase. Half his work is sitting in a warehouse in Greenpoint, and he's asking for his cut of nothing. Thinks I'm ripping him off." She pulled back and looked at

Agnes. Her eyes were glazed with horror at her own admission. Then she laughed.

"You're . . . trying to spare his ego," Agnes justified. She had seen other editors at her workplace lie to authors about how brilliant they were or how well they would do. It was part of courting.

"I should've waited till he was famous to sleep with him. He's fine, but he's a boy, really. Whereas . . ." Charlotte trailed off.

Before Agnes could think about whether she really wanted to know, she found she'd lifted her hand and rolled it forward, encouraging Charlotte to tell her.

"You know that feeling you get down low, just from seeing them?" Charlotte said, smiling dreamily. "God, they walk in the room, and it's like a butterfly releases from your vag."

Charlotte had seemed about to confide more, who he was or what he was like. But then Veronica Orton came in and interrupted them. She appeared in silhouette against the hall light. She was petite and wore her dark hair in a topknot. "I thought I saw you go this way."

"What is it, Veronica?" There was annoyance in Charlotte's voice, a tight tone Agnes had heard before—the time she'd complained about the text from a friend who asked about money. Charlotte stood and pulled the chain on the standing lamp, and the room sprang from half light to full light.

In spite of the jumpsuit Veronica wore, which said *playful*, she was all business. She grimaced, and two wrinkles appeared on either side of her mouth like quotation marks, emphasizing her words: "I'm sorry, Charlotte, but I can't keep chasing you. You know I need the money."

"Really, Veronica?"

"I'm not being unreasonable," Veronica pushed. "You committed fifty thousand dollars to amfAR."

"No one pays those donations right away." Charlotte's voice was icy.

Agnes watched, still feeling faint, wondering why no one here was as courteous as she'd expected them to be.

"You know I'm on the hook for this one." Veronica flapped an arm, gesturing back toward the other room. "Why not sell one of your paintings? Or one Birkin?"

"I invite you here, you look at my things, *price* them, and you suggest I'm broke?"

"You didn't invite me. I found out about the party from Jessica Chu. I call you, and you say, 'Yes, of course, darling, let's get lunch.' But we never do. I call your assistant, and you don't return my messages. It isn't that hard to write a check. And my reputation is on the line." Veronica gestured to the office just off the hall, as though she meant to see Charlotte sit down at the library desk in the other room and make it out then and there.

"I should go," Agnes said.

"No. *You're* good company," Charlotte said but moved toward Veronica in the doorway. As Charlotte passed, seemingly to go sort out the business, Veronica made the mistake of putting a hand on her shoulder like a schoolteacher ushering a child out.

"Don't you t-touch me!" Charlotte slurred, loud enough for the rest of the party to hear. It was the first time Agnes realized Charlotte was drunker than was appropriate. With Agnes herself still feeling the effects of whatever had been slipped into her drink, she felt as though she was watching from a floating place, up by the ceiling corner.

It seemed like Veronica tried to step back, but the women were caught in the small doorframe.

Agnes felt that it was Charlotte who shoved Veronica, but Veronica reacted so violently to it that after it was over, Agnes couldn't say who had started it. Suddenly the women were locked, hands on each other's shoulders, shaking and twisting one another back and forth. Agnes watched in shock as Veronica cupped a hand on Charlotte's throat and seemed to push Charlotte's head back into the wall with a thud. Charlotte yelped.

A man whom Agnes had seen at the party but not yet met came running into the hall at the sounds of the scuffle. "C'mon, stop!" He had a commanding voice, and Charlotte paused first.

Her shriek turned into a cry, and Veronica let her hands drop, too, saying sarcastically, "Oh, really?"

"Hugo!" Charlotte said, turning to the man for comfort. Her fingertips rose to crawl across her hairline. "Help me, Hugo. Look what she's done."

Veronica dropped the decorative clip of Charlotte's that she'd pulled from her hair—several long strands still clinging to it. The top of Charlotte's dress was in disarray.

A few more people came through to see what the commotion was, some concerned, others making wild, tipsy predictions about what might be happening, not realizing how insensitive they sounded. Whitney and Lewis were among them.

"You should go," Hugo commanded a still-fuming Veronica.

"The bitch should pay her debts," Veronica shouted as she turned away and charged out. They heard her slam the door for good measure.

Back at her apartment, Agnes told Hulot, "Mommy feels like shit tonight." She let the dog out on her little deck, then watched him race to release a long stream in the planter. She shook her head. She was lucky there was not much planted yet, or the dog would've killed it. Her head was spinning from everything that had happened at the party. The salon had been nothing like she'd imagined it would be. As she stood on her small deck, looking at the Manhattan skyline, she stared at the same view she'd had with Charlotte—but it was not the same view at all, really. Noble from a distance, the Empire State Building stood, and Agnes tried to recall what else had happened before she'd woken in Charlotte's room.

Agnes's apartment was on the second floor, and she had her own deck, dominated slightly by a large metal awning that extended out just beside her area. **ANAND HOLDINGS**, it said in very serious Trajan; it was a showroom for the building's owners. She had moved from a vibrant neighborhood that was all bodegas, ragged parks, and kids on scooters to an expanse of concrete, like a bleached coral reef waiting for new life. It awakened only at night, though it still felt dark and empty. Her street was more of an afterthought, a one-way where bar-goers circled for parking, little gasps of music as they zoomed past and disappeared in frustration up a side street. She had hoped to meet new people, but she hadn't expected the new start to include neighbors as interesting or odd as Charlotte and her friends.

Now, Hulot jumped down from the planter, trotted over, and flapped his tail three times against Agnes's leg. The air was not quite as humid as it had been—a breeze was coming in from the river. Agnes watched the shapes of strangers ambling through the park, often two by two. *Who would drug me, and why?*

Everyone at the party had hoped to meet someone. There had been a nervous energy, a sheen of optimism over their faces when they'd arrived. They'd each put on whatever they deemed their best. Then they'd done their performances—the politician with his sales pitch; the musician showing off her tattoos and vegan abs you could drop a Plinko chip down; the artist, who dressed too young and whose laughter was a gunfire staccato when his flirtations weren't returned by Charlotte. And yet, no one had seemed to connect. Until the fight had caused everyone to drop their personal brand for one bracing moment of reality.

There had been flirtation, and she'd listened in on conversations where she could tell those involved were attempting to change gear from polite questions to more intimate ones. But it seemed like it was all such hard work. And then, Agnes had been out—hard.

She recalled a lawyer named Anthony, who had told Agnes about his children. It couldn't have been him, could it? He'd seemed so nice. She recalled he'd given her his card. She felt in her pocket. *Anthony Pellerito.*

He'd asked about the article—it seemed Charlotte had told everyone a viral celebrity was here—and somehow they'd segued into Agatha Christie.

"First off, Hercule Poirot, gay. One hundred percent swish," Agnes had pontificated with drunken confidence. "He's allowed in their world, but only because he doesn't talk about Captain Hastings, so obviously his boyfriend." Agnes tapped the side of her temple for emphasis. "He has an outsider's eye for duplicity for a reason."

Was it drunken confidence, or was I high already? Agnes tried to recall what happened next.

Anthony hadn't argued with her. He'd chuckled appropriately and asked . . . what? *Something odd,* she thought. Agnes closed her eyes and thought hard.

"You're not in the club, are you?"

"Club?" Agnes had tilted her head and waited for him to say more.

"Well, everything's a club, isn't it?" He'd gestured around the crowded room with his beer.

"Of course, the salon, you mean."

"Yeah, of course." Anthony had said he preferred watching CSI shows to reading Christie—he was too tired after work to do anything else. Then he said he had his kids the next morning, and he cut out early, leaving a trail of charming normalcy. Agnes watched him saying his goodbyes. Like all the men there, he'd lingered with Charlotte, close enough that they had to have felt the air of each other's laughter. *Was he The One she meant?*

Had Charlotte invited her only because of her fleeting viral status? The magazine article had been mentioned at every turn she took through the party. *Maybe the drugging was someone's idea of a trick,* she thought. *Pull one over on the so-called detective.* She wondered if the comical writer would pull a joke like that. Whitney and Jamie had been the ones to fetch her first drink. Jamie had been supposed to bring it, but Whitney was the one who had delivered it. Chase, the artist, had said he was high when he arrived. Lewis, the journalist, had been in the kitchen when she had gone for her second cocktail, but so were several others. Had they spoken? She thought so but didn't know for sure. It felt like a record skip in her memory. The only thing she was certain of was that the heaviness she felt was abnormal.

Agnes slunk back inside, into her bedroom. She left the door open, the screen pulled across to keep out the giant Brooklyn mosquitoes. The heat had broken, and the breeze was nice. The dog was not a big barker, and he'd be okay there. As she lay down, her phone rang. Even before looking, she knew who it was. Slowly, she scooped it up from the bedside table.

"Please don't judge me on tonight," Charlotte said. Her voice was quiet and husky, like she was lying down.

"Of course not."

"There are other things going on. I'd like to hire you."

"At the gallery? I don't understand."

"As a detective." Charlotte's voice was urgent. This was no simple courtesy call.

Agnes gathered herself as she sat up. "I've only done that once before."

After a long silence, Charlotte answered. "But you don't know any of *them*. That's the key." She said *them* with vitriol. This wasn't the soft-eyed, tender person who'd come to check on Agnes only an hour or so before. This was the woman who'd fought back against Veronica.

"Charlotte, are you alone right now?" Agnes said, surprised to hear the warning coming from her throat. She had a flicker of a thought, which was that the drink she'd consumed maybe hadn't been meant for her.

"I'm okay," Charlotte said. She promised she'd call the next day to talk more but didn't mention a time. Then she hung up. Agnes turned over on top of the duvet to face the window and the sliding door.

Agnes closed her eyes and thought, stupidly, of Charlotte sitting near her in the bedroom—a little closer probably than she'd meant to be—her perfume, jasmine and bergamot. She had an urge to go back upstairs and protect Charlotte. But from what? Besides, she felt too heavy.

In spite of her fatigue, Agnes's sleep was fitful: at midnight she heard a sound she thought was gunfire and started awake to Hulot's typical two barks. This was unusual for a Thursday—Fridays and Saturdays were the nights that the neighborhood was truly rowdy. *Firecrackers, left over from Fourth of July.* She called the dog and slid the door, and he came back into the apartment, then jumped up on her bed instead of going to his own, a fuzzy mat on the floor.

She jolted awake again to the sound of a woman yelling. Agnes sat up. She was sure it was an emphatic "No!" she'd heard. She looked at the clock on the nightstand, its digital green declaration: 4:05.

"Nooooo!"

The word was repeated, but this time as though it was speeding closer to her. Agnes's heart felt like a stone in her chest.

The next noise came four seconds later: a heavy thud nearby, almost like a bomb outside. *The room didn't shake,* she told herself, realizing it wasn't an explosion.

Hulot shot off the bed with a startled yip, then began barking aggressively. He charged out onto the deck, and Agnes followed slowly, realizing she'd forgotten to shut even the screen when she'd let him in earlier. She had been in a drunk sleep. She moved out a step, then stopped, unable to make herself go farther.

"What's going on out there?" she called, as if it might be random New Yorkers doing something stupid and loud. But she knew it wasn't. Hulot was over by the marquee, which jutted out, adjacent to their deck but just slightly above them. It was repurposed from an old theater.

Something, or someone, was there, she knew. Agnes tipped her head back and looked up the flat building. She couldn't see anything.

"Shush, shush," she hissed to calm the dog. As she walked across the deck, she stepped on something flat and cold. She jumped and, beneath her foot, saw a dark rectangle. She stooped to pick it up. In her hands lay Charlotte's onyx necklace. The chain was broken.

She craned her head upward again. Then she crossed the deck in three steps, still holding her neighbor's necklace, and tried to peek onto the marquee. It was an awkward angle. On tiptoes, she could see a crater of tin and just the curve of a hand thrown out. The fingernails were a polished pink.

Oh no, she thought. *Oh no.*

And Hulot barked, and barked, and would not sit. For a full minute or two, Agnes tried to calm him, as though it would help the situation.

"Shut that dog up!" a deep voice hollered, a neighbor coming to the window now. Agnes could see a faint silhouette above that looked like a man in an undershirt.

"Help! Help!" Agnes yelled. *Whoever it is might still be breathing,* she thought.

Then she heard the neighbor—whose outline she could make out, a couple of apartments up and over—go silent, as if the speaker could see what she could not.

Her throat burned, and she felt hot tears as his shape receded. She knew what had happened but couldn't think it.

She dragged Hulot by the collar into the condo and shut him in. She set down the necklace on her patio table, then took a chair from the set and pulled it to her ledge, where the deck ended. She was wearing only a T-shirt and underwear and didn't think to put on any shoes. Agnes had thought she would brace one foot on the chair and use the ledge, which was higher, then from there climb onto the steel awning, in case the woman was still alive. It was the sort of thing Agnes could've done as a tomboyish twelve-year-old, and she convinced herself she could do it now without falling to the street below.

When she stood on the chair, she caught her first glimpse of the body: utterly broken, long hair whispering in the breeze. Face down, but bent to the right, she was smaller, flatter than a person should be. The arm closest to Agnes was twisted in a way that made no sense. There was an indentation in the awning where her face lay. Everything was silent—the kind of noiselessness that left no doubt. The breath was gone from Charlotte Bond on impact.

Chapter Three

Derek Anand was waiting for Agnes when she walked into the Hummingbird, the café in the bottom of the Kentwood tower. He stared out the window, so deep in thought he didn't seem to notice her arrival. It was one of those establishments with tall skinny stools—not a real chair in the place. Derek appeared perfectly comfortable perched on his stool, one sockless loafer on the tiles, the other hooked up on the rung. Whether the shoes were Sperry or Manolo Blahnik, Agnes had no idea, but to her he was the picture of a man of leisure—one who could afford to ignore the phone that lay on the counter beside him, even as banners kept appearing on its screen. A plastic cup of half-drunk ice tea indicated he'd arrived early.

Agnes had already reached him when he shook his head and made eye contact. "What a terrible shock," he said. Agnes could feel him scrutinizing her. He asked what she wanted, then got up to buy her drink.

Her own phone chirped, and she saw it was a text from Mia: How was the party? Meet anyone?

Agnes couldn't begin to answer. She'd consulted with Mia about what wine to bring. In the end she didn't think it had even been opened. Or maybe it had. She had no idea. She silenced her phone.

When Derek returned with her cold brew, he said again, "A shock. We've never had anything like this happen at any of our buildings."

"Do you know what's happening with the investigation?" she asked. She felt more upright today than she had the night before but chose her words carefully. If she recalled right, Derek had arrived *after* she'd gone to lie down in the bedroom. That meant she could trust him, at least a little.

"That's what I wanted to talk about." Derek's tone was serious.

"Okay?" *Talk to me specifically, or talk to everyone?* she wondered. She added sugar and stirred the cold coffee with the paper straw before taking a long gulp.

His phone chimed repeatedly, and text alerts swam on his screen. Derek picked up the phone and turned its screen down as Agnes readjusted her position on the challenging café stool. "I heard the police report was filed as suspected suicide. But you know how to see through those," he said.

"I work in publishing. I edit books for a living. I could proofread the coroner's report. I might be of use then."

Derek sipped his tea and rolled his eyes. "We both know her blood alcohol level is going to come back as *flammable*."

Agnes pushed her thumb around on the counter in front of her, picking up spilled sugar granules. *Charlotte would have laughed at that.* She tried to remember Charlotte laughing—not like the last moment she'd seen her.

"I liked Charlotte." Agnes defended her. "But did I know her?" She wondered if Derek, like so many at the party, had been involved with her beyond being part of the family who owned the building where she lived. Yes, he resided in the Kentwood, too, but he seemed to know a bit more about Charlotte than most would. At the same time, he seemed upset only at the circumstances, not at losing a tenant, friend, and neighbor.

"Of course. You've also had a shock. You found her," he said, nodding and looking in her eyes—yet Agnes felt he was trying to bond with her over something he himself didn't really feel. He cocked his head. "Did it look like an accident to you?"

Agnes shook her head. "I heard her yell *no*. Like a struggle, and you don't yell that at yourself."

Derek's face brightened, and he ticked a finger at Agnes. "You know what the insurance company will do to my premiums if it's *not* a homicide? You cannot imagine."

He had an agenda, Agnes realized. It was nonresponsibility. Homicide had nothing to do with his building codes and meant he couldn't be held responsible.

"I have someone scanning through the footage, so you don't have to worry about that part. But what did the police say to you?" he asked. "They must've questioned you. They definitely questioned *me*. They wanted to know why the windows open wider than four inches. I told them to look at their city bylaws—that standard is only true of windows in units with children. But do they listen?"

"They didn't listen to me much either," Agnes interjected. The police hadn't believed her that she could hear a voice from so far up. Possibly she'd still seemed too groggy to them to be credible. They had questioned why she slept with the balcony doors open and warned her that New York was still New York and she was only fifteen feet from the street. *Don't learn lessons the hard way, lady.* "I told them someone could still be up there, but they weren't in a hurry to get into her apartment."

"Someone?"

Agnes glanced around, but it was a Friday—too soon for the brunchers who swarmed the neighborhood on the weekend. There was only a woman alone trying to take a selfie with a famous pastry. *Ah, New York,* Agnes thought. *Where a dessert will be more famous than you will ever be.*

Derek inhaled a long breath, making his nostrils flare. "No forced entry. No one left from the party by then."

"Charlotte wouldn't do it."

Agnes shut her eyes and for a second saw Charlotte in her mind: opening the window when she'd come into the room to check on Agnes that night. It did open wider than Agnes had expected. And she had been drinking heavily. Who knew if she'd stopped after Agnes left? Probably not, if the party had continued. Maybe she'd gone to close it in the middle of the night, drunk and half-asleep, and leaned too far, misjudged the distance?

Derek supplied the answer. "I agree. She threw a party. No one's suicidal who throws a party."

"Depends," Agnes replied, thinking of Mia's late husband's reaction to the last party that was thrown at his house.

"Regardless, Charlotte is someone who had plans."

Now that they were breaking the logistics down, Agnes felt on the same side as Derek. She had argued the same point with the detective who had talked to her. This was a woman's whole life. Ten minutes, and it seemed the police were ready to fold it up and walk away. Agnes hadn't understood why the investigators weren't taking her seriously. If anything, the detective—whose name was Kowalski and who looked like he had seen daylight only on federal holidays—had seemed too accustomed to women yelling at him at five in the morning.

What the detective had said to her that really bothered Agnes was "You might be surprised how much people can hide their pain. Especially in that world."

The detective's words implied that he and Agnes were the same kind of people; Charlotte Bond was another. He'd asked no details about Agnes, so how could he tell? One of his cops had written down her name and occupation, how long she'd known her neighbor. But Kowalski had just glanced around her unit—in his mind, that was all he needed to do to know a hundred things about her. But Agnes hadn't seen a depressed woman that night, or any of the times she'd spoken to Charlotte.

"The broken necklace."

Derek leaned forward with interest.

"It could have broken when Charlotte fell, like if it got caught." Agnes pursed her lips and squinted in thought. "But it landed far away from her. Isn't it more likely it broke in a fight right before she fell? I mean, we know she had at least one fight last night."

"But do you know why she and Veronica fought?" Derek asked.

"I overheard it. Charlotte hadn't paid a donation yet."

"You heard half of it. Veronica has already fronted the money to save face. So Charlotte is in debt to her, and Charlotte wants to settle with some worthless painting."

Agnes thought of Charlotte in a warehouse staring at Bubble Wrapped painting stacked on top of Bubble Wrapped painting. "And it was by Chase Manhattan?"

Derek's dark eyes lit up. "If this was a job interview, which it is, you'd be doing great. It also helps with the insurance if we say we hired a private investigator."

Agnes shook her head. "But I—don't you need a license for that kind of thing?"

Derek winked at her. "This is New York. License schmicense. I mean, the guy who does our electrical is an ex-con who works under three different names." Something clicked for Derek, and he jumped to another thread. "Did you know that Charlotte was from the Bosch family? That was her real last name."

Agnes remembered Charlotte saying she'd changed her name twice. Once would've been the divorce. When it hit Agnes, it made perfect sense. *Bosch Pharmaceuticals.* The company had pushed opioids onto doctors, and the name was slowly being pried down from performance art theaters across the city. The corrupt reputation could have been a heavy strike against anyone bearing that name in the arts, but Derek complicated her thesis.

"From what I gather, she's estranged from the family and changed her name to Bond at least a decade ago. And they are pit vipers, even for a New York family."

"But why the money trouble with Veronica?"

"Ask Veronica. And ask her today—because this is my point: wealthy family, sensational death—"

"There are going to be articles about this," Agnes cut in.

"Without a doubt already being written." Derek folded his arms across his chest and waited for her answer. "We have thirty seconds to get ahead of this."

Agnes considered it. "I think the police are wrong. But I have three manuscripts that I said I already edited, and my boss knows I'm lying." She didn't say that she'd called in sick and her head felt four steps behind her.

"You're an editor. That's why you're good at this."

"I correct split infinitives," Agnes said.

"It's your job to carefully evaluate and make things make sense. And in no way does this make sense." Derek smiled for the first time. It warmed up his face. "I say I'm a film producer, but my real job is my family, and I will protect them. I'm ready to pay for that."

When Agnes protested that she couldn't take a salary to investigate a friend's death, he solved the issue easily by proposing he waive her condo fees for a whole year. It didn't seem to be anything to him, just a shrug of his polo-shirted shoulders, but to her, it was a bargain she could not refuse.

As they finished up and stepped outside the café, a pickup truck pulled over to the curb, ladders and tools in the back. The driver put the blinkers on and got out to shake Derek's hand. Derek seemed to be expecting them.

"We have to document, then clean and repair the marquee. You don't want to be on your deck while we do that," Derek suggested.

From underneath, the black vintage marquee didn't appear dented, as it was a half-foot thick, but Agnes could see that the impact had driven the seams apart slightly on one side; there were bolts that had broken and a seal that had come undone. The driver and a young assistant in overalls were already setting up the ladder when Derek turned back to Agnes as if he'd just remembered something.

"You know, you're very brave. I was there when the fire truck brought you down from the marquee. When my brother suggested that we needed our own investigator, I thought, *I know who can do this.* You could have fallen yourself. What made you risk it?"

Gauging it now by the extended ladder, Agnes could see that the platform was at least twenty feet up. She could've easily taken a dive into the street. Agnes almost hadn't climbed up, but she supposed in that moment she'd felt she *had* to check, no matter how impossible Charlotte's survival seemed. She remembered only seeing more than she wanted to see.

She had no idea how long she'd crouched beside Charlotte's body, unable to get back down again, like a stunned cat stuck in a tree. She recalled the fire truck coming and a firefighter telling her to stay where she was. He came up and brought her back down the ladder with strong and steady hands while the EMTs examined Charlotte and determined what Agnes had known from one brief touch to her mangled but still-warm wrist—she was gone.

Agnes felt cold suddenly, even though the day was approaching eighty degrees already. "If there was some chance for her, how could I live with myself if I didn't try?"

Derek studied her as if she fascinated him. It was clear from his expression that he wouldn't have made the same decision.

Agnes went upstairs and purchased a YouTube master class on private investigation. She listened to fifteen minutes, then collapsed on her bed for an hour of sleep before starting work for Derek. It felt like she'd only just closed her eyes when the concierge rang her. "An Ethan Sharp is here."

Chapter Four

Agnes had asked Ethan to bring her Gatorade and Doritos to help settle her body and mind. She'd thought he would come later, but since he owed her rent, he'd run right over. Or maybe he'd always been that devoted, but due to the gaps in their friendship, she hadn't anticipated it.

When Agnes took possession of her condo, she'd had five months left on her lease. A well-loved one-bedroom on the third floor of a sixplex in Bedford-Stuyvesant had been her home for years. A railroad apartment only five minutes from a good subway line was like a strong stock: you held on to it. Rather than let the apartment go at a moment when New York rents were skyrocketing, she'd decided to sublet it. Ethan had not been her ideal tenant—in fact they'd been somewhat estranged after each had accused the other of trying to murder Mia. But it had been hard to say no to helping someone she'd known for almost twenty years. When his relationship had dissolved after Mia's party, Ethan lost almost everything. A full year after the remembering party, it was hard to keep up their grudge. In May, he had phoned her out of the blue for help moving his things into a storage unit. She'd explained how she had gotten rid of her car months before, when the transmission went. She couldn't drive his things to the storage locker for him, but she could help another way. Agnes had given him one month free, and then he was supposed to cover the $1,900 cost of rent . . . she'd lived there long enough that it was vastly under market, and the deal had cemented their friendship again. (She supposed she did feel more than a little guilty for some of the snarky accusations they'd traded.)

"It sounded like you needed this pretty bad," Ethan said as he entered. He held aloft a black plastic bodega bag with her hangover supplies inside. They had arrived at the sitcom era of their friendship. *Old friends,* she thought. *When even the wounds are funny now.*

Like her, Ethan was in his late thirties, but his shaggy dark hair harkened back to an era when the Strokes were gods on their bedroom walls. The only difference was that his Ray-Bans had become progressives and there were a few thin silvers snaking their way across his forehead.

"Hey, thanks." She went back to the bed, even though Hulot kept jumping up on Ethan.

"You okay?" he asked as he bent and removed his Converse sneakers. He scratched the dog's ears but kept his concerned gaze on Agnes.

She told him about Charlotte, everything that had happened the night before, and the meeting with Derek.

"And someone roofied you?" Ethan scowled as he sat down in her reading chair. "Who was it?" he demanded, his voice nobly rising beyond his weight class.

"I was still too clear for a roofie. Something else, I think. Xanax? What's Xanax like?" Agnes finished the sports drink.

"Oh, Xanax—I could do my taxes on Xanax," Ethan replied. "But probably different for you if you're not used to it."

"Whoever it was, I think it was on purpose. I have about a thousand snatches of conversations I remember, but everything feels out of order. And I need to go to Charlotte's."

Ethan stood up. "The crime scene?"

His certainty surprised her. Already she felt restored.

Charlotte's condo now had the dullness of a bar in morning light. It smelled stale, though it had been only a few hours since Charlotte had lit up these rooms with a toss of her hair and her throaty laugh. Derek had instructed the concierge to let Agnes in, and now she and Ethan stood in the space. She was holding the key card, glancing around, like a guest who hadn't been properly invited.

"Is she, like, royalty?" Ethan asked, looking around.

"Heiress," Agnes said. "But didn't like to talk about it."

"Very New York."

Things were in nimble disarray: a stack of napkins left on the sideboard, chairs pulled into unique positions, the sectional slightly split, its two sides pulling away from each other like friends who weren't talking. There was one still-full wineglass among the knickknackery, an empty cheese board sitting on the coffee table, a colorful hand-painted ashtray with a half-smoked joint cradled in its indentation, and a couple of cigarette butts besides.

"I don't remember anyone smoking," she said to Ethan. But of course, the party had continued after Agnes had left. She moved across the room to look closer. There was a lipstick trace on one cigarette butt; the other was plain.

"What do you remember?" he asked, moving over to the wall shelves to glance through the books and knickknackery.

A discarded pashmina was draped over the sectional arm as if someone had just set it there, but whether a guest had forgotten it or it belonged to Charlotte, Agnes couldn't say. She lifted it and smelled it; it smelled floral. "That isn't the perfume Charlotte was wearing last night. It's someone else's." Agnes glanced at Ethan, felt self-conscious, and set it down again in the spot it had been.

As she glanced around, she shuffled through the images she could recall: "The musician, Nic, was standing over there with me . . ." She trailed off, remembering: Jamie returning from the kitchen; the journalist, Lewis, on the sectional; Whitney trying to catch someone's attention across the room. Agnes closed her eyes, and the figures moved around the room clockwise in various formations. The artist, Chase, had been over there with Charlotte. Lewis had been staring at them jealously. But

Chase had looked hurt too—his advances weren't landing. The other woman, Tabitha, had been in their huddle as well. "Was that her real name, or did I make it up?" Agnes wondered.

"Should I write down everything you say or just the real things?" Ethan asked.

Agnes moved around the space. "I'm trying. There was a chef named Cody."

Cody Buckley had come up to Agnes and looked her up and down like she was Wagyu brisket. She couldn't remember what they had talked about, only that Cody had eyes that almost projected what he was fantasizing about. Tattooed on his right hand was the word *shef.* The misspelling—on purpose, she hoped—had made Agnes's editor brain recoil. She recalled how he'd quickly moved off after realizing she dated only women. He then had sidled up to a woman who was wearing a clingy low-cut black dress.

She was stalling now, she realized, moving around the main room because she didn't want to go into the bedroom right away. Although it made sense to examine that room first, she didn't want to be in front of that long window again, this time alone.

Ethan went and looked around the kitchen. When Agnes followed him, she noticed nothing amiss. In the fridge: a bag of grapes, a heavy stem still remaining that had not been put out at the party, Greek yogurt, romaine lettuce, a bottle of fish oil capsules, a deli container with limp green pasta inside, a few cheeses, the usual assortment of salad dressings and condiments on the door. A carton of orange juice. "A single woman's last meal," Ethan noted while looking at Agnes.

"Shut up. I'm dating. Lots. So many dates." It wasn't quite true. Agnes usually clutched her phone and swiped left or right. It felt like a game of flash cards in kindergarten where you're shown the same word again and again until you sort of recognize it. Only on apps the alphabet was made of strange faces and flattering angles.

"I'll check out the bathroom," she said as she fled the conversation. *Old friends see through your little lies too,* she realized. But she barely knew Charlotte, so how did she expect to see the inconsistent stories?

In the bathroom, Agnes found an assortment of medications. Three different brands of amphetamines and Wellbutrin canisters lined the shelf. Trintellix—what was that, another mood stabilizer? It sounded like a cell phone provider. There was an assortment of prescription painkillers. A couple of leftover Valium. *Whoever spiked my drink could have just chosen one from this stash,* she thought. Agnes moved a couple of skin creams, tinctures, and vitamin bottles out of the way and found a rolled-up baggie with several loose pills.

The cops must have done exactly what she was doing, Agnes realized as she shut the bathroom cabinet. They'd glanced around, checked the medicine shelf, and determined that Charlotte was easily a danger to herself. A heavily stocked selection of wine, vodka, and rye in the kitchen/dining area and a robust medicine collection. Boom, that was their story.

Did they know more than Agnes? *They see these private last moments every day.* Before she answered herself, another voice in her head told her, *Cops don't do anything, which means you can do everything you need to and no one will stop you.*

The voice was that of Jacob Kroll, private eye and fixer to the stars, in the master class Agnes had purchased. She'd watched it on 1.5x speed, which turned Kroll's avuncular rasp into a chipmunk patter that made dark pronouncements like "I am the court of last resort for people who can't go to the cops" sound cute.

Agnes went into the bedroom and glanced around for something she could use to open the window without leaving prints. All that presented itself was a pair of nylons lying on the accent chair between the bookshelf and the window. She inserted her hand into them and then pulled the latch. Carefully, Agnes pushed the window with her stockinged hand. Far below, she saw the still-dented marquee and her own roof patio. The underside, not the top, had been repaired. The window opened easily, and when Agnes glanced down to the base, she saw the bar that the window was meant to be held by—a gold-colored rod that would've let the window open outward only six or possibly eight inches. It was broken. Had it been that way when she and Charlotte had been talking there?

Agnes closed her eyes and felt a rush.

"I have a secret . . ." she heard Charlotte saying, her voice and the room warm. What had she said about the man she was seeing? It was definitely a man—she'd used the male pronoun. "He seems special."

So the stockings? Agnes stared down at her hand inside them. Were they—she felt the backs of her arms tingle—a *clue*? Had she been getting ready for him after the party? Planning to put on something sexier than what she was already wearing? Did that mean he'd been at the party—or not? But it had been hot, too hot for nylons. The bed was mostly still made, the comforter partly pulled back, as if she'd started to go to bed, then hadn't. Agnes looked under the comforter but left it mostly where it was. Charlotte had sounded like she was lying down when she'd phoned.

Ethan then entered the bedroom with a shocked look. "There's a room, and it's nothing but shoes. That's weird."

"No, it's not." Agnes shook her head and looked at the window again. Did it get broken last night, or was it broken already? She couldn't be sure. To her surprise, there was another ashtray on the bookshelf just a couple of feet away. "The window was broken before. Because Charlotte didn't want the smoke in her condo, she'd have wanted to have it wider for those emergency late-night cravings."

Ethan examined the window. "Did she lean too far out?"

"Charlotte was taller than me. Her balance could have been off."

Glancing at the shelves, Agnes took in the titles of many artist monographs and art history books; when she spotted the Susan Sontag essays, Agnes felt a flutter of recognition. A few well-thumbed novels—the bright-pink spine of Sylvia Plath's *The Bell Jar*. Anaïs Nin's *A Spy in the House of Love*. Nabokov's *The Annotated Lolita*. Charlotte had a love for classic literature, maybe favorites lugged from place to place since college.

Ethan was peering at a framed photo hanging on the other wall: Charlotte at a black-tie event with George and Amal Clooney. He pulled back and said, "She seems like she had things to live for."

Agnes picked up one of the cigarette butts and danced it beneath her nose. She sneezed and set it down. Who had Charlotte smoked with in the room last night—and was it before or after the party dispersed? It could have even been while Agnes was there dozing, but not likely. Most people didn't tolerate smoke, she reasoned.

A book of matches with an image of a wild boar head printed on the cardboard lay on the bookshelf. Absently, Agnes picked it up and put it in her pocket.

The journalist, Lewis, was a smoker, experience had told her. Agnes suddenly was reminded of a brief conversation with him by the kitchen bar, where he'd been ordering scotch. She'd asked how he knew Charlotte.

"No one *really* knows her," Lewis had said. He'd tapped his empty glass on the countertop as if it would help get his drink made faster. "You choose people, or you choose your secrets. She chooses secrets."

Yet Charlotte had paid him no attention, so after-hours smoking with her ex was unlikely, Agnes reasoned.

On this side of the bed was a wineglass, a red resin in the bottom. It hurt her to think about Charlotte's mouth on the glass, her beautiful manicured hand setting it down there, an hour or maybe just minutes before her ending. Ethan flopped on the bed as if he were a kid in a hotel.

"Don't do that," she snapped. Then she saw on the nightstand a distinctive bloodred iPhone—Emmanuel's from last night. She recalled the flashy color from when she'd awakened to him taking photos in here.

"Is that her phone?" Ethan asked, getting off the bed.

Agnes reached out and touched a couple of buttons, trying to wake it up, when they heard the flushing sound.

She and Ethan stared at each other for a long, confused moment.

"We need a weapon," Ethan commanded.

"I'm not a weapon person."

Agnes looked for a wine bottle, vase, candlestick, flashlight, anything. But the candles were votives, and the only knickknackery apparent was a set of small glass jewelry bowls. The game of Clue had lied to her. Not every room held a weapon.

"Check the drawer. There's always a gun," Ethan suggested.

She stepped over to the bedside table and pulled open the drawer. Instead of a small ladies' pistol, a long translucent pink dildo rolled forward in the drawer with a soft thud. *Okay.* She stared at it, hating to encounter such an intimate item in this circumstance, and in front of Ethan at that. She drew in a breath and took it out. "I can work with this."

Someone was definitely in the condo; she could hear movement.

"It could be Derek," she whispered hopefully, lowering her pink silicone baton. But he knew she was there, so wouldn't he call out to her?

She crept carefully through the door where Veronica and Charlotte had started fighting the night before. Ethan followed behind her.

A broad-shouldered man with dark curly hair stood in the main room with his back to her. He wasn't tall but big enough, she thought, that he could possibly throw someone out a window. She tightened her grip on the toy, which had felt hefty when she'd pulled it out but now suddenly seemed comically wobbly.

The man wore a white shirt with the sleeves rolled and tan tailored pants. He set down a laptop bag and began flicking through several pieces of the mail on the sideboard. Mail didn't seem like a killer thing to be concerned about. *Make a break for it, or interrupt him?*

"Hold it!" she said, trying to sound authoritative. She was still holding the toy slightly aloft in case she needed to strike him.

"Yeah. Hold it," Ethan parroted.

The man jumped. *"Mierda!"* His phone fell to the floor with a clatter. "Who the hell are you?" He glowered at them. He had a slight accent. Spanish and regal.

She raised the toy higher in a threatening manner.

His eyes flicked upward, following it. He held up his hands as if she'd trained a pistol on him.

"I'm Agnes. I'm an editor—an investigator. For the building management. Who are you?"

"Was I interrupting something?" He kept his hands up, but his face broke into a smirk.

"Who are *you?*" Agnes repeated.

"Matias Silva. Charlotte's husband."

"Charlotte was single."

"I am still her next of kin." He dropped his hands to either side of himself, as if to say *She calls, and I come.*

Agnes looked at the giant pink dildo and lowered it. She handed it to Ethan, who took it with a confused look.

Matias bent to pick up his phone from the Moroccan rug. When he straightened, he smirked again and said, "I thought you might be one of her artists. Or is it possible you are one of the puppies?"

"The puppies?" Agnes echoed.

"The people she collects. Strays. Very sweet people, but those who do not quite . . . fit in."

Agnes felt a horrible sinking feeling. Matias smiled. "There is no shame in this fate. I was Charlotte's *perrito* once. At least I got to keep the place in the Hudson Valley."

Matias Silva wasn't shy about moving around Charlotte's condo.

"It's his place. Maybe we should go?" Ethan muttered to her. He set the toy on the back of the couch cushion.

Agnes thought about leaving but realized this was a prime opportunity if she did want to find out more about Charlotte. Matias's hands looked strong, like they could rip up an unsatisfying carpet if they needed to.

"I live downstairs." Agnes pulled the pashmina over the toy.

"You're the one who found her? Was it bad?" the ex-husband asked.

The cops had tracked him down, Agnes realized, and given him the basic facts. She wondered who else knew by now. "It was horrible to see her like that," she answered.

"I wonder if she suffered?"

Agnes glanced at Ethan and could see they both had the same thought. Matias asked it without concern in his voice, more like he was asking about the afternoon weather. He then turned to enter the bathroom and shut the door with a polite "Excuse me."

Agnes and Ethan quickly conferred.

"We have that friend's phone," he said. "We should leave. He could totally call the cops on us if he thought about it for a second."

Matias exited the bathroom one minute later. Agnes looked at him and asked, "Do you think Charlotte could have been suicidal?"

"Oh no, never. She loved life too much," Matias said. "It is clearly a horrible accident."

"What makes you say that?" Agnes peered at him. His eyes were a flinty hazel gray, and he was a stubbled handsome. When she thought back to the men at the party, it was easy to see Charlotte had a type.

"On my father's ranch in Caracas, there was a horse no one could break, one we called Huracán. Charlotte was like Huracán."

Agnes could see that spirit. Charlotte was warm and giving, but she had fight.

"Did you know her family?" Agnes asked.

"Her friends were her family."

"She was estranged from her own, though?"

"I have money. I was never after the Bosches', if that's what you're getting at," Matias said. "Don't look for any sense about what happened with her family. It's different for the rich—they always end up swearing to never talk to each other again over a Chippendale chair or some real estate snub. It's stupid and boring." He stretched and yawned. He picked up his laptop bag and said he was going to go to her lawyer's office. He would be putting out a statement through the gallery.

Agnes realized that he and Charlotte still had business together despite being separated.

"You're very calm, considering everything . . ." Ethan probed.

"I am sad. But I didn't love her anymore. She was impossible to love, and I am not alone in that. Big club, you know."

"Where were you last night?" Agnes asked.

That smirk came back. "And who did you say you are investigating for? The building? Or yourself?" He shook his head. "Maybe the fan club has a final member?"

Agnes was caught off guard because it was probably truer than anything else.

"Well then, *la detective*. I was upstate, with my girlfriend and our baby. Four months old." Agnes must have blinked at the addendum to his alibi, because he added, "Don't be shocked. I'm happy now. Why would I ruin what I have for Charlotte?"

He looked around one more time before leaving, asking her to lock up when she was done as though she were staff to him.

After he'd gone, Ethan sat on the couch and did breathing exercises to calm down. To describe Ethan as *anxious* would be an understatement on an ordinary day. Agnes went back through the condo and returned the toy to Charlotte's drawer. A bottle of folic acid capsules, vitamin C, and Saint-John's-wort were clustered on the bottom shelf of the nightstand. Natural remedies. *So who are the pills prescribed to, then—Charlotte or someone else? And which doctor prescribed them?* Agnes wondered. She quickly headed back to the bathroom, where, opening the cupboard, she was confronted with only glass shelf and white space. The yellow prescription canisters were all gone. Just the skin-cream jars and a couple of loose pills remained. He'd taken them.

How was it possible Matias had stood there with them and had a calm conversation, not even blinking or letting on that he'd cleared out all Charlotte's meds and filled his bag?

Chapter Five

Downstairs at her apartment, Agnes pointlessly googled *Veronica + rich + fundraiser + New York*.

She couldn't remember Veronica's last name, and the encounter with Matias reminded her that sorting out who was deep into Charlotte's world and who was shallow was something Agnes had to figure out. A moment later it occurred to her that searching through Charlotte's followers on Instagram instead would be much more effective. It was like a DMV records search but for the people who make duck face.

"We should have thought to take pictures in her place," Agnes said to Ethan. "If I'd done that, I'd know if all the medications in Charlotte's bathroom had her name on them—or who prescribed them."

Ethan stopped petting Hulot and began pacing, something he often did when excited. The dog turned in circles, following Ethan with his gaze. Agnes's space wasn't really big enough for it. "You know what you need to do? Make a list of everyone at the party. Interview them one by one, catch them in little lies," Ethan said.

Agnes looked at him in surprise.

"Oh, I watch *Miss Marple* with my mom sometimes," he clarified.

"It was a big party, though. And the ex-slash-not-ex-husband wasn't even there."

"Matias? I don't think it was him. All he did was take some drugs. Anyone might. They're drugs. Last time I got high, I did this." Ethan pulled up his sleeve. A black outline of a small ray swam over his pale muscle. "I wanted an ilu—from the second *Avatar*. Manta ray was the only fish the guy knew how to do. The irony? I don't even swim."

"That's not as bad as some," Agnes acknowledged, remembering how Ethan had paid to remove several bad band tattoos from their youth. "In fact, it's sort of cute."

Ethan shrugged and let his T-shirt sleeve cover it again. "Regret is a great long-term relationship."

"So you think Matias took them for personal use or to protect her?"

"Either way, it's no indication of their relationship or his motives," he said. "We can't say if he's a good or bad person because he took the drugs." Ethan drank the coffee she had brewed. "Jealousy, vengeance, or financial gain. That's what you need to find for motive. We know that from the other case," he said, meaning Mia, as if they'd been an odd couple, detectives in bad suits working together late into the night.

Agnes tapped her lips in thought. "One of those might fit for him."

"And all three fit for Veronica, given the fight you told me about. And the actor—all he did was take photos out the window—"

"Playwright," Agnes corrected. "But it was a window she fell from only hours later."

"True, but it was a nice view. And he left the phone. Only a very stupid killer would leave their phone behind *twice*."

"No, he isn't stupid. He won a Pulitzer," she finished. She realized Ethan was right on all counts. She also realized her friend was systematic in a way that was useful. *A part of you made Ethan come here because you knew you needed him,* she thought. He saw flaws where others saw a regular story playing out.

"Write down as many of the guests as you can remember. They're all the last ones to see Charlotte alive. I'll google them and see if I come up with anything useful," Ethan offered.

Guest List

Agnes Nielsen, struggling detective
Whitney Astor-Barnes, author
Nic Kelly, musician
Jessica Chu, communications
Rachel want to say Efron? real estate agent
Veronica Orton, fundraiser
Tabitha, concerned partygoer
Sofia Stone, fashion editor
Madi, nice woman, assistant to someone important

Agnes looked over her list. She struck *struggling* from behind her name. She seemed to have unconsciously chosen *detective* as her descriptor instead of *editor*. She typed the names out and searched through Charlotte's social media profile for others she wasn't sure of. Photos had gone up, tagging Charlotte just hours before. That told her not everyone knew yet.

Lewis Grant, journalist
Chase Manhattan, bad artist
Jamie Metzger, politician
Emmanuel Haight, playwright
Cody Buckley, horny chef
Anthony Italian name, nice lawyer
Alexander Russian name, wouldn't say what he does
Dr. Hugo De-something, doctor?
Jonathan Somebody, CFO
Derek Anand, real estate mogul / film producer
Blaine or Blake? bartender

On her nightstand, a phone started chirping out notifications. It was Emmanuel's, now plugged in and recharged enough to come to life with delayed texts.

Char! This is Emmanuel. I'm using Wyatt's phone, pick up!

I left my phone at your place. Text me if you get this, Charlotte.
Or whoever sees this.

Charlotte, put down the bottle and text me back. Plllleeeessse!

As Agnes cradled the red phone, a final delayed text came up on
the screen: I hope you're okay. Will try in the morning.

She thought about Charlotte's own phone, wherever it was, and
texts coming in that would never be answered. People didn't die like
they used to—unequivocally. Now Facebook accounts lingered on and
shared memories; IG preserved final days and nights. *Being plugged in
makes for slow power downs after our cords get pulled,* she thought.

Then the red phone rang. Agnes glanced at Ethan, whose eyes widened. He nodded for her to pick it up.

Agnes took the call. "Hello?"

"Charlotte?" Emmanuel asked on the other end. "Are you okay?"

"This is Agnes."

"Sorry. This is my phone. Who has it?"

"Charlotte does. She did. Now I do. I met you at the party."

There was a long pause on his end, a feathery hitch. Then Emmanuel
exhaled. "Is she okay? I'm hearing there's something going on at her
building."

"Charlotte's dead." Agnes sat down on her bed as she said the
words. It was the first time she had said them aloud.

"Oh my God . . . It was a fall, wasn't it?" Emmanuel asked.

Agnes felt the saliva dry up in her mouth. She stuttered out a
"Y-yes." She locked eyes with Ethan but didn't think he could hear
what Emmanuel said on the other end.

"Yeah, that's what I heard. I have so many people to call. And I lost
my phone."

"I have it," she said, thrown off and shaken. "We're speaking on it."

They were both taken aback by Emmanuel predicting Charlotte's manner of death. They weren't sure how he would have heard about the fall but not about Charlotte specifically. Ethan said he had to make his way home for a work Zoom but asked Agnes to check in immediately after going to meet Emmanuel to drop off the phone. They hadn't managed to locate Charlotte's phone that morning. Agnes wondered if it would've been in her purse, though she hadn't seen that in the condo either. Probably the police had it.

Agnes found her way to the East Village and the theater where Emmanuel had said she could return the phone. It had a modest marquee above a simple brown brick facade. Inside the Garland, a manager greeted her and waved her in, but Agnes entered the jewel box of a stage space to see it was empty. When she returned to the main desk, he said to try the rehearsal room. It turned out to be a large plain room with black floors, chairs around the edges, and a few scattered music stands bearing scripts. A beautiful young woman in a leotard was stretching, as if getting ready for a big game, while several other actors in overalls or sweats sat cross-legged on the floor, consulting their scripts and whispering. Emmanuel was with them. He had changed since the night before—he wore tan shorts, a loose button-up, and Nikes—but he looked as though he'd barely slept.

As Agnes waited, she read one of the Playbills.

DECOHERENCE
By Emmanuel Haight

The same breakup scene is played by 12 different New York couples. In each there is a subtle change in direction and events, mimicking the constant threats to the fragile quantum state that underpins the universe and our memories of discrete moments. Runtime: 3.5 hours

"Good Lord," Agnes breathed when she saw the length of the play. It was the kind of epic cultural event New Yorkers would tell everyone to see, but they themselves would never get around to it. *You definitely have to experience it. Me? No, I haven't yet. My cat gets upset when I'm gone that long.*

A moment later Emmanuel saw her and came over. He was already extending his hand for the phone. "You don't know how happy I am to have this back."

Agnes eyed his outstretched palm, wondering if there might be incriminating things on the phone she was about to pass back. Though she'd itched to take a crack at his password, she hadn't wanted to get locked out. Seeing him again, she realized he certainly had the physique of someone who could pick a woman up and drop her out a window. He'd been helpful to her the night before, but he hadn't come back with her water: maybe he *had* been rattled at being caught documenting the window. Emmanuel met her gaze, and she let the phone fall into his hand.

His fingers closed over it possessively. He stared down at it, then at her. His mouth made a firm, flat line. "Did the cops give it to you?"

It wasn't the first question Agnes would have asked if she were in his shoes. She might have started with a simple *What happened last night?*

"We found it right after you left the party," she said, which, although technically true, implied she'd taken possession of it much earlier. A half truth often served better than a lie.

Emmanuel didn't seem to notice or question it, and Agnes watched as he scrolled through the messages and call log, then quickly clicked the screen to dark, perhaps as if there was something there he didn't want her to see.

"I just can't believe it," he said in a hushed tone, and she could tell he didn't want the others in the practice space to hear. But unlike Derek or Matias, Emmanuel's eyes showed his emotion; they brimmed. Behind his square-framed glasses, he blinked rapidly. A moment later the shine subsided. "How long did you know her?" he asked.

Agnes startled. She'd been planning to question Emmanuel, but it was already the other way around. *This is how writers maintain their control over the world,* she thought. "A few weeks. What about you?"

"Oh, since I was a waif." Emmanuel's voice changed now. His shoulders seemed to relax as he spoke. "Honestly, Charlotte called my mother to tell her. Almost midnight, half-wasted at an after-party. They talked for half an hour; then she handed the phone to me. That's how I came out." Emmanuel dashed a hand through the air as if he were going way back in time, ancient. "You know," he went on, "Char and I haven't been that close the past year or two. That whole salon scene could get ugly if you stayed too late—too adult for me, once it's just the chain-smokers and the alcoholics left, hanging on."

Agnes couldn't tell if he was just filling space or if there was something behind it—something he knew, a story he desperately needed to share.

She invited herself to a seat on the vintage velvet couch. "Did you know anything about her and Veronica? They fought. You had already left?"

"I don't know what happened, but Veronica should be declawed." Emmanuel tucked a strand of his blond hair behind his ear. He squeezed in beside her on the two-seater, putting one arm behind her since it was the only way they'd both fit on the small settee. His body language said the gossip was clear for landing. He was wearing a heavy cologne— smoky and citrusy. Agnes didn't recall smelling it lingering in Charlotte's room that morning, when she and Ethan had investigated.

"Veronica used to be married to the CFO of Whitestone. She even auditioned for *Real Housewives of New York* a couple years ago— they didn't take her. Didn't pass the required psychological testing." Emmanuel raised an eyebrow. "I'm sure it's sad to get left and still be raising his first wife's kids. Since her divorce, she'll pick a fight with anyone: prince and waiter alike."

"I tried to find her online, but she isn't listed." Agnes pulled her phone out and went to Veronica's Instagram. Although Veronica didn't have an enormous number of followers, Agnes now noticed she was followed by several celebrities.

"Of course not," Emmanuel said. "She lives in the *bubble*. Full-service building, doormen in epaulets. She's the richest ex-wife in New York."

"So I'll just DM then?" Agnes deadpanned.

"No." The word was small and hard, like an ice cube.

At Emmanuel's reproach, she put her phone back in her pocket.

"Charlotte told me she has Halston's old suite. The one that looks down on Saint Patrick's Cathedral," he said.

"And she's still not happy?"

"She's . . . incorrigible. Charlotte banned her for a while. She hit on my boyfriend right in front of me. I also saw her put Whitney Astor-Barnes in a headlock two salons ago."

"A headlock?!"

"Well, Whitney does gossip. And she steals all the tens," he admitted.

"I thought that was Charlotte?" Agnes asked, stupefied by the unending supply of information Emmanuel now poured out.

"You know girl talk. Whatever Whitney said about Charlotte is true of herself." Emmanuel rolled his eyes.

"Was your friend Wyatt at the party last night?" Agnes didn't remember seeing Emmanuel with anyone. But that name was among the texts that had risen in bubbles across the red phone's screen. That meant Emmanuel hadn't gone home alone. *What if he and Wyatt returned to the Kentwood? Two people can commit a crime easier than one,* she thought.

Emmanuel shook his head. His large knee began to jostle up and down with energy that shook the couch slightly. "Veronica can't share. She hoards money, she hoards contacts, she hoards her, uh, children. Charlotte was generous. She *gave*. She knows that if you want love in New York, you pick up the tab on someone's dream."

"On someone's dream?"

"She *made* people. My God, what a loss." Emmanuel launched up, removing his glasses and rubbing a massive hand over his face.

The actress who had been stretching nearby now came over, her back straightened, limbs pointed, her body radiating her distress. The woman's voice rose as if she were already on the stage. "Charlotte's dead? This is over?"

"No, Zora, we were just—" Emmanuel protested, but his face betrayed him.

For such a slight young thing, the actress could project with incredible force. "It's true? She's dead two weeks before previews?! There's no play."

At the commotion, the other actors at the far end of the room stopped what they were doing. Many rushed over, demanding answers from Emmanuel.

"What was Charlotte's involvement?" Agnes asked one of them as she was bumped away from Emmanuel, but she didn't need the answer. *She was an investor,* Agnes realized. Emmanuel had nearly admitted as much, and there was also the text Charlotte had gotten when Agnes went to the art gallery. *My needy gay,* Charlotte had said. Emmanuel definitely did need her, and it wasn't for friendship or reassurances. A 3.5-hour play would be a commitment.

"How much was she funding?" Agnes asked a bearded man in the throng. Emmanuel had been swept to the far side of the room.

The actor's face was full of concern. "She was funding it all, of course."

Several people in the group were asking Emmanuel questions, and Agnes realized that actors, strangely enough, didn't have the biggest capacity for empathy. They all seemed to talk over each other: "We have the theater, but for how long?" "What about our salaries?" "Will the show still get written up? She promised to get me a profile in *Vanity Fair* with a writer she knew."

Agnes's phone vibrated in her pocket. She squirmed out of the throng and pulled it out. Mia had texted: What happened last night??? Are you okay?

There was a link to a Gothamist story. The headline read:

WHO DIED AT THE KENTWOOD LAST NIGHT?

Before Agnes could click, there was a hand on her back. Emmanuel guided her toward the door.

"The actors are upset, so thanks for that." As he guided her through the space and into the main theater, he continued, "You know, I did have some concerns about Charlotte."

What concerns, Agnes wondered, *about someone whom he said he wasn't around much? Someone he wasn't close with anymore, who of course just happened to be funding his current project.* He had been performing for her for the past twenty minutes.

Emmanuel touched her forearm as they walked back through the theater space. "Look, Char's marvelous, but also always a bit flighty."

An enormous gold frame stood on either side of the stage and went across the top, making a picture out of the blue-black curtains behind. Agnes and Emmanuel perched themselves under it on the stage's edge.

"Have you heard when the funeral might be?" he asked. In this quieter space, she could hear the tightness in his voice.

"I don't know. I met her husband this morning. Is he the one who would organize it? Do you know him?"

"You mean Matias? He's so ex he may as well not exist."

What if she and Emmanuel had had a disagreement or she hadn't been able to pay to fund the production? *Just like she didn't pay Veronica,* Agnes thought. *Why did Emmanuel pick at Veronica like a scab? He could have expressed his dislike, then moved on. Why the kicking up of so much dirt?*

Agnes glanced around the theater. A man in coveralls carried a ladder across the back of the stage. She could hear him talking to someone else. A spotlight above them turned on, then off.

"How were things going with the play?" she asked.

"Fine," Emmanuel said a bit too quickly.

"If you don't mind my asking, how much does it—"

A theater tech interrupted them with a holler. "Backdrop coming down!"

Agnes and Emmanuel both turned to look over their shoulders as a painted New York skyline fell with a thud. It had an Edward Hopper feel to it, the buildings brown and the windows all boxes of creamy-yellow light. Agnes stared at the Empire State Building. She thought of the skyline from Charlotte's window.

Agnes turned from the backdrop to Emmanuel. "On the phone you said, 'It was a fall, wasn't it?' Why did you say that?"

Chapter Six

Large, fluffy, golden. Almost perfect, if Agnes overlooked the frugality of blueberries. She eyed the pancakes she had ordered around the corner from the theater at a tiny restaurant that seemed intent on keeping itself a secret. She balanced on a stool at the bar, the plate taking up most of the space in front of her. It felt wrong to eat—Charlotte had been her friend; shouldn't she be grieving?—but she had stepped outside of emotion into a more analytical headspace. It was already 2:00 p.m. Agnes didn't want to leave the city to go back to Brooklyn until she'd figured out how to deal with Veronica. So all-day brunch it was.

A Google Images search for *Veronica Orton* showed her in front of logo walls at red-carpet events and private corporate parties. Yet Veronica looked even less fun than she had at the party the night before. Her slit skirt might show a well-toned leg, but on her face there wasn't a smile—more something an angry child might draw. The historic building Emmanuel had mentioned for Veronica turned out to be accurate, the Olympic Building on Fifth Avenue, now turned into luxurious apartments. If Veronica wasn't expecting her, she'd be turned away. Nothing he'd said really illuminated what might have happened. But the fight plus his opinion of Veronica made her a suspect, even if Emmanuel himself was holding something back.

She'd quizzed Emmanuel on his knowledge of the fall, and he'd said that the video installation at her gallery had made him nervous for her. Charlotte could be impulsive. Just the week before, he said, she'd mentioned having "too many problems to cope with." Emmanuel had stressed, "I was actually checking that the window wasn't broken when I went in there."

Agnes had fixed him with a solid stare and said, "Are you sure it wasn't?"

When Agnes arrived in Midtown, the fifty-one floors of the Olympic Tower seemed to glare, indifferent to her. *Indifference is good,* she reasoned. *Being ordinary makes it easy to pass by unseen.* Glossy brown glass rose out of the Armani store. Longchamp and Versace huddled beside. The atrium was open to the public, and people were gathered there drinking coffee at steel tables. Agnes walked in with purpose.

Why do this? Agnes simply had to. She was the person who put the sentences in order, the one who corrected mistakes. If she stopped now, who would she be?

When she reached the concierge desk, she stood behind an expensively dressed silver-haired man and waited her turn. He kept trying to interrupt, but the concierge only held up a gloved finger, nodding, phone pressed to his ear. There was a slight glance of reproach, as if interrupting was something that had never happened at his desk before. As Emmanuel had stated, he was wearing an old-fashioned doorman's uniform, black with gold piping on the sleeves, a tobacco-colored tie from the days of chic brown on brown. She heard the doorman say into the mouthpiece, "Yes, the yacht launch is for seven p.m. *today.* Getting the bottle of Diana '61 is a matter of life or death, and I mean it. You're dead to me."

"Excuse me, but this is important," the other man tried to interject.

Expertly nodding, the concierge said "Absolutely," both into the phone and to the man.

The second the phone call was disconnected, the two began to argue, in polite tones implying respect but nonetheless imbued with disgust.

"We have a code of conduct here," the concierge replied.

"So does the world. It runs on preference and bias."

"Of course it does. And your client is the *second*-richest person in the building. Now, what do you need?"

"I've just come from Ms. Orton's," the suit said importantly, extending a card while flashing his Rolex.

At the mention of the name *Orton*, Agnes stepped back reflexively, trying to disappear. But both men were laser focused on each other.

"If the police show up, call me. Do not let them in. She is *not* to be questioned unless I'm present."

"Absolutely, sir," the concierge said, smiling with a pleasantness that was diamond hard. "We're not the kind of building to let anyone in."

The lawyer turned and left abruptly.

After filing the card, the concierge looked up at Agnes. He squinted at her usual summer uniform. She was wearing khaki shorts and a black polo-style shirt.

"*How* may I direct you?" He emphasized the *how* as if there was no help for someone who appeared as she did.

Think Fletch, she told herself. It was her older brother's favorite movie from childhood, and he had made her watch it a dozen times until she could lip-synch the jokes she was too young to get.

"Delivery for Veronica Orton." She pulled her Fjallraven knapsack from her back and held it up with both hands as though it were heavy.

The concierge glared. "I'll take it." He extended his hand.

Agnes upped the improv. "It's cave-made French butter. With all respect, I just got off a red-eye from the fucking Alps, and the dry ice is gone. Do you want to deal with Veronica when she finds out I left it at the front desk, melting?"

On her way there Agnes had stopped off at H&M Home to pick up some curtains for her place, which made the knapsack look quite full—though if he called her bluff, all he'd find was a $29.99 two-pack of linen-blend curtains in olive green. No blocks of artisanal butter anywhere.

His gaze flicked across a log. "You're not on the list."

"Of course I'm not. It's a gift, from *Gwyneth.*" She lowered the knapsack and tried for a disbelieving air. She knew from scoping Veronica's social media it was halfway believable.

There was strident ringing from the phone in front of him, which was lighting up with requests, every one likely as impatient as the lawyer before her had been.

He nodded okay and buzzed a door open. "The service elevator is around the corner."

The elevator opened directly into the apartment. The doors slid back to the sound of children screaming, and Agnes found herself looking into a long open space, lavishly decorated. It didn't seem the kind of place where two children—perhaps nine and ten—should be chasing each other, but they were. The smaller one was currently hurdling over a green velvet ottoman as if it were part of a steeplechase. Behind them Manhattan itself draped, blue and bright, at the floor-to-ceiling windows. It was true what Emmanuel had said; the space perched at a vantage where it looked straight down at Saint Patrick's. A second later, seemingly unaware of her intrusion, the kids crashed with a distressing *ka-thunk* into a large sofa that had to be Italian, the older one throwing fists. A third child, a tween girl with large glasses, appeared from another room to yell their names, which Agnes heard as one word: "DanielandAlma, stop it!"

The doors dinged a closing chime, so Agnes stepped out of the elevator, narrowly missing a fourth kid, a toddler on a PlasmaCar. He pulled the wheel hard like he was at Nascar but still zoomed across one of her sneakered toes. Agnes dropped the knapsack and yelped in pain.

The tween girl looked at it and said, "Give me my brioche donut."

Agnes shook her head. "Wrong delivery."

The girl pointed—"Kitchen's in there"—before turning away with disinterest, going back to her iPad now that the other children had quieted down. One was still sitting atop the other, but it seemed the smaller one had flipped the dynamic, so perhaps there was less to be concerned about.

Agnes made her way into the kitchen, where Veronica barely glanced at her. Her hair was in a looser chignon than last time they'd met, and her cell phone was cradled against her cheek. She leaned against the marble counter in a pair of Versace jeans and a white blouse. "It's not the right time for this conversation." She glanced at Agnes but didn't react. "I'm having a day here. AJ just left, my first assistant has Hungarian Covid, Franklin turned away two reporters already." She placed two fingers in the space between her eyebrows. "Honestly, I wouldn't talk to anyone right now, except I know you need it."

Tentatively, Agnes raised one hand in a wave.

Veronica glanced at her. Lowering the phone, she said, "Are you my second assistant?"

"Kind of?" Agnes decided to go with it.

Veronica went back to the phone call. "Well, tell me who the male lead is. Is he sexy?" There was a pause, and then she said through gritted teeth, "Ensemble, huh. Yeah, but they can't all be sexy. I don't know. Theater is basically setting money on fire."

When Veronica said *theater*, Agnes realized it was Emmanuel. *After trash-talking her all morning, did he just reach out for a new benefactor?* Agnes was both impressed and repulsed.

"I'll think about it. My new assistant's here." Veronica clicked End without a goodbye. Turning to Agnes, she said, "Trish sent you? And your name is . . . ?"

"You met me at Charlotte's," Agnes said.

Veronica's body went rigid. "Oh. You're that girl."

"Agnes." She stiffened at being called a girl.

"Why did Franklin let you come up?" Her tone had gone cold, and Agnes realized Veronica might be afraid of her. She turned and hurried into the great room, where the children seemed to have settled down. She urged them both to go to their rooms, *now*. Amid protests, she handed the boy a handheld video game. "Here, screen time," she told him, and, like saying *treat* to a dog, he immediately did as she'd asked.

The younger girl, Alma, scowled and refused to budge. She'd clearly won the right to the plush leather chair away from her brother. "I'm *reading*," she said like she had just invented it. "I'm supposed to read."

"You can read in your room just as easily."

"Fuck you, Veronica. Where's Darcey?"

"She's in isolation!"

Shocked, Agnes gestured to the book's cover. "I met that author. Really great. She gave away signed posters when the new edition came out last fall."

The little girl looked up. She glanced between the two women, assessing. "Veronica says we aren't allowed to have posters."

"Fine. If you go read in your room, maybe we can see about a poster. To look at. Not hang up." Veronica glanced at Agnes.

"Sure, still have it, mint condition." Agnes hoped it was true.

The girl smiled and slid from the chair, taking her book with her.

Veronica turned back to Agnes and shook her head. "My step-kid, and she always gives me such shit over nothing. This one's my real kid."

Veronica gazed at the toddler who remained as if he were a small and beautiful creature, sitting on the Persian rug, slobbering and chewing on a remote control. Veronica knelt and took it from him, then replaced it with a plush brown bear; the toddler smiled and immediately bit its face and gummed its nose.

"Specialty butter," Agnes said, changing the subject since she knew little about children.

"What?"

"It's why the concierge let me in."

Veronica's eyes narrowed at the mention of nonpaleo fat. She sank onto the sofa in front of the long windows. She suddenly looked smaller. "You can't just come here with butter."

"I didn't know what else to do," Agnes said. "I've only known Charlotte a few weeks, and everyone is looking to me for answers." It wasn't entirely true, but it wasn't entirely false either.

"Well then you should hear what they're asking *me*." Veronica hunched her shoulders and rolled her neck.

"Because of the fight?" Agnes kept her tone light like it was nothing. Like she herself hadn't come there to ask that exact thing.

"People go to fundraisers and pledge one hundred thousand, and it's not because of the chicken. They get to do business. Make deals at the bar. Be seen. Sometimes they pay the pledge. Sometimes they don't. It's a dance we all do." The tension fell away as Veronica described the things that were familiar to her.

"Did you crash the party to confront her?" The words came to Agnes almost out of nowhere. She remembered Veronica's interruption: she'd mentioned getting the party details from someone else.

"I don't crash parties. I make them." Her nostrils flared. "And they are transformative experiences. Give me an ex-governor found in a dungeon with a feather duster up his ass, and I can get him sainthood in three charity appearances." Veronica leaned against the cushions and extended an arm across the sofa's back, the cathedral below her as if for emphasis.

"Quite a statement." Agnes raised an eyebrow.

"Don't give me the normal-person look." Veronica sighed. "You don't understand—shame is a feeling that stops with your first million."

Agnes had no idea what the price tag was that swallowed shame, but she did know what she'd overheard the night of the party. "But this time you were on the hook."

Veronica nodded. "Yes."

"You fronted her the money for amfAR," Agnes continued.

"She told you?"

"You said it in the bedroom."

"That's only one part of it." Veronica leaned back. "Look, I loved Charlotte. I really did. There are only so many ballsy women like us in this city. And for the most part she could handle my big Scorpio energy."

Agnes bit her tongue. She had seen Veronica tear out Charlotte's hair. Veronica's problem wasn't her birth sign. It was more likely her drinking and unprocessed anger issues.

"Then Charlotte came up with a new scheme. She asked me to make a donation to Jamie's campaign with her. We each put in fifty thousand, and I get that back and the money she owed me."

"I don't understand that," Agnes said. "You'd be paying a hundred thousand to get what?"

"It's called free money, honey. New York State pays matching donations to political campaigns. Someone donates a hundred thousand to a candidate like Jamie. New York matches that amount. And Jamie quietly returns the original donation, plus a kickback. Charlotte could use that to pay off her debt to me, and Jamie gets to keep fifty thousand in free money for his campaign. The real secret to the rich not paying for anything is no one understands how we do it."

"Why did she want to boost Jamie Metzger's campaign?" Agnes asked.

"Honestly, I don't know. Maybe he was her latest pet? But she started sounding like her father. He thought he was a kingmaker. All the men in this world do."

Charlotte liked being powerful; Agnes could see that. It showed in how she curated the guests, how she was in charge of her own gallery. It was what had made Agnes admire her: the fact that she was a woman in control of her destiny. When she spoke, men actually listened. But at this moment, Agnes felt both terrified and entranced. It was the same feeling she had when watching rich women on reality TV.

Agnes sighed loudly. "Why do I suddenly feel like I'm in a ten-page *Vanity Fair* article?"

Veronica ran her hands over her forehead and her hair. She loosened her bun and redid it absently. She looked exhausted. Veronica may have lived in the bubble in the clouds, but she was still a single mother in New York.

"I said no to Charlotte's donation scheme, and then these darlings showed up." Veronica pointed across the space with a clawed finger to three Chase Manhattan paintings against a wall, still with cardboard spacers on them.

Agnes hadn't engaged much with his work the day she'd gone to Charlotte's gallery, but it was recognizable. She walked over to study them. They were a combination of paint with collage. Two were oversize, featuring cartoon characters with erections and dabs of hyper color, jagged seams of paper attempting to cobble the image together. *Yep. That's art all right,* she thought.

The third painting was different, and it was the one Agnes responded to more. Although it featured the same neon green and bright blue and was full of slashing brushstrokes, there was a figure in the far distance that appeared to be a blindfolded man. There was something haunting in the stillness and the distance, the one lone figure.

Charlotte's taste ran toward the eerie and transgressive, Agnes reasoned. But she was older than Agnes and had come of age in the nineties, when that *was* art.

"What are they worth?" she asked Veronica.

"Before? Nothing. I once saw a dealer throw one of Chase's paintings in a dumpster outside of Art Basel Miami. But after leaving them here, Charlotte could say, 'Veronica is cornering the market on Chase Manhattan.' Amazing, right?" Veronica craned her head back and looked at the cathedral. "I really did love that tricky bitch."

Agnes couldn't tell if the words were regretful or if there was some glee in them. Both, maybe.

Chapter Seven

Agnes leaned her head back against the leather seats of the Uber. The car she'd decided to get after Veronica's was creeping across the Fifty-Ninth Street Bridge, the ride home longer than she'd hoped. Maybe it was the adrenaline of interviewing Veronica after being up, more or less, since 4:00 a.m., but exhaustion had set in. Although she hadn't expected Veronica to do any of the things Emmanuel had hinted at—there was no headlock or reality TV scratches directed her way—Agnes had been on guard, and she could now feel her whole body winding down.

Veronica had lost money—would she kill over it? Agnes had once read in one of the books she'd edited that five thousand dollars was the average unpaid debt that could lead to a murder. She closed her eyes and wondered how the rich stopped themselves from murdering each other more than they did.

The Uber driver was saying, "Bit busy up ahead. You want me to let you out here?"

Agnes opened her eyes, leaned forward, and peered through the windshield. It had felt like only a moment, but they were back in Brooklyn and a couple of blocks away from Agnes's condo building. As her car crept slowly closer, she saw the front of the Anand Holdings marquee was clogged with people and cameras and microphones. Traffic on her one-way street was having to edge over slowly to go around double-parked vehicles. A man in cargo pants was aiming his wildlife-size Canon lens up at her deck. She bet Hulot was not loving the commotion outside. A news van was parked in front too. NY1, the free news channel.

She spotted Derek Anand wearing a suit and speaking to a group of reporters. Another man with dark hair and a beard stood behind him, looking solemn. Would they give the media Charlotte's name or just a basic statement from the real estate company? Derek had been right that morning—they'd had thirty seconds to get ahead of it, and that time was up.

"Turn here," Agnes instructed, pointing at the next narrow one-way. She directed the driver back through the side streets of Williamsburg toward downtown Brooklyn.

It was after six when Agnes got out of the car and approached her old building, the place she had lived for almost a decade. She saw that the garbage and recycling had spilled outside of the enclosed bins. She remembered how much her landlady used to yell at her while digging through the trash receptacles. *You're the one with the black garbage bags! I know this hummus container is yours. They'll fine me!* Agnes tried her best, but sometimes—usually right after a giant sink-roach visit—she just wanted the garbage out of her place. But why had her landlady known which apartments used which trash bags? And didn't everyone use black ones? Why did she dig through them? It had been creepy.

And yet, here she was, taking refuge in what she knew. Agnes climbed up the stoop stairs and, although she still had a set of keys, pressed the buzzer for her old unit.

Ethan's voice came over the intercom and asked who it was, and a minute later she had climbed the two flights of stairs inside and was standing at her old door, its battle-scarred brown paint that hadn't been redone since she'd first lived there. There was, however, suddenly, a camera positioned in the hallway, pointed directly over her. She eyed it warily. There had never been security before.

Before she could knock, Ethan opened the door to her. "How did it go?"

"What's with that?" Agnes pointed over her shoulder to the camera.

"They're so cheap now. I thought it would deter anyone thinking about breaking in. I wasn't going to wait for the landlady to do it."

She nodded. "Good idea. So you're going to stay then?" She realized they hadn't discussed any of their ordinary life details that morning. They'd gone from hangover Gatorade and Doritos to investigating a crime scene.

"Yeah, I like it." Ethan stepped out of her way for her to come in.

Looking around, she saw Ethan was out of place in the apartment. The slightly salty smell of *boy* collided with her candle-and-crystal collection, odds and ends she'd left behind. The low-backed plum-colored couch had been the right size for Agnes to stretch out on, but with Ethan's height it seemed as though he'd borrowed a hobbit's furniture. He hadn't changed the main room much. She did like the hardwood and the crown molding compared to the featureless features of her new place. At the far end of the apartment, she could see his mattress on the floor of her old room.

"You know, you're welcome to change things in here," she said.

Ethan offered her a coffee and brought it over in one of her old chipped mugs. WELL-BEHAVED WOMEN RARELY MAKE HISTORY—a script font wrapped the cup. Mia had given it to her many birthdays ago.

"Shit, I just realized I never texted Mia back," Agnes said, sinking down onto the couch.

"It's okay. I updated her."

Agnes raised an eyebrow.

"My therapist gave me some guidelines. I can text her three times in a month. If she texts back, I can continue the conversation. But if not, that's it. It works okay."

Agnes was genuinely impressed. Ethan had always taken medication, but he also needed to stick to routines and avoid becoming overly involved. In their friend circle, that had sometimes been a problem.

"Well, that's good. I was just so busy today . . ." she said.

"Oh yeah, I barely had time either." They were having a contest of "Who's the busiest?" They'd always had a kind of fraternal competition.

Ethan pointed at his computer. "I just finished a work meeting before you buzzed."

Agnes brightened. "This morning you didn't tell me much about your job."

"It's for Sony." Ethan smiled. "I can pay you the rent next week."

She was impressed. "Wow! What are you doing?"

He nodded. "I serve takedown notices to YouTubers for copyright violation. So, in a parallel universe, I guess I'm serving myself." In the past, Ethan had created a show about films, playing clips and pointing out their story flaws or continuity problems.

"It's an O. Henry story." Agnes took too large a glug of the coffee. She'd forgotten Ethan brewed it at bend-your-bowels strength. She set it down. "Speaking of stories . . . Emmanuel was inconsistent. Whereas Veronica's totally consistent but untrustworthy."

As evening came, she detailed everything that had happened. She held out her phone and invited him to look at the photographs she'd taken at Veronica's of the paintings.

"Was the artist fourteen?" Ethan cracked wise.

"I'm wondering if Chase could be involved somehow," Agnes said as he passed the phone back. "She owed him money too. And I feel like there was some weird tension between Chase and her at the party, but I can't remember why I think that." She pressed a palm against her temple.

"Could be. I was thinking the theater guy—"

"Emmanuel," she supplied.

"Right. Emmanuel. He wouldn't do anything to cut off his funding supply, so that's illogical." He flipped open the computer. "This woman, Rachel Efron, she sold Charlotte the condo."

Agnes snapped her fingers. "I talked to her! She knew Emmanuel Haight, the playwright, too. She said that half of New York's real estate agents are former actors."

Agnes recalled Rachel leaning back on one uncomfortable heel, arms crossed over her ample chest, saying, "You have to be able to act to get someone to drop millions on two doors and four windows." Agnes had done a quick tally on her own doors and windows and found them slightly less.

"It might have been just after that I felt woozy." Agnes closed her eyes for a moment. She had asked Jamie for the first drink, and he'd gone to the bar, but Whitney had actually been the one to fetch it. The second drink had been when she was talking to Lewis, who seemed to have stationed himself at the bar permanently. The lawyer, Anthony, had also been nearby. Bartenders often had access to drugs, too, which meant they couldn't be ruled out either.

Ethan had pulled up a picture on social media. The woman who'd called herself Tabitha was standing in the gallery with Charlotte. He pointed. "This woman, Tabitha Lane, works with her."

Agnes felt her forehead crease. "Since she fell, do you think I should limit our suspect list to those who knew about that gallery piece . . . the video of the woman falling? Emmanuel mentioned it." She felt the skin on her arms rise in goose bumps.

Ethan shrugged. "I think we look at everyone. But it's good knowing how they might overlap."

She nodded. She reminded Ethan about how Charlotte had called her last night, wanting to speak to her today. "And now, she's just . . . gone. I asked her why, and she said, 'Because you don't know any of them,' like she needed to confide something." Agnes wondered if something else had occurred after she'd left—something that had provoked Charlotte's fears. Had she suspected what was about to happen? *Like the video woman. Walking toward the edge, unable to stop it.*

"Yeah," he agreed, "making future arrangements. Not what I'd do if I were suicidal. *Charlotte: not a suspect.*" Ethan took the computer back to his desk, and without looking up, he said, "Why don't you stay a bit, take a hot bath, give Mia a call. You need to take care of you right now."

Who is this person? Agnes wondered. Aside from the mattress on the floor and the two months since his last haircut, it was like Ethan had become a grown-up. Like her, he had been working on himself in the time since they'd last seen each other.

Agnes yawned and stretched out on the small sofa. "Actually, I am really tired."

The voice that woke her was low and urgent. "Agnes . . ."

She stretched and found her socked foot going over the arm of the sofa. It took a moment for her to remember she was in her old apartment.

"Agnes, come here!" It was Ethan, a whispered call from the bedroom.

She stood up and moved through the place by memory; her eyes were open, but the lights were out. The bedroom was dark, though it was barer than when she'd lived there and easy to navigate around the bed to the place where Ethan had called her. There were two long windows, both with translucent shades that were pulled halfway down, part of the window exposed. He was standing beside the farther window, looking out, unmoving, his back to her, shoulders stiff.

As she crossed the room to stand beside him, Ethan put out a hand to stop her from moving too close to the glass.

"Look, but don't let him see you."

"Who?" She moved closer to the wall.

At first she saw nothing unusual. It must have been nine or ten now. Under the streetlight, teenagers were trading taunts outside the corner deli. Music from open car windows. The thrum of air conditioners. Two friends dressed like Guy Fieri were sharing a joint as they walked. A woman with a Chihuahua in her bucket purse was clearly waiting for an Uber, her phone held out, illuminated in her palm. The neighborhood was busy enough. Agnes glanced at Ethan and followed his sight line. The man's stillness should have attracted her gaze right away.

Across the street, standing, not against the wall, not beside any particular stoop, nothing to distract him—no phone, no friend—only a lit cigarette for company, was a mountain of a man. He wore a full tweed suit in spite of the July heat. His head was round and stubbled. He must have been at least six-five. He wasn't young but was as wide as her and Ethan standing side by side. He was staring at the building they were in—not at them, more like the foyer and door below, the place she would be expected to exit from.

As the orange glow of the cigarette flared, she felt a burn inside her guts. "I see him."

"He's been there for almost two hours."

Agnes lightened her voice and tried to joke: "No chance you put one of those security cameras up out front there?"

Ethan said no but that maybe he would order another. He squeezed her shoulder, a touch that was rare. Like brother and sister after all the years, they could say anything to each other but seldom touched.

"Who do you think he is?" she wondered. Being followed couldn't be a coincidence.

"Oh, he's hired." Ethan sounded certain.

Old-school muscle. Agnes nodded and moved away from the window. "Then the question isn't *who* but *why.*"

Chapter Eight

Agnes wanted to leave, but Ethan argued that Agnes needed to *remain alive* to return home, and what was piddle on an IKEA rug in comparison to an emergency room bill at Mount Sinai?

"Good point." They decided that Ethan should go to Agnes's condo and walk and feed Hulot, then return.

She watched out the window as Ethan went—ready to film whatever happened using her cell phone. *What if he has a gun?* It was something she and Ethan hadn't even discussed.

She couldn't see but knew Ethan was unlocking his bike right there, only twenty feet from the large suited man. He must have seen Ethan come out, but he barely blinked. The man obviously had no idea Ethan lived in her apartment. *Why would he? Ethan's name isn't on the mailbox downstairs.* The big man continued to keep his eye trained on the doorway below as Ethan made his way down the street on his bicycle, a bit quicker than he usually rode.

He eventually texted her photos of Monsieur Hulot frolicking in the park. The dog was a dark blur under the streetlight. Agnes felt relief and a fast flicker of sadness. It was the only time her fur baby had been with someone else.

What motivated someone to jealousy? Agnes's last relationship had fizzled, but she hadn't spent so much time wondering if there was someone else as she had wondering what else she might have done or said differently. Her ex, Lise, had been different from her, and they'd been in different life places. That became clear over time. Jealousy seemed pointless. Of course people went on to date others. What mattered was what they'd shared with you, and what had always concerned Agnes was whether she'd shown up, listened, and been honest about who she was and the things she wanted from the romance. But maybe that was an unusual attitude. Television and novels ought to have schooled her that there was more finger-pointing than self-reflection in the world. *And it does make for better entertainment,* she thought. There'd been plenty of surliness at Charlotte's party and energy flowing in many directions. Whitney had seemed jealous of Charlotte's ability to pick up men. Nic had seemed vaguely jealous of her painting, her things. Veronica had outright cataloged them. Lewis had seemed jealous of everyone. Chase had seemed to attach himself to Charlotte's side as if she were his new mommy.

Was Charlotte's death about money, or anger?

Thinking about who might have sent this six-five intimidation factor, she realized it had to be Veronica. She possessed the wealth to have someone following her within minutes of her leaving the Midtown building—*God, she probably has an app for concierge muscle service.* Emmanuel definitely didn't. They were the only ones she'd talked to so far. Or maybe Matias? Agnes thought he would be more direct, though. Besides, Matias knew she lived in the Kentwood. Whoever was responsible for the man outside had only Agnes's old address.

Ethan returned without incident around eleven. She'd told him to spend some time with Hulot and that she would text if there was any status change. She'd tentatively looked out every ten minutes or so. Ethan came back with a change of clothes for her, her laptop, and her toothbrush. Also, a container of pad thai.

Agnes hugged Ethan surprisingly hard. As he set the takeout down, she gazed at him with admiration she hadn't felt for him in decades. The day's fear-sweat had gotten rank. Agnes reached gratefully for the fresh T-shirt he'd brought. Then to keep it from getting weird between them, she said, only a bit facetiously, "You're kind of my hero right now."

He put his arm up and flexed a muscle. It might have been comical except his spaghetti arms had almost turned into man arms sometime recently. Agnes realized he'd actually been working out. What if all these years, she'd gotten it wrong and his ex, Zoey, had been holding him back—or they'd both been holding each other back? She felt suddenly glad she'd given Ethan the apartment. Lise had seemed exciting, but by the end of the relationship, she'd realized they had become trapped. As Ethan divided the container between their two plates, Agnes scrolled through her phone and the photos she'd taken during the relationship that were left on Instagram.

Still standing, he peered at the phone over her shoulder and broke a set of chopsticks with an intruding *crack*. "Why are you doing that to yourself? *Now* of all times?"

"Because I have an idea." Lise didn't look threatening enough in the photos for what Agnes wanted to do, though. Agnes began scrolling for someone else's photos to use. "Do you remember when Catherine Zeta-Jones confronts the surveillance cops in *Traffic*?"

"Don Cheadle and Luis Guzmán." Ethan shook hot sauce all over his plate.

"Mm-hmm." Agnes chewed through a mouthful. She felt scared but also pleased with herself. "I'll just go talk to him."

"Brilliant. Except that was a movie. This is real life," Ethan said.

Agnes walked outside, clutching the tools she needed for this scene. They'd agreed Ethan would call 911 if anything went wrong. The man was a bit farther away, sitting on a wooden bench around a sidewalk tree. He looked tired but watched her warily. As she walked up to him, he got to his feet. His shoulders and chest seemed to expand as he drew himself up to his full intimidating height.

"I know we're not supposed to talk, but I thought you might want a coffee," Agnes said, extending the extra-large takeout cup of bladder-challenging dark roast.

"No, that's—" He put his hand out to stop her, and since he was quite a bit scarier and bigger than she'd realized from the window, she paused.

"Oh, I understand if you can't take it. It's just . . . since you're out here, I wondered if you could keep an eye out for me."

She tried to juggle the coffee and her phone. She hadn't thought about how to show him the photo if he didn't accept the coffee. But she managed to swipe her screen and bring up a picture of St. Vincent and flash it at him. "My ex. She's been stalking me," Agnes lied.

The guy stared at the phone, assessing. The rock star, whom Agnes had obviously never met, was thin and pretty with an asymmetrical haircut. She didn't look frightening at all, but she was giving the camera the finger. He said nothing.

Agnes went for the dude-to-dude act. She may have even lowered her voice. "You ever date a crazy girl? You know how it is. Just, if you see her hanging around, would you tell me?"

He didn't say yes or no, but he gestured for the coffee, as if he would accept it.

Ten minutes later, he left his post, no doubt to find a nearby bathroom at a bodega or bar.

Agnes used that moment to hop in a cab back to the Kentwood. As she sailed through the city, she sent an email, calling in sick again to her publishing job for the next week: sorry, all, finally got the Covid. She thought it was possible Derek had been right about her skill set. Detective work might be her real calling.

Chapter Nine

Agnes woke early the next day, walked Hulot, and then put her list in order of most-likely suspects. Veronica was still at the top of it, but Agnes also wanted to explore the jealousy theory; she included the men Charlotte had been known to be involved with. She realized that this actually took Emmanuel off the list. She had just finished writing *Lewis Grant* when her phone rang, displaying his caller ID.

She drew back, shocked. *Do people actually still do that? Just call someone—someone they don't know—out of the blue?* It felt like a tiny invasion. Nonetheless, she knew she was going to pick it up. Her finger moved toward the phone screen. If anything, it saved *her* from having to reach out to him.

After a tentative hello from each of them, Lewis launched into an unexpected spiel. It was clear to Agnes that he was at a desk in a bull-pen, if such things still existed, or possibly in an office or room where someone else was. Either way, Lewis was in professional mode, nothing like the caustic man she'd seen at Charlotte's party.

"I know it's short notice," he said, "but the paper is working on several pieces on Charlotte, and I'm thinking you might help us fill in some holes. It's not just my article, though, you understand—we have several writers—so I might need to circle back a few times, if that would be okay?"

"Okay," Agnes said without hesitation. If she could think of Lewis as both a possible suspect and a source, the whole thing might become easier. *This could be a gold mine.* "Actually, I'm running around a lot today. Let me think." In reality, she had not figured out at all what her next move should be.

"Oh, uh . . ." There was a long pause. "Where are you going to be?"

Before Agnes could come up with a lie, she heard Lewis speaking to someone else. "You want me to . . . ?" She could tell he was asking their permission, even though she could hear only part of it.

Rather than jump in, Agnes waited. It was something that had been said in the master class she'd ironically played on fast-forward. "When in doubt, pause. Live with the silence. People will reveal themselves. A pot can't wait to boil." She had rolled her eyes at that—because pots didn't boil, water did—but the advice seemed salient.

"Uh, it looks like I might be able to pop across to Williamsburg," he said.

She could hear Lewis tapping on a computer. He knew what building she was in. *Did we talk about that at the bar in the kitchen, when we talked about Charlotte?* She couldn't recall. She scratched Hulot behind the ears and suggested a coffee shop she didn't normally go to but that had a large walled-in garden patio. It would give enough privacy that they shouldn't be seen by anyone. At the same time, it was public and not far if she wanted to make a fast exit. Also, they had great sandwiches, and she figured that Lewis would never judge her over ordering carbs. In her experience, writers were almost always hungry.

Agnes was there first. She brought Hulot with her; he behaved himself, and no one seemed to mind. Her thought was that the dog added a layer of protection. Even if he was mostly prone to hiding and whimpering— no one else knew that. She chose a picnic table where she could have her back to the wall and see anyone who came into the café or the garden.

Lewis looked more disheveled than he had when she'd met him at Charlotte's. He had not shaved, and his T-shirt wasn't tucked into his jeans. She'd been right that he saved the button-ups for events—this was his working uniform. Black T-shirt, loose-cut denim, laptop bag. And since it was too hot to wear it, a faded blazer over his arm. He was carrying an iced coffee and looking nervously around the patio. It occurred to her at that moment that he might not remember what she looked like. They'd talked about scotch, she remembered. Maybe he'd had more than a few scotches.

She recalled she'd wanted to like Lewis, as an intellectual adrift in that sea of sociability and proper skin care, but his mood had seemed resentful. *We were waiting together for ice,* she now realized. She remembered the bartender had come back with a bag of ice on their shoulder, which they'd set in the sink, then ripped open. Their ear had crawled with piercings and plugs, and a white collared shirt exposed a lotus flower neck tattoo. She now wondered if they knew Charlotte or had simply been hired from an agency.

Agnes had tried to fill up the space: "I read an article in the *Atlantic* recently—" she'd said to the journalist.

Lewis had cut her off. "Oh no, I never read the *Atlantic*. Used to write for them. That's like sleeping with an ex all over again." He said it with disdain. He picked up his fresh drink. "Do you know the difference between scotch-neat drinkers and scotch-on-the-rocks drinkers?"

Agnes shook her head.

"The latter are infinitely more social. The former are happy with the burn and don't need the conversation to go with it." He'd taken her drink from the bartender and passed it to her—politely, she'd thought at the time, though now as she recalled it, she wasn't sure. "Good talk." Lewis had tipped his glass at her, the four cubes he'd waited for clinking against the sides, and moved away.

She'd thought writers were supposed to be better at listening. In spite of his ice theory, it hadn't been much of a conversation. He'd mostly just talked at her.

Now, as she watched him scanning the garden, she felt her guard go up.

Agnes gave it another second, observing him, then stood up. His gaze found her.

"You choose people, or you choose your secrets," he had also said to her at the party. Agnes knew which she chose. And now she knew what Lewis chose too—it wasn't people, or they would make more of an impression on him.

Before he sat down, he saw Hulot under the table. He paused for a second.

"He's friendly," she said, hating to have to give up that information so quickly. But Lewis looked extremely apprehensive. "And he's not that much of a dog, really."

"I was once bitten by an off-leash Chihuahua in a Laundromat."

"What had you done?" Agnes asked, then was aghast at herself for jumping to the conclusion that it was Lewis's fault.

Lewis shrugged and said he hadn't done anything but he'd had to call the owner's vet to confirm the dog was vaccinated. The vet had been terse with him and tried to plead doctor-patient confidentiality until Lewis impressed upon him that it was a *dog*—they didn't feel shame when you discussed their medical history.

She brought Monsieur Hulot over to her side of the table and pulled the leash tighter. The pup didn't seem to mind being closer, an excuse for more ear scratches. Lewis positioned himself at the farthest corner of the table. That worked to Agnes's benefit, and she was glad she'd brought him.

"Charlotte loved dogs," he said. "But she also had two rehomed. Which is fancy New York speak for 'She got rid of them.'"

"It's like you take that personally," Agnes let slip. She sat up a little straighter. Was he there to work on his article or there to unload? That wouldn't be the worst for Agnes, except she knew there was a small part of her that didn't want the shine of Charlotte to fall away. Some of what he said might be true, but it was also only his perspective. She remembered the warmth of Charlotte, her voice as she spoke to Hulot—or to

Agnes. There was love there, even if it had the touch of performance—she embraced the world with a warmth and openness.

Lewis took out his notebook and pen. In retaliation, Agnes did the same.

"Was the party the first time you met any of her friends?" Lewis asked.

Agnes felt bumps appear along her arms, as if a breeze had swept into the sheltered patio. But of course, none had. Charlotte had said she wanted to talk to Agnes specifically because she didn't know *any of them*.

Agnes waited a second, then decided to state the obvious. "You don't like them, do you? Her friends?"

Lewis brushed some crumbs off the table and drank his coffee. She couldn't tell if he was going to answer. He had a face like a chalkboard, where many things seemed to get written and erased very quickly.

"Some of them are okay, but there is one circle. A clique very into intellectual games in this undergrad kind of way. You sort of strike me as someone who might be into that kind of thing." Before she could get offended, he elaborated. "Are you into games?"

There were board game clubs and things like that people at her office were into. Ethan had been a Dungeons & Dragons guy when they were at college.

She went with the easy answer. "I'm a monster at Wordle."

"How did you meet her?" Lewis was tapping his pen, as if to say *I hope you can give me something I can write down*. They were doing the same work: compiling data about Charlotte and her associates, hoping it was going to mean something. A giant constellation of a dot-to-dot that might eventually make a picture if you could locate the next point, give the wandering pencil line some order. But she didn't trust Lewis enough to think about working with him.

"I met her a few weeks ago. Just around the building."

"And you don't work for her? Her new assistant, maybe?"

Agnes shook her head. *Veronica mentioned an assistant during the fight.* A good source, if Agnes could figure out who. She picked up her pen and asked him back, "But *you* knew her a long time?"

"I met her last year at the first salon." Lewis looked contemplative for a moment, but then he tapped the notebook with his pen and said what the newspaper was really interested in were her business dealings and her family. What had she done since becoming estranged from the Bosches? There was the art gallery, of course, but also the fight with Veronica and those rumors of fundraising improprieties. He asked her if she had Nic Kelly's phone number by chance.

Agnes did—the musician had insisted on putting herself in her phone. But Agnes wasn't going to give it out and wondered to herself why Lewis wanted it. As a feint, she scrolled through her texts, passing by a chain she'd had with a woman named Evie from a dating app—she hadn't thought about her since before the party. Dating seemed like an alien concept now, reserved for those with free time after work and no crime to solve.

Lewis pressed for several other numbers, but Agnes genuinely didn't know them. Only two or three of the people she'd met had even followed her back on social media.

"For someone who wanted out of the most infamous family in America, Charlotte really was, I hate to say it, a fame whore." He tapped the pen on the notebook and looked at Agnes. "That's why she invited you. *New York*'s DIY Detective. That's a joke, right? You don't really do investigations?"

Agnes took a large swallow of her drink to avoid answering right away. She let his sexism hang in the air for a blistering minute. "Where would I even start?" she fake laughed. "Me? Doing that kind of *real* work?"

Lewis chuckled in return.

She leaned in and added, "But if I had to, maybe I would start with you?"

"What are you saying?"

"Does your editor know that Charlotte had, um—"

"Been intimate with me?"

"I was going to say 'slept with you because of who your employer is?' But that would be so demeaning." It wasn't the first time it had occurred to Agnes that Charlotte had chosen her party guests, and her boyfriends, based on their clout. But she wasn't going to judge her for it: this was New York City, and many people dated using their Rolodex. The jab was really there to see what reaction it might tease out of him.

"Look, her business was a collapsing house of cards, and that's what's going to come out. Maybe I can save some people some embarrassment." He closed his notebook. "Maybe not."

Agnes thought of the three paintings at Veronica's. Charlotte was also funding Emmanuel's play—enough that he had to find a new patron within an hour of learning of Charlotte's death. What if the donation to Jamie's campaign wasn't because she couldn't donate herself but because she simply wanted *more* donations for him? But why—what allegiance did she have to him and/or how did it benefit her? *Some of it adds up, and some doesn't. What else is Charlotte involved in?* But to know that, Agnes realized she'd have to let go of any adoration.

Agnes decided to share a little to keep Lewis talking. "She didn't sell any Chase paintings. Half his work is sitting in a warehouse in Greenpoint. She told me that at the party, but apparently even Chase doesn't know that."

Lewis opened his notebook and scribbled with a lefty penmanship that looked like he'd never be able to reread it. "Half, she said?"

Agnes nodded a confirmation.

"I'm not surprised it didn't sell. I'm not a fan—for many reasons." Lewis took out a crumpled package of cigarettes, and Agnes leaned in to see what brand. Had he been the one smoking with Charlotte in her apartment? Most people Agnes knew vaped. Lewis fumbled in various pockets but couldn't locate a lighter. Sitting across from him, she realized Lewis possibly wasn't large enough—even with the broken window in the bedroom. But then, did possessiveness take priority over size?

Agnes reached into her pocket and found the matchbook she'd taken from Charlotte's bedroom the day before. The cardboard bore a black image of a wild boar head.

Lewis reached for them, then stopped, looking down. When he glanced back up, he had a different expression—one that was supercilious. "Tusk?"

"What?" Agnes asked.

"Cody Buckley's new restaurant." He showed her the image. It must have been the logo, but Agnes hadn't realized it. "Eaten there yet?"

"Do they have Groupon deals?"

"Not likely. But he's catering the memorial. Try the ostrich sliders." Lewis got up and gathered his notebook. "Can't smoke here anyway. I've got to go."

"What? There's already a memorial?"

"Thursday. You don't know everything, do you?"

"Who else is organizing it?" she asked, but he was already out of the courtyard and heading into the street.

Chapter Ten

No matter how hard she tried, it seemed Agnes could never be fashionably late to anything. Even when she had waited as long as she possibly could, she would always show up at the party to find she was still only the second person there. But this time, she contemplated a new approach: be at the memorial early as a death hag—and see who was first. She felt it would say something about who was the closest to Charlotte, who was inner circle.

Lewis hadn't responded to her text when she'd asked for more details, but Nic, the musician, had given her the address freely and said she'd be on the list. Agnes had immediately roped in Ethan as her date. He had promised he'd be her eyes and ears. He'd had to work that day but said he could come after.

In the days between the Lewis meeting and the memorial, Agnes had gone to the New York Public Library, where the Bosch family had their own room for science, history, and the family archives. She'd looked up and seen the name over the doorway covered in taped-up poster board. *It's why the rich always choose marble—it's hard to change,* she thought. But Charlotte's father's business history was like any other: some guy was really good at buying other businesses. Agnes felt she'd learned nothing that helped her understand what impact any of it might have had on Charlotte.

Except maybe that Charlotte would know how to select a better wine than the one Agnes now held in her hand. At least she had a perfect view of the main doors to the lobby where the memorial was being held. It was in an industrial building that had now gone posh event center. The event was to be hosted in a rooftop space with a view of the skyline, but the ground floor had several sidewalk businesses, one of which was a wine bar. Agnes planted herself on the patio, keeping her sunglasses on. If anyone she knew spotted her, it made perfect sense that she was there, fortifying before the event.

She was halfway through her sauvignon blanc, and although several bold names like Chloë Sevigny had entered the large brick building, Agnes had yet to see anyone from Charlotte's final salon.

Quite a few celebs here, she texted Ethan. But it would be better with you! And the address. Just in case. He longed to be helpful, but she knew from years of experience that he could also be forgetful or have a sudden attack of nerves and ditch on obligations. He had once hidden in the bathroom while his friends gathered for a screening of his college film and hadn't come out until halfway through.

They had spoken a couple of times since the night at his apartment. It was Ethan's opinion that the big man outside must have wanted to be seen. He'd intended for Agnes to know he was there as a warning. Even so, it couldn't hurt to make sure she wasn't alone in case there was trouble. Ethan wasn't much of a protector—he weighed as much as an empty DVD case—but he *was* smart.

Agnes took another sip of her drink. For a second, she thought she caught a flash of tweed out of the corner of her eye, but when she looked over, she saw it was not the big henchman. Instead, she saw a full-figured woman in a skirt suit.

When she took a longer look, she recognized Tabitha, who had been at the party. The research she and Ethan had done told her Tabitha was on the board of Charlotte's gallery. If what Lewis said was true about Charlotte's business problems, Tabitha might know them. She strode along with two little girls, identical twins. Though they wore different-colored dresses, they were the same style, and each child had her hair in pigtails.

It was weird that Ethan didn't text her back right away—it was almost 6:00 p.m.—but she put the phone down on the table and surveyed the sidewalk.

Hugo from the party was the next to pass her. He was the one who'd broken up the fight. He was dressed sharply in an olive suit and was walking from the direction of the Kentwood with purpose. She didn't know much about him except that when Ethan had googled him, he had been listed at the Kentwood. She couldn't recall having run into him or passing him in the lobby in any of the time she'd been there, but his location definitely gave him proximity. *Access,* Agnes thought. His earliness might mean they were more familiar friends, or it could have been simply because he lived nearby. Regardless, it was time to mingle.

Before she could go in, she got a text from Ethan. On my way, it said, and she felt relief settle over her. She finished the wine and stood to leave.

"Agneees!" a voice drawled from the sidewalk with surprising familiarity. She turned and saw the chef, Cody, standing there with a young woman who could have been either his date or his daughter, which was a distinctly New York problem.

She suddenly recalled that Emmanuel had said she'd been talking to him at the party right before going to lie down. But she wasn't sure. The sequence of events was still fuzzy: she knew she'd talked to Lewis, Anthony, and Rachel too. *You have to let your apprehension go if you're going to learn anything,* she silently scolded herself.

Cody introduced the woman he was with, whose skin was as perfect as a doll's, as Keira and asked if Agnes wanted to walk in with them. She figured it would be rude to say no, so she nodded, and the three of them walked toward the doors. Cody and Keira had a looseness to them that told her they'd already had a couple of pre-event drinks. The young woman was wearing a black poplin skirt and a black top that was slightly sheer, as if she'd gone shopping for a sexy funeral outfit on purpose. Agnes complimented it, and Keira touched her arm and said thank you.

"Don't steal my date," Cody warned her, but before Agnes could take offense, both he and the girl laughed, and she realized it was easier to just laugh with them.

Inside, they found the elevators and pressed the button for the fifth floor.

"How do you know Charlotte?" Agnes asked Keira as the old elevator whirred upward, though she considered, before asking, that the girl might not know her at all. Emmanuel had labeled Cody a letch, she remembered. Maybe Charlotte's memorial was just another excuse for a pickup. She had seen an Instagram photo of Jessica and Cody the night of the salon where they'd looked chummy.

"The restaurant," Keira said.

"She had some points in the business," Cody said.

"She was your partner," Keira countered.

Agnes thought it was a bold correction to be making in front of her. *What did Emmanuel say? "If you want love, pick up the tab on someone else's dreams."* Lewis had mentioned not having a full picture of her businesses. Yet it couldn't have been a huge secret if Cody's date was telling her. Then again, they were weaving when they had walked up together.

"You work there too?" Agnes asked the young woman, putting it together.

"I'm the hostess," Keira said.

"She's modest. You're the glue," Cody said. "Especially this week."

The elevator opened to a hall, and beyond it was a long room with finished dark wood floors, set up with chairs and tables. At the far end, the windows showed them the skyline and the Queens ferry going past on the East River.

Cody feigned chivalry and gestured for Keira to step off the elevator. He watched Keira's butt as she walked ahead in her spiky black shoes. He raised his eyebrows at Agnes, as if to invite her to agree with him, silently, that the girl was *fine*. Their relationship was more than business. What about his relationship with Charlotte? Agnes thought of the clique Lewis had mentioned as she watched Keira walk toward a lineup of several people in the doorway.

A young couple, overdressed, were clearly trying to get in but were being told they weren't on the list. The girl was wearing a shiny dress, and where Agnes stood behind them, a corded tag was visible just inside the neck, as though she planned to return it. Agnes cringed. It was like looking at a version of her younger self. Disappointed, but trying to hold their heads high, the couple walked past them toward the elevator and probably back to art school.

Now it was their turn, and the young employee with the man bun consulted his digital list on the iPad.

"Exclusive till the end," Cody remarked as he waited for his name to be found.

"Agnes Nielsen." Agnes wasn't sure how they could all be there. Nic had texted her a link through an invite app, and Agnes had clicked the appropriate button, but she still had that sinking feeling that any of them might be turned away. What about Ethan when he showed? Keira was clearly Cody's plus-one. Could she get a plus-one? "My date is coming after me," she said, to try to pave the way for him getting in.

A few clicks and keystrokes, a nod, and it was uncomplicated—if you looked like you belonged, she supposed. But what made her look like that? *Age,* she decided. *And maybe taste.* She prayed Ethan would be wearing his best sneakers.

As they walked into the long room, Agnes asked, "Does this affect Tusk?"

Quickly, Cody's manner sobered. His voice dropped. "Charlotte was a silent partner. I mean, I'm devastated, but Tusk will be fine. We make food. We sell it."

He crossed his arms. *He didn't mean for me to know.*

"It's strange we were with Charlotte just a week ago tonight." Agnes tried to inject a tremor into her voice and found it surprisingly easy. Maybe she wasn't acting.

"I know," Cody said, picking two already-poured glasses of wine from a table that was serving as a bar. He handed one to Keira.

"Excuse me. I have to get a shot of the view," Keira observed, unable to contain her juvenile joy.

Agnes watched her dance across the large space, a little too happily, as if she were at a wedding instead of a funeral. The room held only a few scattered groups of people.

"Were you there when she and Veronica fought?" Agnes added an explanation. "The party's a bit of a blur for me."

"I definitely left with someone."

"Awesome!" Agnes said, as if they were bros. *Cody Buckley and Jessica Chu—I knew it.* Jessica was one of the women in the bedroom who'd said she wished men wouldn't pretend they were serious if they weren't.

"Don't tell Keira. We're not, you know, exclusive. But she's jealous. Younger girlfriends are like that. All that new raw emotion. Like a volcano in an A-cup."

"I get that," Agnes said as her stomach roiled.

"Knew you would. Anyway, that's why me and Charlotte didn't work out. Too much the same. No one's going to be the one to change us." He lifted his drink in a silent toast.

Cody's world was as dank as a closing-time pickup. Agnes scanned the room for an out and saw Hugo near the bar area. Cody noticed her looking.

"Hugo. He was Charlotte's new one."

Agnes stared at Hugo Desjardins with new eyes. They'd found his name online, but not his social media. He was talking with Tabitha and her children and appeared to be making the girls laugh.

"Oh yeah, I think she mentioned that." She nodded. This was the man Charlotte had said might be the one, a flame for all seasons? Agnes hadn't seen that he was handsome, but of course she saw it now. To her, he'd just been a man in a stiff shirt across the room.

"Looks like a nice guy, but he does not mind closing out a bar. He can party too." Cody smiled with the knowledge of someone who has seen humanity at 4:00 a.m. too many nights. He excused himself to go join his date.

Agnes took out her phone and googled Hugo again, careful to have her back to the wall so no one could come up behind her and see what she was typing. Dr. Hugo Desjardins. She had assumed he was a medical doctor, but now as she scrolled through the results, she realized he was a psychiatrist. The prescriptions in Charlotte's medicine cabinet. She had a feeling she knew who had prescribed them now.

There were more people arriving—among the strangers, Agnes noticed Jessica and Madi from the party. They were standing off to one side, consulting quietly.

Emmanuel was there with a smaller man with a blond mop of hair, metal-rimmed eyeglasses, baggy black trousers, and a yellow man purse slung on his back. Emmanuel had put on a white button-up with his khakis. He'd always worn sneakers, but now she saw he'd swapped them for a pair of cherry Doc Martens oxfords. The outfits were not funereal. They looked more like they could have been snapped by Bill Cunningham walking through Madison Square Park. After Emmanuel saw Agnes, he claimed a couple of chairs quickly. She wondered if he was now avoiding her.

At the front of the room a tech was setting up a microphone, and Jamie stood there, giving him instructions, as if the event's hire didn't know what to do. The sound system came on with a sharp buzz, and everyone looked around, wondering if the event was starting now. Then the sound cut.

When did Jamie get here? Agnes hadn't seen the politician come in when she was downstairs waiting.

She glanced around for Ethan and then saw a familiar-looking face weaving through the crowd. It was Evie, from the dating app. They'd exchanged a few pleasant texts and talked about a coffee or drink, but then neither had followed up with the other to confirm a day or time. Typical dating-app behavior. Was it possible she had known Charlotte? If Agnes remembered right, Evie was a Canadian actress living in New

York. Charlotte was immersed in the arts; circles in Brooklyn could be small, even in a borough of over 2.5 million. But Evie looked lost, standing near the bar as though she couldn't decide whether to get a drink or bolt. It was then that Agnes realized she couldn't recall her last name.

Agnes had a choice: go over and introduce herself and see if the shock of IRL wasn't too awkward, or catch Jamie as he finished with the sound tech. She chose the latter.

Jamie's eyes narrowed when he realized she was going to interrupt him. His head swiveled around, gaze taking in the room, as though he had something else he'd been about to do. "Hi, uh . . . give me a minute."

The appeal-to-the-ego approach, Agnes decided. "Sure, I just wanted to say hi and ask you more about your campaign."

It worked. Jamie's expression changed, and he patted her shoulder and promised to return in a minute.

When Agnes turned around, dating-app Evie was at her elbow. She said hi and leaned in for a quick cheek kiss that caught Agnes off guard. Evie had obviously been expecting to find her here.

"Evie!"

"Agnes! You know, a funeral is kind of weird for a first date, if you don't mind my saying so." Evie glanced around the room. She had an inquisitive face, long curly hair framing golden brown eyes. She was cuter and younger looking than she'd seemed online, and both things made Agnes feel suddenly nervous.

"I—I don't understand," Agnes stammered.

"You invited me?" Evie took out her phone and waved it back and forth.

Agnes glanced down at her own phone. Evie. Ethan. She'd gotten her texts wrong. Ethan had known it was that day and hadn't needed her reminder. She'd accidentally sent the address to Evie. When she looked, their contacts were both *ES*: Ethan *Sharp*, and Evie *South* Williamsburg, punched in under the neighborhood she'd given Agnes.

Because, of course, dating has more to do with a geographical radius than it does actual attraction or even common interests.

"It's really more of a memorial," Agnes tried to explain.

"What's the difference?"

Onstage, Jamie was now showing someone where to set up a moody black-and-white photograph of Charlotte on an easel. Flower stands had been brought out, white roses and lilies. There was no denying it was a funeral.

Evie was attractive—a men's vest and no blouse, Freebird heeled boots, paired with a light citrusy perfume—and if Agnes really thought about it, they probably did have common interests. She just hoped the list checker at the door would let in *two* dates. Rather than confess, Agnes said, "Listen, you didn't meet this woman. Her funeral is going to be better than most people's birthday parties."

Evie smiled. "I have to admit, this is more interesting than another iced coffee on another patio."

"You're an actor, right? There's Emmanuel Haight. Do you know who he is?" Agnes waved across the room. "Emmanuel!"

Evie looked instantly impressed when Emmanuel looked in their direction. But his eyes unnerved Agnes. He looked scared at someone shouting his name. The thought was broken when Evie clutched her arm. Agnes liked the whisper of their skin touching as they moved together across the large space. Evie leaned in with a conspiratorial whisper. "Who else is here?"

"So many people. Charlotte was connected. Do you drink?"

As they approached the bar, Agnes saw Ethan coming toward them. She was used to seeing him in a hoodie and Chuck Taylors, but for the memorial, he had pulled a suit jacket from somewhere in the far depths of his closet. It was a gray windowpane pattern and looked as old as he was. *Thrifted? Or bought for him by mother or girlfriend?* He'd paired it with long navy shorts and camel oxfords in the typical I-don't-care fashion that had always worked for him and tech billionaires but no one else.

"Hey, got stuck on the G train." He complained about his transit like a New Yorker instead of just saying hello. It seemed to take him a moment to register that a woman had attached herself to Agnes's arm, and when he did, he squinted at her and said, "You're not . . ." Ethan ticked a finger at her. "I've seen you in something."

Evie smiled expectantly.

"*Wolf Island.*"

"Oh my God. You saw the werewolf movie?"

"I saw it at Sundance Midnight, two years ago."

What was happening? Suddenly Evie let go of Agnes's arm, and all the bright energy seemed to pass instead between her and Ethan. *Oh no, actors.* Agnes should have known better than to think she stood a chance. Now Agnes was scrambling to catch up. She didn't even know this woman's full name, let alone what shows or films she may have appeared in.

Evie cocked her head. "What's your name?"

"Ethan." He put out his hand to shake.

Did he just use a voice that was lower than usual? Agnes wondered. *Is Ethan . . . trying to steal my date?*

At that moment, there was a tapping on the microphone, and everyone began to turn toward the front of the room.

"Chairs?" Evie whispered. She pointed to a small table along the side of the space. Agnes and Ethan followed behind her. Ethan leaned into Agnes and whisper-exclaimed, "How do you know Evie Mallon? She was kind of the Parker Posey of indie horror for a few years."

"Totally," Agnes said, covering things well enough. "Evie Mallon. I've known her forever."

No one had taken these seats because the table was wedged awkwardly between one end of the bar and a large speaker. *At least we'll hear everything.* As they edged around and pulled out chairs, Agnes tried to do one final survey of the room for who was there and who wasn't. Cody and his date were sitting at a table with Chase, clad in leather pants in spite of the heat. He peered, red eyed, from under untidy hair. Jessica, whom Cody had almost confirmed he'd left with that night, was sitting alone at a table directly behind them, wearing a puff-sleeve dress with a sweetheart neckline. Agnes noticed many of the women were dressed as if they hoped to catch some eyes . . . *Is everyone here looking for a grief grind?*

It was hardly fair for Agnes to judge, seeing as she herself had inadvertently tricked a date to come meet her.

Anthony Pellerito was sitting with Lewis Grant, Whitney Astor-Barnes, and Emmanuel Haight and his friend. Agnes's gaze flicked back to him. Why was the lawyer sitting with the writers? The grouping made sense aside from him. They were all in different worlds—journalism, comedy, theater—but Anthony didn't fit here in his sober Ralph Lauren suit. She tried to gauge any energy between Anthony and Whitney, but it was impossible to say, since almost everyone was now watching the stage, where Matias was about to speak.

Matias looked uneasy as he shuffled a few white cue cards between his large palms. "Charlotte . . . what can I say about Charlotte?" He paused and looked at her photograph. He shook his head. "I wasn't ready for her. Who was? The world wasn't."

The room chuckled.

"By the end, we realized it was not love that we had. But we respected each other," Matias said, "as two predatory animals in the jungle might."

Beside him in the picture onstage, Charlotte's expression was one of distraction. She looked slightly surprised, as if she never expected to be present at this gathering. But there was something magnetic there—the way her head was turned toward them as if at just that moment a friend had said her name. *Which friend?* Agnes wondered. *Who took this photograph, and is it the same person who selected it for tonight—or someone else?*

Scanning the room, she saw a woman sitting at the back with a stroller—Matias's new girlfriend. She was wearing black pants and a lilac wrap blouse appropriate for nursing. *Hardly Lady Macbeth.* Hugo and Derek were at a table close to her. Nic and Rachel, the real estate agent, were there too. Agnes realized almost everyone was there, except Veronica.

There were also people who looked important, but Agnes didn't know them. Older people who looked like character actors in someone else's life. The men whose hair had been kept in the same styles for years, no doubt, and the women whose large jewelry distinguished them, whose hair dye somehow looked natural, who laughed because it was preferable to tears. People with expensive, comfortable shoes. People who mixed easily with those around them and never used their phones as social crutches. The task of narrowing down who was a suspect here was almost impossible.

"Charlotte had the willpower to walk away from anything she did not like. She despised the hypocritical and the boring," Matias declared. "I respected that. She also walked away from me, but . . ." He laughed, even though the audience didn't. "She had *conviction*. You must admire that."

Agnes looked at Ethan to see what he thought of Matias as a suspect. Ethan shrugged. People were clapping, and Matias let go of the microphone and said he would open it up to anyone who wanted to speak. "She loved parties and people speaking their minds. So please do so." He walked to the back of the room.

Below the table Ethan passed Agnes his cell phone. Agnes expected him to show her something about Matias, some bit of info he'd found, but instead the screen was open to Evie's page on IMDb. She was twenty-seven and had four recent credits on popular TV shows. Agnes had heard of them but hadn't watched. There were also appearances on several shows she'd never heard of at all and a lead role in the horror movie that had made Ethan drop his voice an octave and stand up straight for the first time in a year. In the photo, Evie was wearing only a black bra, and rivulets of fake red blood ran across her skin.

She glanced back up to see Ethan smirk and wriggle his fingers for the phone back. Agnes clicked the side button so the screen would go dark and Evie wouldn't see what they were sharing. Agnes didn't like how much he was enjoying taunting her.

Cody got up. This was unexpected. He seemed to waver for a moment as though he couldn't decide, then headed toward the stage. He stared out at the room a little longer than was comfortable. He licked his lips. "I'm so sorry for our loss."

It was a weird statement. There was a long moment, and then Emmanuel clapped, and a few others joined in.

"Charlotte . . . she was the one. She was real. Right here." Cody thumped his chest with a fist for emphasis. "She was an artist in her own way, but with people. She molded so many of us. Like terrines." He seemed lost for a long moment before jumping right to a toast. "To Charlotte." He raised his glass, which was already empty.

The crowd echoed: "To Charlotte."

"That was bizarre," Agnes whispered.

Ethan debated. "I wouldn't say he's the next Anthony Bourdain, but it was heartfelt."

A woman Charlotte had worked with through La Musa—not Tabitha—took the stage. Her speech was printed on a piece of business paper, and she read it woodenly without looking at the audience more than once.

"A lot of adjectives but not a lot of emotion," Ethan noted to the table.

"Please stop!" Evie interrupted them a little too loudly. The disturbance at their table caused a couple of heads nearby to turn. Evie leaned closer to Agnes and whispered, "You two are being really shitty. You're not reviewing this like it's a show, are you?"

There was muttering at the table beside theirs, and before Agnes could respond to her, a man with a plate of sliders in front of him leaned over to his wife. "Great, and now here's Mr. Bike Lanes to tell us all how to be better citizens."

Onstage, Jamie was taking the mic: a true politician, looking more comfortable there than anywhere Agnes had seen him. "There's a reason we are all here," Jamie began. "And that's because of Charlotte. More than brave, she was courageous. And her gift was making others courageous. I wouldn't have gone from tech to running for office without her strength."

Agnes turned back and leaned close to Evie. "I've been asked to investigate Charlotte's death. She was probably murdered."

"Very likely by someone here tonight," Ethan added, arching his eyebrow like he was hosting a murder-mystery party.

Evie stared at Agnes, as if she were waiting for the punch line. "Wait, you're serious?" she asked. When Agnes didn't answer, Evie rose from the table with the look of a woman escaping a weird date before dessert dropped. "I'm just going to go to the restroom."

Both Ethan and Agnes watched Evie's exit with hangdog looks until Ethan broke the silence. "Who's going after her?"

Without answering him, she stood and hustled after Evie.

When Agnes entered the restroom, Evie noticeably stepped back from the sink, away from her.

Agnes put her hands up. "Let me explain."

"I don't like dates with someone where that line is spoken. Like, who are you even?"

"I am exactly who I say I am in my profile," Agnes began to assure her, then stopped. "No, I'm not." She grabbed the part of her forehead where the wine sulfates seemed to collect before continuing. "All right, here's who I am. I'm from Michigan. I sang carols and wore dumb sweaters. I was the top of my class; then I came to college here, and I realized everyone else was the top of *their* class. Now I work in publishing, and I'm mediocre at best. But then this thing happened. Someone tried to kill my best friend."

Evie's golden brown eyes widened. "I want to be sure here. It wasn't you?"

"No," Agnes said. "I solved it. And I think I'm good at that, and I'm going to go with it. Have you ever had a friend who was a lawyer, then they opened a bakery and they were happier?"

"But instead of scones, for you it's murder?"

"I like scones too." Agnes laughed. "I'm normal. Maybe I should stop falling in love with the victims, but you know, baby steps with a new career, right?"

Before Evie could say anything else, Whitney entered. She looked at the two women with an acknowledgment that some kind of discussion was occurring. Whitney smiled, walked past them, and disappeared into a stall.

Evie followed Agnes's sight line. It was clear she knew that Agnes wanted to wait. Whitney knew Charlotte well and would be worth talking to.

Evie reached in her backpack and handed Agnes foundation. She whispered, "Look natural. Be doing something when she comes out." Evie kissed her on the cheek and ducked into the other stall, leaving Agnes to her performance.

For a brief second, Agnes felt the wet smudge, like a badge of courage on her skin.

Then, as Whitney emerged from a stall, Agnes pumped some of the foundation into her hand and spread it over her face. Agnes rubbed it in gently. She glanced over as Whitney washed her hands in the sink next to her. One finger bore a ring with a large black rectangular stone and looked very similar to the necklace Charlotte had worn. "I love the ring."

"Thanks. It was a gift." Whitney gave a thin smile, as if she was having a hard time making small talk.

"Didn't Charlotte have something similar? Was it a set?"

"Oh? I don't think so. A good friend brought this to me from Brazil. You know, onyx is a very popular stone."

"It's very pretty."

Whitney seemed to soften. She stretched out her hand in front of her and admired the ring. It had a silver setting that took all the space to her knuckle. "I love that it protects me from evil intentions."

"Sorry, what?"

"Onyx. One of its properties is spiritual protection. If you believe in that?" Whitney arched an eyebrow in the mirror.

Agnes could roll with astrology and sage smoke easy enough, and crystals were pretty, but her generation's embrace of commercial occultism was getting to be a bit too much. Maybe this group of friends needed an exorcist, not a detective. But she found herself nodding. "Yes—and I'm a Pisces, so I totally feel that," Agnes offered as a bonding point. "I'm very into being protected, spiritually."

"Be careful. It's a Sagittarius moon this month." Whitney dried her hands with a paper towel. "You don't think that had anything to do with Charlotte's death?"

For a moment, Agnes hesitated, unsure if the comedic writer was making a joke. But Whitney's expression said she took astrology as seriously as Agnes took grammar—something that was the underpinning of the universe.

Agnes shrugged. "Can't rule anything out, and we'll see what the coroner says."

"I told her not to wear so much blue," Whitney said, shaking her head. "Not when her aura was so green."

"Let's not victim blame."

"You're right. And there is a connection with the jewelry. But it's personal. I can tell you more at the after-party." Whitney smiled more genuinely as she left the restroom.

There's an after-party? Agnes thought. *As if the memorial isn't exclusive enough.*

Evie popped out of the other stall and looked at Agnes. She gave a thumbs-up.

"I did well?"

"That was improv 101. You agreed with her and used 'Yes, and' statements. Keeps the scene going! What is the deal with the ring?"

"Charlotte had an onyx necklace. Exactly the same."

Chapter Eleven

The speeches were over, and people were milling about in semiconfused formations while the sun set over the Manhattan skyline, visible through two walls of windows. Agnes had noticed the rituals of life and death had gone freestyle recently. Baby showers that came a year after the baby was born, weddings where the cake was ditched and first dances were done last. Now she found herself at a funeral with a rumored after-party that was going to separate casual mourners from the insiders. She desperately needed to find out the address.

"I get 'Yes, and' *onstage*, but how do I really apply that to a nonacting situation? I can't just go around spouting BS at this thing," Agnes said to Evie as they wove around looking for Ethan.

"BS is actually a beautiful tool. You're just building on what someone else says. Think of it as *being creative*." Evie nodded, then said she was going to duck out and find a place to smoke.

Evie went downstairs to vape while Agnes continued looking for Ethan. She was thinking about more *yes, and* statements to try out on some of the other people there.

Peering across the room, she saw that Lewis was looking worse than when she'd seen him last—didn't look like he had slept since Saturday. He'd put on a suit, but his manner was one of agitation as he spoke with Emmanuel. Lewis kept pulling a hand through his hair. At first, Agnes thought he was trying to restyle it; then she realized it was a habit, a *tell* of his frustration. She slid through the crowd, hoping to hear what had irritated him.

"When would I have time? You *know* I was out of the state," Lewis was retorting as Agnes wedged herself into a cloister of women, trying to blend in, her back to the men.

She bet Lewis and Emmanuel wouldn't notice her—and they didn't. She nodded as Madi talked about a shopping app: "You get the box, try things on, take what you want, put back anything that doesn't work for you, and just send it back!"

Behind her, Emmanuel had folded his arms across his chest. "I know that a five a.m. flight to Austin doesn't cover your ass between eleven and four—that's what I know."

Lewis ran his hand through his hair again. But in spite of his agitation, he dropped his voice and leaned in, hissing, "I was on assignment. I literally didn't know she had died until *twenty-four hours later*."

"I feel like *twenty-four hours later* is an exaggeration for a journalist. You may have been out of the city for work, but I doubt you were away from your phone for more than ten seconds." Emmanuel smiled, but not in a kind way.

"I wasn't here, and I'm not dangerous. What's dangerous is what *you* started."

Behind her, she felt as though the conversation had ended, but she didn't understand why. Then she saw Lewis storming out onto the balcony, pushing the door open so fast it bumped Whitney, who was standing outside in the orange light with Hugo.

Emmanuel turned and, seeing Agnes, grabbed her arm. "Come with me."

Oh Jesus.

He pulled her quickly out of the event space and into the coat check room across from the elevator. Just from his grasp she felt how big he was—he would no doubt leave bruises—and it took a second after she tried to pull away from him for Emmanuel to let go. He was cross and sweating. "You've been kicking hives, and you don't know a honeybee from a wasp, do you?"

"I don't know what you mean," she protested, forgetting all about her *yes, and* breakthrough.

"I see through your whole H&M disguise. You went to see Veronica after I told you not to! Everyone is talking, and everyone is on edge."

"Yes, maybe I did. You practically pointed at her in a lineup," Agnes said.

"No. I said she's a wild card. That's not the same thing."

"You're parsing now because she's funding your play." Agnes noticed he didn't correct her. "She's buying up friends from that night."

"She's not even in the club," he said.

Agnes felt a chill run down her arms at the words *the club*. She'd heard that phrase before from a few of the men. She hadn't thought enough about it . . . a golf club, a social club: it could have been anything. A *clique*, Lewis had called it. But now, with Emmanuel glaring down at her, his eyes shiny and his body practically vibrating, it clearly carried weight.

Emmanuel knew he had let something out. He audibly hissed the word "*Shit*."

Agnes drew in a breath and remembered it wasn't lying; it was *being creative*—at least according to the two or three improv tips Evie had tossed her way before going off for her vape. Agnes fixed him with a stony stare. "I know about the club."

"You do?" Emmanuel seemed momentarily relieved. He leaned back against the wall, then stopped himself since it was mostly coat hangers holding linen suit jackets. "Of course you do. People underestimate you. They trust you because they think you don't see the angles to play."

Agnes nodded. "It has strangely worked out well for me." *Do I really believe that? Or do I just want him to talk?* She supposed she did believe it. "Maybe trust isn't overrated."

"No, don't say that." Emmanuel raised his head. "Don't trust anyone here, especially the men."

Agnes had a flash of who had been at Emmanuel's table: Lewis and Anthony. She imagined circling their names in a thick red marker.

"It was only a game," Emmanuel was saying. "A creative-writing thing for Sunday nights instead of being hungover."

Agnes remembered her YouTube master class training. *Let people talk. A pot can't wait to boil.* She nodded like a therapist and said nothing.

"You already know Charlotte was pushed, don't you?" Emmanuel whispered.

Agnes's mouth went dry. She tried to say *yes, and,* but Emmanuel stopped her with a sound—a large, moist sniff back that didn't seem as if it should come from someone as styled or gym hardened as he was. His eyes had misted. He put out a hand and waved it around as if he couldn't breathe.

"Lewis?" she asked.

When Emmanuel could speak, he said, "It's not him. It's *me.* This is all my fault."

Then he sobbed hard, a mushy hiccup. She gripped his shoulder. Two people passed the coatroom and looked in: they saw a man grieving, a woman giving solace.

In Agnes's ear, Emmanuel shuddered out, "I didn't kill Charlotte, but I wrote her death. I swear it was only a game."

She grabbed Emmanuel by the forearms. "Tell me all of it."

He took a shaky breath. "*I* was the one who wrote the plan this time. After a party, because then the scene is already compromised. There are too many prints. The toxicology is going to show it *could* be an accident. Everyone will be drunk, which means we're all unreliable witnesses. But I didn't do it. I was *plagiarized!*"

"You can't copyright a murder." Agnes glared up at him.

"I was inspired by Thomas De Quincey. His essay 'On Murder Considered as One of the Fine Arts.' It was only a mental exercise. I mean, at the time."

"The window in her place was broken. You knew that," she accused.

Emmanuel nodded, acknowledging his lie at the theater. He had known she had fallen—one of the first things he'd said to Agnes. Even more than getting his phone back that morning, he'd been concerned about Charlotte.

The playwright pulled out his phone and spent a moment tapping. Then he passed her a message, already open. Agnes scanned it quickly.

RE: JULY VICTIM PROPOSAL #3

My Magnificent Murderers!

All the proposals this month were nefarious and scandalous! They truly heeded the most important rule of The Perfect Murder Society: *There is no such thing as the perfect murder.* But it seems like Proposal #3 has garnered the most support, and that means a lot to me! (Tee hee). I've collated below the strongest feedback from the chat to help inform our final vote.

"A single woman in New York with some fame and money and too many people declaring themselves her BFF. AKA: She's a needy, walking disaster. Then there's the messy dating life. That increases the pool of suspects exponentially. And that's only if they even think it's a murder, and this plan is really good about obscuring that."

"After a party! Brilliant! She'll be drunk, and, knowing her, there'll also be some other surprises in the tox report. Detectives can be assholes about victims, especially at 4 a.m., and this proposal rides that bias right to shore. Her 'lifestyle' alone will be 50 percent of getting the cops into the 'doomed woman' narrative as quickly as possible."

"1. Very New York. 2. The method of death will play into the narrative that this is one more tragedy—not a murder."

"What I really like about this proposal is it incorporates mistakes into the plan. Like we say in our meetings: *every murder has one*. This one is a game changer."

P.S. I don't mean to end this email on an uncomfortable or weird note but I did float everyone's registration fee last year to get this started and an encrypted server and message board is not cheap. I still haven't received all the funds back. My Venmo is linked below. Have a great Fourth this weekend!

"You wrote this to the club?" Agnes stared at the screen in her hand. She'd had his phone and *given it back*. The police could have even had it from that first hour onward . . . if they'd believed her that it might have been foul play. But just as one of the members had predicted, the cops loved their doomed-woman idea.

"Last winter, we started with celebrities, but we got bored with fake overdoses," he whispered.

"You had fun making these plans?" She could hear her voice rise.

"It was fun until people we knew were put into the fantasy list. I didn't start the trend, but I played along."

He chose her to play the victim because she didn't get back to him quickly enough, Agnes realized. It was Emmanuel who had texted Charlotte that time at the gallery, wanting the funding. She had the funds, but she took her time with these things. *With Veronica. With Chase. With Emmanuel.* Charlotte was dead because he'd been impatient. And because someone else had stolen the idea.

The notion of a secret social circle who knew Charlotte and had taken delight in details of her imaginary death, and then hadn't come forward with them after the fact, was disgusting. Agnes ran her fingers over her lips as if she wanted to wipe away the conversation itself. But Emmanuel kept talking . . .

"I don't know why I put Charlotte in there. Maybe I was angry at her; she was always stalling on paperwork, and then I had to chase her, and when I saw how good the plan was . . . Do you know the feeling of being proud of your work?"

Emmanuel had seemed nervous at the theater when she'd returned the phone. *It was because he was hiding this. When he took me away from the cast into the theater, did he want to tell but then held back?*

"After she died, I didn't know what to do." Emmanuel breathed in through his nostrils, and they flared. He was summoning his ability to confess more, but she could see it was a struggle. "The club members are anonymous, except for me. We both know how that looks right now."

"Was Charlotte pulling out of your play?" Agnes said, hoping he'd tell her she was wrong.

"Some days it felt like that. But I didn't kill her," Emmanuel said, his voice now steady and clear.

"I need to see the actual plan," she stated firmly. "How did you invite people if it's anonymous?"

Emmanuel nodded. "I started it. Then the next person invites someone in. It's a chain, and it's all encrypted."

"That's a lot of effort to hide something you think is just a fantasy league."

"Do you know how hard it is to be creatively free right now? Secret societies were always about the thrill of getting away with something. People joined the Perfect Murder Society for the same reason they joined Dead Poets Society—for the joy of being a little shit again without it ending up on Facebook."

"Wait. The acronym is PMS?"

He sighed. "We only realized it after."

Pays to have women in the room, Agnes thought. But the idea was so bizarre, like a dark-universe Wes Anderson trope, it had to be something close to the truth. "Can you tell me the one thing you know for sure?" Agnes asked.

He shook his head. "Don't ask me that."

"Emmanuel, you have to. Who was the first person in the club other than you?"

Chapter Twelve

Anthony Pellerito. Agnes was trying to imagine the polite and normal father as the second member of the Perfect Murder Society. Coming up with a victim's name, devising the method, when, where, how you'd get away with it. Then, like a marketing meeting, circulating ideas, work-shopping, arguing, and voting. Hadn't she been talking to him at the party just before she'd felt the room go sideways? They'd been talking about her article and DIY Detective status.

Could I have been drugged specifically to keep me out of the way? As if I would've donned my professional detective fedora then and there?

There were a million things Agnes needed to know about this club, not least of which was who the other members were. But Emmanuel's friend Wyatt had come into the hall, swinging his head in one direction, then the other. He spotted them in the coatroom and walked toward them.

Agnes could see by the way Emmanuel straightened, his whole countenance shifting into a blank wall, that his friend didn't know anything and he wasn't going to discuss it further now.

"He knows I'm going through something," he said to Agnes. "But he's not in it."

Saving face in front of his friend didn't matter for her—telling Ethan did. And she could see the conversation with her was over.

Emmanuel's expression was unreadable. Wyatt was asking if he was all right, and they were standing close, as if she had ceased to exist.

Emmanuel had come clean and unburdened himself; Agnes knew she could find out more later, and for now she had to will herself onto a balcony to find Ethan. She veered back through the main room toward the side door.

She had a terrible memory of Charlotte's scream the night she fell twenty stories: a balcony was the worst place to be. As Nic tried to hand her a flyer for her music show, Agnes slid past her, and although she nodded and grabbed it, saying "Thanks," she kept moving swiftly. She jammed the flyer into her purse. Heads turned as Agnes burst out onto the balcony.

Standing against the railing, the politician, Jamie, smiled when he saw her. Before she could weave away, he flicked his sneaked cigarette over the edge and stepped toward her.

"Were you looking for me for that talk?" Whereas before the event he'd been preoccupied or annoyed by her, he now seemed eager.

"*Yes . . . and* I, uh, think we should do that. Maybe alone. Another time?"

He raised an eyebrow. "You want to hang out?" Although he hadn't put out vibes at the party, he now looked intrigued.

"Yes, and . . ." Agnes nodded and felt like her head might come unhinged from her neck. She had no interest in a date or being alone with any of the men now—but she also didn't want to lose opportunities. Until she could find out from Emmanuel who else might actually be in the club, it was worth keeping doors open. "Give me your number."

Jamie reached into his suit coat and took out a pen. He fumbled for a piece of paper, then produced a small card. He wrote his number on one of the paler-colored sections of an abstract image. When he handed it to her, smiling, she saw it was a postcard for the Chase Manhattan art show. The number was written in a cloud above the head of a cartoon with *X*s for eyes. Chase's art was as creepy as it was simplistic. She'd seen him inside earlier, at the back, but he hadn't seemed to detach himself from his drink long enough to socialize. Were he and Jamie friends, or was the card like Nic's music flyer, just a tactile bit of spam floating around?

"Okay then," Agnes said, touching Jamie on the shoulder before dodging away. "Looking forward to it." She couldn't believe that to get more information, she was exploiting the male inability to turn down a date if it might lead to sex.

Agnes tried not to jostle elbows of those milling around with their drinks. There were several stragglers out on the wraparound balcony, but the space was narrow for socializing—four feet wide at most. It was eight thirty now, and the sky was bruising with purple and black. It felt too similar to the night of the party, when she and Charlotte had sat, talking intimately, beside her large windows.

Someone was sitting there reading a newspaper, even as the light was fading. No one would throw someone off a balcony when there were people just around the corner, she told herself as she headed for the other end of the terrace.

Near the far end, she saw Evie was against the railing, talking with Lewis, who looked calmer now than he had inside. *So there's Evie; where the hell is Ethan?* she wondered.

Lewis's back was to her and blocked her view. But their body language told Agnes it was casual conversation. The actress looked surprisingly relaxed with a man she'd never met before. Watching Evie's skills in practice gave Agnes pause. She hoped the small flirtation they'd shared in the bathroom earlier hadn't been an act . . . that had been real for Agnes, even if it was just a conversation and a cheek kiss.

Just then, a hand grasped her firmly around the arm, and she felt her body go rigid.

"I've been watching," a voice said in a whisper.

When she turned, she saw it was Ethan. He pulled her back apace, taking her farther away from Evie and Lewis. How had she walked past him without noticing?

"Give them space," he said. "We have things to talk about."

Agnes nodded. "Yes."

In one hand Ethan still gripped a newspaper. She followed him a few feet back toward the small bench where he had been sitting. He'd been holding the paper up, open in front of him, and she'd walked right by, mistaking him for a stranger.

"What's the idea? Are you channeling the Pink Panther?" she asked.

"I love Inspector Clouseau."

She hedged, unwilling to admit she'd been duped. "Original or Steve Martin version?"

Arguing about film detectives was easier than admitting how scared they should be, that she could have made a fatal error, leaving her friends milling on a balcony with a secret society of murder experts. She felt sure Lewis must know about the club based on things he'd said, even if Emmanuel wouldn't confirm it. She wanted to unload to Ethan about the club, but Whitney and Hugo were only a few yards away from them, both holding empty glasses, talking closely as though they'd had too much.

"You're not listening," Ethan insisted. He smacked her with the newspaper like a dog getting trained, but not in the proper way. It drew her gaze back instantly. He whispered, "Rachel said she may be reselling Charlotte's place. The ex-husband has already been talking with her."

"How did you find that out?" Agnes asked.

"Reading the real estate section at a funeral in New York. Classic icebreaker."

Agnes thought of the complexity of Charlotte's finances. Maybe the husband was a co-owner of the condo, but the rest had to be a tangle of trusts and foundations. *The rich don't live like us, and they sure don't die like us,* she thought. There were also Charlotte's active businesses. The art gallery. The restaurant. *Cody said that Tusk would be fine.* Yet business interests seemed irrelevant, in conflict with what Emmanuel had told her.

Unless it wasn't. *Who can be in a fictional murder club and also profit? Why do they need to be mutually exclusive?*

For Emmanuel to be on the phone with Veronica within hours of Charlotte dying—no matter who called whom—his stage production wasn't any viable part of Charlotte's business. He wasn't safe. He wasn't covered; her passing jeopardized him rather than benefiting him. That meant he *had* to be telling Agnes the truth. He was thoughtless, but not vicious. In a word, an artist.

Ethan had his phone raised. "Before I forget, I videoed the speeches. Let me AirDrop them, and you can see if anything jumps out at you."

When she peered over at his phone, there were several circles on the AirDrop screen under the word *Devices*: some just names, others with photos. A partly bald, partly silver head—the nose spread out like a boxer's—appeared in one of the circles. She gasped.

"The heavy," he said softly.

Agnes looked around but didn't see the guy. The muscle they believed Veronica hired. They peered back through the glass to the event hall. The man wasn't there, and yet his phone was obviously close by, maybe just around the corner. He had an unmistakable face.

"You can't use that word. It's . . . loaded," she corrected. "There are a lot of large-framed men who don't do the bidding of wealthy villains."

"Let's hope so." Ethan swiftly moved toward Lewis and Evie. He was as scared as her and wanted to get far away from the digital ghost of a guy whose iPhone was apparently *BearDen78*. Somehow the handle didn't make him any less threatening.

"Goon . . . is that word any better?" Ethan asked while striding toward the far end of the balcony.

"*Goon* is fine, culturally speaking." Agnes attempted to sound rational as they rushed along. "*A Visit from the Goon Squad*. I mean, that won a Pulitzer."

She couldn't think whether there was another door on the other side or if the balcony was about to abruptly stop. A door to get back inside was a long shot. As they hurried past, Evie raised her head questioningly. Lewis was rubbing her shoulder in a familiar way now. Agnes fleetingly hoped she didn't *yes, and* too much. Around the far corner, the balcony went three more feet, then stopped. But there was a ladder going up one more level, steel built into the brick, in case of fire.

"There's a gym on the floor below us in this building. Maybe that's where he is?" Ethan argued.

But Agnes's hands were already grasping the metal rungs. She stepped on the first rung and looked back. Beyond the balcony, it was five stories down: below them, a weed-studded rectangle of concrete and, beyond that, the East River.

"Agnes!" Ethan's voice was panicked. "Let's check one more time. I think capering in real life can lead to death."

Ethan popped open AirDrop again. Only one circle appeared—the one with Agnes's face in it.

As they made their way back inside, Agnes carefully monitored the remaining milling guests. She saw that the neon flyers Nic had been passing out now littered the tables. She was using the memorial as a networking event, the same way the other women had continued to use it as a dating pool. With no trace of the goon—that was his acceptable name now—Ethan left to do work at home. Lewis and Evie had disappeared somewhere.

Agnes noticed Anthony looked as though he was flirting with a petite brunette at the bar. Agnes felt her eyes narrow. She saw Anthony differently after Emmanuel's confession. The woman had been at the salon, but Agnes couldn't remember her name. She was sure she was a fashion editor at a magazine; she now recollected she'd overheard Jamie pressuring her to write up the salon that night: "Art and fashion have always been friends. Add a dash of 'finding love in the city' to that, and you've got a perfect article for your audience."

A slideshow of Charlotte's face was projecting on the wall like an installation video, and some of the women seemed to be gathered there, watching and signing a guest book on a gallery-style plinth. It was like two rituals meeting, mourning and art exhibition all at once.

The crowd had thinned substantially. The celebrity guests had left, and now it was likely those who knew Charlotte more intimately. A server was picking up empty glasses and asked Agnes if a vodka shot sitting on the table closest to her was hers. It looked untouched, so she picked it up and downed it. Agnes closed her eyes and felt the fire of the drink lick her throat as images of Charlotte danced across the room. Charlotte in a suit. Charlotte on a horse, maybe on vacation. Charlotte in a short skirt. Charlotte in a selfie with Whitney. Blonde Charlotte. Brunette Charlotte. Charlotte in a creamy-white blouse, her clavicle like music. Charlotte laughing with her head thrown back.

Agnes breathed deep, feeling renewed purpose. She surveyed the room for who else was left: Chase was slumped at a table, his head down, a glass clutched in his hand, though the alcohol was probably the lightest drug he'd done that night; Derek Anand was standing nearby, in conversation with Alexander, a Russian party boy she had met briefly at Charlotte's.

"Ah, you tried my vodka," Alexander said. "It's good, yeah?"

"Yeah. Did you tell me a story at Charlotte's about the TV show *Friends*?" she asked. It was just a whisper of a memory.

"Yeah, yeah."

"Tell me again?"

Alexander said in heavily accented English, "I went out to LA. I said I want to act. They said, 'You can't act. You have an accent.' I said, 'What do you mean—I spent one whole week watching *Friends* marathon; now I sound like Joey Tribbiani, no?' They say there is only porno and hopelessness for me in LA. So I come back here. Now I'm businessman. No regrets."

"That's it." She smiled. "I knew it was funny." But she could see that in fact he was quite serious about it.

"How is your work going?" Derek asked, catching her gaze, raising his thick dark eyebrows.

Agnes startled that he would be so open about it. But when she met his assessing stare, she saw he wasn't really asking. He was signaling her that he wanted a check-in. She nodded. "Good. Busy."

"How many stories do you think there are in your building?" Alexander said, watching the various Charlottes dance on the projection wall across the room.

"Oh, there are twenty stories," Derek said. "It is one of my family's largest buildings in Brooklyn. Twenty-one if you count the rooftop garden."

"No, my friend." Alexander's lips parted in a smile, and he lifted his glass, as if toasting Derek's confusion. "Stories, um, what is the word I want? Experiences? I mean about *her*." His eyes glanced up at Charlotte's image. "Everyone has one. I met Miss Bosch at a club. She danced with me even though she was there with . . ." Alexander gestured vaguely, as though he didn't remember. "Someone else."

The idea of Charlotte dancing with Alexander, even for fun, made Agnes's head spin. Or perhaps it was the vodka, which she'd drunk too fast.

Miss Bosch, she realized he'd said. Alexander had called Charlotte by her old name. Her discarded family name. "What do you do again?" she asked Alexander. "You're in business?"

Alexander exchanged a glance with Derek and said in a cagey way, "Party promoter."

Hugo joined the conversation just as her phone chimed. The text was from Evie South Williamsburg: Waiting for you at after-party. It's at TUSK. Leonardo DiCaprio is here! Big into art.

"Sharing stories about Charlotte?" Hugo asked. "I could talk all night," he said with a subtle head nod.

"It seems like there's another party?" she asked the three of them, but their faces were blank.

Then Hugo said, "Sign the memory book first."

"Oh yes," Agnes said. "Of course."

"Do you know Hugo?" Derek asked her. "He lives at the Kentwood."

Hugo nodded. "Five Twelve."

Agnes realized the condo number meant he was a few floors above her unit. *It was him at the window that night,* she thought. Hugo must have been the one who yelled down at her to shut up her dog. The one who had to have called 911. But did that mean he couldn't have been with Charlotte? Or did it mean she hadn't actually fallen twenty stories? If he was her latest love, it made sense she would have been with him, didn't it?

At the book plinth Agnes picked up the pen. She paused. On the opposite page was a long description that the fashion editor—who she saw now was named Sofia Stone—had written about Charlotte's impact on her career. Jamie had written: *Friend, anchor, nonchalant nonpareil. Mentor, muse, immutable. You will be missed by so many.* And his name. She turned the words over in her mind. She supposed a politician ought to be able to conjure a bit of trite poetry if he expected to stand on city stages.

I need this book, Agnes thought, flipping a few pages and seeing that others had taken time to write recollections, often about how they'd met her or her impact. It would help her untangle Charlotte's web—who knew whom and how. She looked around. The room was definitely dwindling, probably due to word spreading about the after-party. She shook her head thinking of Evie, invited out of the blue and already there. *Some people fit in no matter where they are.* Agnes wondered if they knew how lucky they were.

She looked up, scanning the event space for cameras. The building was reno'ed but old. Hanging from the wooden ceiling were painted pipes and sprinklers. No cameras.

Her purse wasn't going to be big enough. She took off her linen jacket and draped it around the hardcover book.

Chapter Thirteen

As the Uber left Greenpoint behind and headed up toward the Queens-Midtown Tunnel for Manhattan, Agnes tried to think about who had been left in the room at the end and who might have been in Emmanuel's deeply nerdy and potentially lethal club. Unfortunately, *deeply nerdy and potentially lethal* described most of the men at the memorial, if not her life. Matias had started the speeches but was gone before they were even over. She hadn't seen Jamie since their balcony exchange. Hugo was still there in the final hour, and Charlotte had been dating him. She didn't know if his aside that he could talk all night was an offer or threat. Whitney was there at the end too—and she'd been at every salon since the beginning, probably as in-house astrologer.

"I'm starting to feel like I don't know anything." Agnes muttered the thought as she flipped through the pages of the guest book. The light was limited in the car, though.

Agnes pulled up Emmanuel's number. I need more, she typed.

The men in the club mattered, but she couldn't stop thinking about the jewelry Charlotte and Whitney both had. It was a simple detail, but one that nagged at her.

Above the door of the restaurant was the boar's head icon that appeared on the matchbook Agnes hadn't known was from Tusk. It was a suspended heavy-looking metal head, two piercing tusks on either side of the long metal snout. Eye catching. The kind of thing you definitely wouldn't want to stand under in a windstorm. Though tucked into the first floor of an overpriced hotel, the restaurant wasn't discreet in any way. Cody clearly wanted to stand out. She recalled someone at the party the week before telling her the approach was punk butcher shop, though at the moment all she could hear was the thump of Top 40 dance music. Marketing versus reality was the daily battle in New York.

Unlike at the memorial, here there was no greeter and no guest list. Inside the restaurant, the vibe was a curated eclecticism. As her eyes adjusted, she saw the walls were an unexpected deep brown, and a taxidermy head hung over a bar in the back. Although there were touches of pale green to lift the room (velvet avocado-hued curtains, the banquette's seat cushions) and one wall painted with large leaves in a kind of chunky tattoo style, the overall feel was masculine tough. An old-fashioned leather-covered door with a round window separated the kitchen. This felt like a contradiction to Agnes, as she would've thought Cody might be the type with an open prep area—longing to be seen. As it was, he was just coming through the door to set down a large tray, heaving with meats, at a table near a circle of familiar faces.

Gathered around were Sofia, Anthony, Nic, Lewis, and Chase, whom she was not expecting to see, as he'd looked about to fall asleep on the table at the memorial. She spotted Jonathan, the finance bro who could moonlight as a model. She'd seen him only upon arrival at Charlotte's, and now he was standing alone, bopping his head while scrolling his phone. His word had been *indelible*, yet although she had put him on their long list, he'd fallen entirely from her memory.

The lights were dim, and the DJ in the corner was playing to a room not packed enough to justify the volume. There were perhaps fifteen people there—a sliver of the number at the memorial—and not one of them was Leonardo DiCaprio. As Agnes watched Cody carefully remove his strong hands from the tray, laden with the chunks of roast, potato, and tomatoes, she realized he would never have been in the Perfect Murder Society. As much as he ran in the world of money and media, he knew what real work was. His hands showed it. He would never be into the club's schoolboy games. *Besides, if Cody murdered someone, it would be with knives.*

Agnes suddenly felt she understood what it must have been like to be in the society Emmanuel had described: to fixate on the macabre and explore its logic. She disliked how easy and human it was. She startled visibly when Evie touched her shoulder. She gave Agnes a confused look.

"You okay?"

"Um, yes."

Evie gestured to the book under Agnes's jacket. "What's that?"

"It's a long story."

Leonardo was long gone, but according to Evie, he had seemed genuinely upset by the death of Charlotte, one of his favorite art dealers. He'd then flirted with Evie and asked who her agent was. Agnes could see she was still on cloud nine. Evie said she'd go up to the bar and get her a drink.

Agnes watched as she went over; the bartender from Charlotte's party worked here, she noted. She saw that Anthony, the second member of the club, was there and talking up Cody's girlfriend, Keira, at the bar. Anthony came off as nice but was clearly one of those people who came with fine print that needed to be examined. She watched as he wrapped up his conversation with Keira and collected two new drinks from the bar. Agnes was about to follow when she felt a hand on her elbow. It was Lewis.

He leaned in. His breath smelled burned, like scotch and cigarettes. "Who do you think you are? You seem to get everywhere, whether you're invited or not."

For a moment, Agnes wondered if Lewis considered her a threat. But he wasn't wearing his investigative reporter hat just then. He was drinking, not pawing through his notebook. If anything, he looked exhausted, and she thought back to Emmanuel's words at the memorial: "Everyone is talking, and everyone is on edge."

What was it about her being here that made him nervous? Agnes decided to use his concern to her advantage. If she operated on a presumption of innocence for Lewis, it might be beneficial. Unlike the others, she hadn't yet come up with a way to link him to Charlotte in business, and out of all the party guests, he knew her the most intimately.

She nodded at Anthony. "I'll tell you more about me if you tell me about him."

"Him? Not much there. Charlotte's lawyer. Lives on the Upper West, works in Midtown," Lewis said.

This was no trade. Agnes pressed, "What kind of law? Estate?"

Lewis lurched, spilling a bit of his drink. He shook his hand off and set it down on the bar. How had it not occurred to him that Anthony could be a useful contact? Especially if he was interested in Charlotte's assets. Maybe Lewis wasn't as bright as she'd thought he was. Maybe he was like all the men who'd been at Charlotte's—more interested in his own story and hoping it would weave once in a while around some beautiful woman. Or was he hiding something about him and Anthony?

"Her estate's more than he could handle on his own, I'd guess," Lewis said. He was fairly drunk but still talkative. "I knew Tony when he was at the DA's office. The corporate stuff isn't his strong suit."

The DJ was spinning something more ambient now, but it still wasn't easy to talk. Agnes decided to keep the trade of information going and pulled out her phone. Evie was still caught at the bar. For whatever reason she seemed determined to end this crazy night with Agnes.

"Could Matias still be involved in the art dealing?"

Lewis didn't blink. "Could be. He's on payroll, though that doesn't mean he actually does much." He paused, then divulged in a way that told her he'd been wanting someone to share with: "Turns out Chase's work is likely stored at the building we were at tonight. Charlotte's company, La Musa, leases half the second floor. I'd like to take credit for that discovery, but it was one of our other writers. You helped with the tip. Only been leasing it for six months. My question is: *Why* do you know this stuff?" Lewis looked at her with suspicion.

He was asking her about her work; the underlying question was why she was scouting around and who had hired her. She shrugged. "People talk; I listen."

Lewis glanced at Evie at the bar, where she was nursing a drink and holding the other. "Your friend barely seems to know you. What are you using her for?"

"A mistake—she just showed up," Agnes admitted, though his expression said he thought she was playing a game. If she let him ask the questions, she'd learn nothing. Agnes decided to be bold. "Are *you* in the society?"

"No." Lewis's voice went cold.

She waited. The silence pressured him. He talked.

"They *invited* me. An anonymous email. At the time I thought it was dumb. Like an emo version of Soho House."

The music softened and then stopped. The DJ took off his head-phones. He seemed to be wrapping up or taking a break.

When Agnes glanced over at the bar, she saw Evie exchanging phone numbers with Keira.

"*Actresses*," Agnes audibly hissed.

Lewis picked up his drink again and cradled it in his palm. "You mean Charlotte? Don't fall in love with an actress. It will only end tragically," he advised.

Why did he think Charlotte was acting? She'd kept things from him—but wasn't she still herself? She'd noticed he had sidestepped, avoided saying whether he thought the murder society was responsible for an actual murder. But Agnes didn't get a chance to ask more. Lewis's face had taken on a stony look as he stared across the restaurant. When she turned, she saw that Veronica had come in, her hair styled down this time, a long black dress floating around her as she moved across the space.

To Agnes's eye, Veronica looked uncomfortable, as if she wanted to keep to the edges of the party and not get stuck talking to one person. It was hard to say whether a hush had come over the room or if it was just the absence of music after having had it pounding for the past hour. Agnes was still a bit afraid of Veronica—she'd seen what she could do to a good coif—but she'd already had several spikes of adrenaline in the evening, and now her mood steered toward curiosity. She was interested in seeing what others thought of Veronica's presence. In her mind, the group of people who had been at Charlotte's salon were starting to form a Venn diagram. There were places where the social circles overlapped and places where they didn't touch at all. Charlotte-Jamie-Veronica, that was one piece because of the financial. There were others where it was sexual—Charlotte-Lewis-Chase. That also meant Hugo was adjacent. Then there were the women. Veronica-Charlotte-Whitney: one of those trios of women that always seemed to have a life span, shifting from being powered by joy to being powered by jealousy.

As Veronica swept past her without a glance and reached the bar, Agnes took a look to see who was still gathered and who was missing. Jessica had found her way there, which Agnes registered as bold if she and Cody had hooked up only a week ago without Keira's knowledge. Hugo hadn't come. Neither had Alexander, Tabitha, or Whitney. Derek, similarly, wasn't there—likely he'd never been invited. Agnes had noticed her old landlady kept being recommended to her as a friend by Facebook, and Agnes kept clicking past. She suspected people maybe felt that way about Derek too. No one wanted to be friends with the person who literally had the keys to their homes.

Keys. Who else has a key card for Charlotte's? Agnes wondered.

She turned and watched as Veronica now argued in a low tone with the bartender. It was obviously a disagreement, because Veronica bent forward over the bar, and her expression never lightened. Agnes couldn't hear what they were saying, but Evie was still standing at the bar. She tried to give Evie a look that said *Listen in.* But sending commands with her eyes wasn't working with a woman she'd met only that evening.

Evie only smiled at her with those large liquid eyes that had no doubt earned her such decent jobs. Agnes wasn't trying to flirt. She needed her to pay attention—an unfair expectation, of course. Evie wasn't a detective's widow yet.

Agnes would have to do it herself, she decided. Making up her mind not to talk too much, or at all, she strode to the bar and stood just a couple of feet away from Veronica. The bartender turned their attention to Agnes, which told her immediately that they didn't want to continue to argue with Veronica. They were avoiding something. Agnes ordered a margarita. She was sure this time they'd have the ingredients, but more than that, it took time. And she wanted to see what exactly Veronica would do in that gap of space.

The bartender's hands were fast but shaky—Veronica had that effect. Agnes pretended to watch the preparation, but out of her peripheral vision, she noticed Veronica scrolling through her phone. If she'd recognized Agnes at all, she was pretending not to. Thankfully Jessica and Nic were in between them, Jessica leaning back against the bar for support as if her three-and-a-half-inch heels had become wearying. Now that the DJ had stopped playing, the air felt oddly still and flat—there was a Janelle Monáe track, "Only Have Eyes 42," playing from a small bar speaker, but it was mellow, and the volume hadn't been cranked up, as if the bartender had also wanted to spare their hearing.

Nic was saying, "I swear . . . she had sex toys hidden around the place the same way Republicans have guns hidden everywhere: under the pillow, nightstand, wicker baskets, in the bread box."

"Bizarre to know that about your boss," Jessica said.

Agnes's gaze flicked past them. Veronica had now put the cell to her ear. "Matias, you said you'd be here," she said urgently. "I have the SUV outside with the paintings . . . Can I get your shit out of my home and my money back now, pretty fucking please?"

As the bartender handed Agnes her finished drink, she missed what came next in the conversation. Veronica had already clicked off. Why had Veronica brought the art with her?

Anthony waved Agnes over before she could move to rejoin Evie, who nodded down at the drink she held for Agnes, then shrugged and took it for herself, having already finished her own.

When Agnes approached him warily, he asked if he could get her number or email. He said he had a cousin who had written a book and might like some editorial advice. "Isn't that your business? When you're not, I don't know, making celebrity appearances?"

She realized she was now more than a little uncomfortable with people referencing her new line of work, given Lewis's earlier interrogation and Emmanuel's warning for her to stop talking. She suspected Anthony knew what she knew and, in a lawyerly way, was hoping to get ahead of any fallout. She gave Anthony her number but kept her glass close against her chest and her eyes on his hands at all times.

"Hey, Burning Man!" Veronica screeched over at the bar. "Are you going to give me a fucking drink or what?" The bartender put their hands up in defeat and left. This wasn't Veronica working her daytime charm in a pied-à-terre. This was Veronica of uptown legend: a flame-thrower full of gin that no one says no to.

Anthony raised his eyebrows at Agnes. "Quitting time," he said. "I'll text you." He set his empty beer down.

Cody was there now, inserting his body in between Veronica and the bar and subtly pushing her away. It was done with precision, but Veronica was now stumbling back into Evie. Agnes moved closer.

"I'm the reason you got that *Grub Street* review, and you won't even serve me?" Veronica kept balanced on tall Fendi heels as if she were willing herself not to be drunk.

Evie looked at Agnes. *Can we go?* Agnes held up a finger. *One moment.* On the plus side, they had already achieved nonverbal communication with each other on the first date.

Cody rolled his eyes like an annoyed parent. "Blake won't serve you because you stiffed them on your New York Film Festival party. Pay them," he scolded.

So Blake is the bartender's name, Agnes realized. She was also beginning to realize the rich sure had a problem paying their bills.

"Why don't *you* pay that *ass-faced* twink? Use her money. She was laundering it here," Veronica slurred, and if Agnes had learned anything that night, every *she* referred to Charlotte. No one was talking about anyone except her. It was as though her party had continued—she was still the host, laughing, at the center of things, even if they couldn't see her. "Or did you spend all of her money?" Veronica added, a drunk beat too late.

"Go home," Cody said.

"Go to hell." Veronica wound up her arm for a punch, but her elbow crashed into Evie's nose.

Evie cried out, and her hands covered her face, blood streaming through fingers. Agnes led her away as Veronica, undeterred, jumped on Cody, trying to claw at his face.

Cody twisted Veronica into a bear hug and lifted her off the ground. With his size, he could have thrown her. Agnes might have. But she saw Cody's focused and cool side that likely came out of years spent around knives, fire, and alcohol. He silently and carefully hauled Veronica toward the front door like an entitled hundred-pound sack of flour. At the front windows, red and blue lights were now flashing. Cody kicked the door open with a heavy boot and took her outside. Agnes could see the appeal of Cody in that moment.

Outside the door, she spotted the goon. He put out his hands and lumbered forward to stop Cody from tossing Veronica out. The door swung shut, and Agnes couldn't see what happened next.

Blake came over to where she and Evie were standing, going through a stack of napkins, then handed Agnes a bar towel. "The cops are here."

Chapter Fourteen

On the L train home, Evie tilted her face at Agnes, showing off her swollen nose with touches of dried blood. "How does it look? What if Leonardo's people call me? Am I a character actor now?"

"I don't think it's broken," Agnes assured her.

"You're right. It would probably hurt more. I didn't really expect to go ham tonight," Evie said, smoothing her hair back from her face with her palm.

Agnes had no idea what the phrase meant. It was probably an acronym Agnes would need to secretly google. *Go ham*: Was it sexual? Did it pertain to food?

Not knowing what to say, Agnes just looked into Evie's light-brown eyes. They gazed back, unshy. She leaned in and kissed Evie. "Did that hurt?"

"A little. But you can do it again."

Agnes did, but then she pulled away. "Why did you spend this entire insane night with me?"

"Honestly, I have a callback for a series. It's an all-female reboot of *Moonlighting*."

"Great show. Private detectives. So I'm research?"

"That. And you're kind of exciting. That's what I realized after our talk in the bathroom."

"Are you playing the Cybill Shepherd character or the Bruce Willis character?"

"I don't really know those names. They're not in the script."

Agnes kissed her again. Evie tasted like salt, honey, and blood. She was surprised that after everything that had happened, the idea of making human contact was still there. Agnes knew it was partly the alcohol, the whirl of her thoughts, and the half-empty train hurtling forward through the night. Agnes missed her stop.

Getting out a stop too far, she felt a strange tenderness as they separated fingers, and she left quickly, hopping onto the platform without a real goodbye. She waved but didn't know if Evie saw.

Agnes thought of Ezra Pound's poem about the subway, the strangers whose faces were "Petals on a wet, black bough."

She climbed the stairs and exited into the hot, clamoring mouth of Williamsburg, scenesters still drifting past, 2:00 a.m. buzzy. She had to weave through a few extra blocks, but soon she was home and could walk an eager Hulot. She watched her dog's head dart toward invisible smells. She thought about how powerful the invisible was. How everyone was letting go of their love for Charlotte that night. Everyone except Evie, who had no clue what they were all so caught up about. Maybe that was what made Agnes feel like Evie was so beautiful. That bit of distance from the Charlotte mystery.

When she and Hulot trotted tiredly back through the lobby, she thought anxiously of where the goon might be, especially with Veronica busy at some precinct with her lawyers. Although she was the type who would never get arrested for a bar scuffle, Agnes realized. Her people would handle that for her. Agnes then looked up for the small white dome cameras on the ceiling that made her both secure and anxious. That's when she noticed the red dot on the side entrance camera.

She then stood directly underneath it. A red circle sticker was affixed over the camera's lens. She swiped fitfully at it, but it was still far out of her reach.

The next day Agnes woke, rolled over, grabbed a pencil, and made a top-five list. She made it from her gut—intuition—more than logic. After all, she was barely awake.

a) Veronica
b) Anthony
c) Hugo
d) Lewis
e) Whitney

Something about Anthony had stuck in her head—his lingering at both the memorial and the after-party. Maybe he'd returned after Charlotte's salon. *Lawyers literally invented lying.* The fact that he was in the club also bumped him up onto the list.

She couldn't say why Emmanuel wasn't in the top suspects. He had started the Perfect Murder Society; yet she believed he was deeply unsettled by the loss of Charlotte and the use of his plot. That alone made her think someone else. Lewis was assigned to write about Charlotte, but there was something deeper to his questions: a worry beyond Agnes finding out things before he did. Veronica and Chase both had serious financial issues with Charlotte. And Chase may have also had a jealousy issue. But . . . was he a member of the club? He was part of the arts industry along with Emmanuel, but Chase was not the most verbal of thinkers. She had found an old article Chase wrote for *Vice* about smuggling MDMA in his butt while traveling. It was only a few paragraphs, mostly photos of him and members of *Jackass* wearing rubber gloves.

Agnes blinked, and Hulot jumped up beside her and curled against her thigh. She had left some people off entirely. Matias, for instance, and Jamie. Matias had mentioned her being a member of the club, but when she replayed the conversation in her mind, she thought he meant it more generally, Charlotte's "fan club." She'd left out Rachel, whom Ethan had said could benefit. She stared at Hugo's name, ranked at an impressive but still noncommittal number three. "It's always the boyfriend or husband," she said aloud. "Except when it isn't." The fact that

Hugo's windows faced the same side of the building as where Charlotte had fallen was an interesting coincidence, though.

At number five she included Whitney Astor-Barnes for gender balance as much as the jewelry she shared with Charlotte. Whitney had also been the one to bring her the first drink, though Agnes couldn't say whether it was that one or the second that had knocked her sideways.

Should I be looking at the bartender? she wondered. But Blake had not struck her as untrustworthy at all at the after-party. They could easily have spiked her drink the night of the salon, but they'd done nothing at Tusk to arouse Agnes's suspicion, so she left them off.

After pulling on clothes and snapping Hulot's leash on his collar for his morning outing, Agnes went out into her hallway. As she did, she looked up at the cameras. On her floor they were red-dot-free. But as she and Hulot made their way into the elevator, there it was on the elevator's camera, stuck over the lens. This one she could reach, and she plucked it off. She examined the red sticker on her fingertip before placing it on her wallet for safekeeping.

She and Hulot had their regular park jaunt, and as they returned from their walk, she chucked the dog's poo bag into a trash can along Kent Avenue.

There's another thing that keeps a record besides cameras, Agnes knew. Trash cans. The landlord at her old apartment building had always gone through the trash, looking for recyclables, but also to keep tabs on people. And so, after putting Hulot back inside her unit, at 7:05 a.m., Agnes pressed the "B" button for the basement.

The garbage room was a series of dumpsters, some positioned under the chutes that led in. Agnes stood, listening to a faraway *thump* and *whoosh*, then watched as a bag emerged from a chute and landed with a dusty thud in the large green bin. The place stank like cat litter, old tuna, and death. The smell of single people. It wasn't a place she'd normally choose, especially after staying out late the night before, drinking.

No woman is worth this, she thought. *Not even Charlotte.* She pulled a face mask up and began gingerly picking through a bin, tearing open bags enough to pick through the detritus. Identifiers. That's what she'd need. *Disregard any bags that might be from strangers' units.* It wasn't hard—people tended to throw their junk mail and bills into the trash rather than recycle them, so their names were all over their waste.

After thirty minutes, she found that Hugo used green bags, which he had fastidiously double tied. Most people used tall white kitchen bags or large black garbage sacks. The color distinction helped considerably. Hugo had a lot of takeout orders for someone so slim—it was from these receipts Agnes deduced his trash from the others. He favored mango salads from a Thai place and sandwiches from a nearby deli. Banana peels and orange rinds and coffee grounds. *A condom wrapped in toilet paper, ew.* She stared and tried to shift the contents of the bag without touching that. She was glad she'd thought to grab a pair of yellow kitchen gloves before coming down. A pill container that ought to have been recycled was among Hugo's bags. It bore Charlotte's name, which indicated she'd sometimes stayed in his place. Surprise, the prescribing doctor wasn't Hugo but a Dr. Schwartz. Could that mean Hugo didn't know how many meds were in her cupboard? Paper towels, yogurt containers, a disposable razor. There were other hard, pointy objects in the bottom of the bag: crumpled empty tubes of oil paints in many colors. Takeout lids used as palettes. She'd had no idea Dr. Hugo Desjardins was secretly an artist, likely an amateur if the cardboard and paper remnants he'd sketched on, then discarded, were any indicator.

There was something else of interest—a crinkled photograph of Charlotte. It wasn't current, though—more from an era when people did that, printed out pictures at pharmacies. Was that why it was in the trash? Because it held no significance to Hugo? Or because it had a slight line of indigo paint on it along the bottom? He couldn't have known her when it was taken. She'd described him like someone new in her life. Charlotte looked young here—a decade or more ago. She might have been Agnes's age. She might have still been a Bosch, even.

Her hair was lightened, parted differently, and curly. She was wearing a plum-colored top with a draped collar. Agnes removed a kitchen glove and held it carefully in one clean hand.

Why would Hugo throw this out, especially now that she's gone? Hate? Or is he like most of Charlotte's friends? They loved her easily, but liking her was . . . more difficult.

It was a sad thought. After all, Agnes had known her only briefly but had found her infinitely charming, even *likable*. Even with all she'd since learned about Charlotte, her many flaws, it seemed hard to dispute that fact. Yes, she became excited by people, then lost interest in them. Yes, she didn't always do what she had said she would, or at least not in a timely manner. She overspent, overindulged, overcommitted, and maybe overloved everything. But . . . at the end of the day she had charisma. She was like Agnes's friend Mia that way. Everyone had loved her, and she'd always been at the center of things too.

Staring at the paint-smudged photo, she wondered if people tended to draw the same energy to them again and again. Agnes looked for bold women who were spontaneous and self-assured. Charlotte had sought out challenges, thrills, and even, on occasion, danger.

Agnes had barely spoken to Hugo, but her impression of him was only getting worse. Finding the photograph alone made her mentally boost his name up her list. She smoothed out the picture and placed it in her purse.

Then a bag thumped and dropped into the dumpster next to her, and Agnes tried not to hurl. Whatever was inside it was truly awful. Thankfully the bag wasn't green, as she had no intention of opening it.

Chapter Fifteen

After a long shower, Agnes dressed nicer than usual, as if it would help her shake off the garbage room. Then she went out to nurse her hangover with a watermelon salad and Starbucks. Sitting in a café, she answered emails from work (playing sick was great—why had she never thought of it before?) and listened to another episode of the investigator's master class on headphones, this time without fast-forwarding. She was starting to wonder if she'd always been meant to do this kind of work instead of copyediting mysteries and memoirs. She'd grown up on Nancy Drew, and *Harriet the Spy* had also been one of her favorite novels as a child. In fact, she'd used it to justify constantly creeping through her neighbors' backyards. Luckily for her, she grew up in small-town Michigan, where that sort of behavior was acceptable in twelve-year-olds. The one time she'd been caught, she'd been yelled at, and nothing more, by a grad student one block over whom she called "Billy" because he looked like Adam Sandler. She'd seen *Billy Madison* way too many times.

"I'm spying," she'd whispered back when he'd snapped the screen door open and yelled at her, "Little boy, get the fuck out of that rose-bush." Being misgendered stung because she'd chopped her hair into a short boyish bob after seeing Angelina Jolie as supermodel Gia Carangi in *Gia*, a movie that was definitely too mature for her and left her with the impression that dating women must be terrible. She'd long admired Angelina—ever since *Hackers*. How humiliating to be outed as a spy. Of course, the rosebush was in fact far too bedraggled to provide adequate coverage, probably owing to the fact that it was a student's apartment.

Majoring in psychology and statistics, "Billy" seemed to care more about means and medians than miniflora. He was not the most interesting person she spied on, since he largely sat on a secondhand sofa, smoking and reading, but she was fascinated by the fact that a beer bottle could become an ashtray and a flag a makeshift curtain. Agnes kept a meaningless log of how many bottles could accumulate before they would be cleared from the coffee table. The longest "Billy" went was twelve days and thirty-six bottles. (Though it was hard to count from the porch through the window, the closest she ever got.)

If she used this same methodology to understand Charlotte, or her friends, she reasoned, she had to take judgment out of the equation. As a child, she didn't judge "Billy" for his drinking habits—she was simply fascinated by them. They were facts she could measure.

What are the measurable facts of Charlotte's circle? she asked herself. The similar jewelry Charlotte and Whitney had was a fact. Hugo living in the building, fact. Emmanuel writing the plan after seeing the art at La Musa, fact.

But her head was still spinning with everything she'd learned at Charlotte's memorial, from the weird random snippets of conversation to the kisses with Evie, to the heart-thumping realization that the Perfect Murder Society contained several of the most-ordinary-seeming men from the party.

Social rules said she ought to follow up with Evie, but it was hard while also concentrating on the evidence. *Hi, I had a nice time with you while also completely putting you in danger?* No dating articles would ever advise following up with that kind of text. Maybe *Gia* had prepared her more than she'd thought. In that film, they kissed through a wire fence and wound up falling in love, and because it was old school, there was only voicemail—no phone calls or messages until Gia was dying.

She decided to text Emmanuel again instead. She got a notification that he had silenced his messages. She hadn't gotten that before, which meant he'd seen her last message at least. Emmanuel had left before her on the night of the salon, but Hugo had been there to break up the fight with Veronica.

She texted Derek Anand that she needed access to the camera footage, and later when she returned to the Kentwood, she asked the concierge if he knew where Derek was. The concierge tried to phone, and when Derek didn't pick up, he said to her, "Wait here," and he disappeared for a moment into the Anand Holdings offices.

Agnes stayed, standing at the desk. Behind it was a large painting of flowers—three panels of different colors and different styles of flowers etched in each one. Similar to wallpaper, but it wasn't wallpaper. *Who selects lobby art?* she thought. Then she took her laptop out for a moment and went to Charlotte's gallery's social media account to see if there were any photos of those who had attended the opening of the falling-woman video. Maybe Emmanuel wasn't the only one who had seen it.

As she was standing there, peering at her screen, a man came in, looking around. He was carrying a black folder and a set of keys.

"I have something to leave for Charlotte Bond," he said, walking up to Agnes while bouncing the key fob in his hand.

She realized he'd mistaken her for the concierge because of her open laptop on the station, even though she was on the wrong side of the desk.

"What is it? I work for Charlotte," Agnes said. It wasn't a lie. She hadn't dug through garbage or snuck into an after-party just because Derek had asked her to.

"And she didn't mention that it's drop-off day? We spent all spring working on it," the guy said before offering Agnes paperwork to sign. He opened the folder. He began to spout off all the work that had been done on Charlotte's car. Apparently it was fully restored.

"Um, I hate to ask, but has this—has she already paid you?"

"Sure. Paid in full . . ." He consulted the paperwork and tapped a line at the bottom. "Ten days ago. My associate has been calling all week. She knew we were supposed to deliver it. Why didn't she pick up?"

"Italy. Last minute," Agnes covered.

"Well, I guess if you can, you do." The man handed Agnes the keys and the folder, keeping only the signed receipt for himself. "1965 Alfa Romeo Giulia Spider. Sweet car. You want me to park it for her?"

"No, I got it," Agnes said, her fist closing around the keys.

She saw the concierge reappear at the end of the lobby, but she walked outside to look at the car. It was svelte, red, and perfect. Like something out of an old movie. *The little red dress of the car world,* she thought. It was easy to envision Charlotte in its driver's seat. So she'd had the money for this. *You don't pay off debts to strangers and leave debts to your friends if you're thinking of ending things.* Even through her haze that night, she had never thought the death was anything other than suspicious, but here was definitive proof. Agnes positioned herself in front of the car and lifted her phone for a selfie. She texted it to Ethan. You were right—she had things to live for, she typed.

It was a laid-back little drive. Just around the corner and through the alley. She felt the car purring through the stick shift. Then Agnes found her way into the parking garage and eased the Alfa Romeo into a spot she'd used only for a rental panel van the week she'd moved in.

When she walked back into the Kentwood, Derek was at the desk with the concierge. "There you are. We need to talk," Derek said shortly. He'd been fetched, and then she'd kept him waiting.

Agnes followed him through the lobby. She'd planned to ask him in some covert way whether he knew about the society. But now he seemed so abrupt she put all plans on pause. She hoped he hadn't seen her park Charlotte's car.

Derek walked with intention. He went through a side door into the real estate showroom and then to a small, surprisingly cluttered office at the back. His demeanor didn't invite questions. He gestured for her to sit, and only when they were both seated did he look at her grimly. His eyes were dark and somber. "It's the dog."

"What happened?" Agnes could feel alarm in her voice, and when he didn't answer immediately, she wondered if Hulot had somehow gotten out of the condo or if some accident had occurred.

"Chapman in Three Ten. Upstairs from you. He says there has been . . . a problem."

"Is Hulot okay?" Agnes tried not to jolt out of her seat.

"A barking problem." Derek peered at her as though she were dense.

Agnes felt her face redden. Separation anxiety. She'd had Hulot only a short time, and already she was failing him. She hadn't needed to go out to work that morning.

"Of course, I know you have been busy for good reasons," Derek said, nodding. "But I have to tell the occupant that we spoke about this issue and are working to resolve it." He then held his palm up. "This is your written warning." He then wrote on it with his finger. "And I signed it." He then fluttered his hands as if after a magic trick.

"Oh . . ." Agnes realized Derek was not really warning her—he was simply making her aware. Chapman in 310, he'd said. *Who's Chapman?* she wondered. *Could that be the finance bro who was at Charlotte's salon?* He'd been there at the Tusk after-party. *Jonathan.* She remembered his name, though she hadn't had a chance to speak to him.

"Maybe I could arrange for a friend to come by when I'm out to keep him company?" she tried.

Derek smiled, his whole face changing now. "Probably helpful."

"How many of us live in the building?" she asked him.

"Number of units? Number of people on the leases, or . . . do you want spouses and children?" he asked.

She could see that here Derek Anand had a different mindset than when they spoke elsewhere. Here he was efficient, mathematical. There was none of the casualness she'd seen at the memorial, or when he'd hired her at the Hummingbird Café. Behind him on a crammed set of shelves were many bibelots among the office supplies: a wooden sign that said RELAX, I HAVE A SPREADSHEET FOR THAT, a brass elephant, framed photographs of family members in traditional Indian dress, a dusty snow globe from some vacation. At the same time, in the small chaos, he seemed single minded.

"Just the number of us who were at Charlotte's salon that night who live here in the Kentwood," Agnes pressed.

"Ah!" Derek leaned his head to one side, contemplating it. "This is why we must keep you working." He pulled open a drawer and took out a checkbook. He leaned in and carefully wrote on it and slid it across to her. It was a company check for $10,000. In the memo it said: *Pet deposit return.* Agnes had not paid a pet deposit. "That is separate from the condo fees we agreed to cover. Spend whatever you need."

She looked at the check with uncertainty. Even though he'd set it in front of her, she didn't pick it up right away. It was interesting how Derek had avoided her question by pushing money at her. *Payment, or a bribe?*

"Uh, thank you. I can. And . . ." She didn't want to press, but at the same time, she wanted to know. "There's me, Charlotte, *you*, Hugo on five, and . . . Jonathan Chapman. Was he at Charlotte's late that night—do you know?"

Derek wagged a finger at her. His smile returned. "You know, I think he may have been."

"You don't drink," Agnes said, remembering he'd had soda at the memorial.

Derek shook his head. "No, it's true."

"So you have a clear memory. Clearer maybe than anyone else who was at the salon."

Derek laughed and said he wouldn't say that. He turned in his chair and reached behind him, and for a moment Agnes felt herself grow jumpy. The space was almost too private. There'd been hardly anyone in the showroom when they came through, and this back office seemed purposefully tucked away, with only a high window that showed her the brick wall of the alley. But Derek wasn't reaching for anything unusual. A laptop in a black case was set down on the desk between them.

"This is the only real memory one can count on," Derek said. What if he was going to show her something about the Perfect Murder Society? If so, should she play dumb and pretend not to have heard of it yet? Even though Derek had hired her, there was no saying he wasn't involved.

Derek was wearing a short-sleeved shirt, and she noticed the small dark hairs that covered his forearms as he opened the computer and pulled up an application. Its icon was shaped like a remote control. "Last week, after the police did literally nothing, I asked the concierge to review the footage and tell me if he saw anything unusual. He didn't, except that a couple of cameras weren't working now."

On-screen, an image appeared of a hall. It was hard to say which hallway she was being shown. Agnes was aware that there were many cameras, at least a couple on each floor, plus the stairwells and entrances. From the rounds she'd made, she knew they were located about seven and a half feet up, high enough that no one would bump them but not out of reach for someone who was trying. She watched as people exited the elevator, and a door opened and they disappeared. The angle distorted them slightly, but all the guests would be captured. There was Whitney, here came Jamie, now Nic, and then Lewis. Derek nodded. And here was Agnes, standing, shifting the wine bottle she'd brought from one hand to the other.

"Watch this," he said, pointing to the screen.

Agnes watched herself look up directly at the camera.

"You're the only one who did that. Observant."

He fast-forwarded to the footage where people began to leave. Anthony was first—Agnes remembered again he'd mentioned having his kids early the next day. The time stamp on the bottom showed 8:32. Agnes tried to stitch together the night: she must have been talking to Charlotte in the bedroom not long after. She could imagine it. Emmanuel left next, just after 9:15. He lumbered away from the camera. He'd been in Charlotte's room when Agnes had woken. He'd left his phone. Charlotte had come to check on her, and they'd talked. Veronica would have come in to interrupt Agnes and Charlotte shortly. Then . . . the footage showed 10:10, when Agnes left. She'd felt like it couldn't have taken that long—everything had seemed to happen quickly. Had she really spent an hour talking to Charlotte, or had the argument between the two women gone on much longer than she'd realized?

Time had been undone for her. She wasn't reliable.

Emmanuel had said that none of them were good witnesses. It was why he'd planned the murder to follow the party—even if he'd conceived of it only as a game, a riddle.

The camera was just at the right height and angle, she realized. That was why you could tell who everyone was and see their expressions, even if they all looked slightly squat.

At 10:15 in the footage, the condo door opened, and then there was a flurry of white. It looked like a hand in front of the lens. Immediately the image went gray—not as if someone had knocked the camera down but as though they'd covered it with something.

Agnes was sure she'd stopped breathing. She met Derek's gaze. He looked as uncertain as she was. Then he backed up the line along the bottom of the image and played it again.

A glove. It was a bright-white glove on a hand. It was frustrating. She couldn't see the wrist. That meant they couldn't see any identifying body features or what they were wearing otherwise.

Agnes felt like she'd been punched in the gut. "Did you tell the police?"

"I only discovered this an hour ago, after you asked for the footage." He shook his head, and his expression clouded. "You know they were done in her unit in all of forty minutes. I'm not ready to hand this over to them." For the first time, Derek's voice contained a tremor of empathy for Charlotte . . . or was it actually disgust at what he considered shoddy workmanship?

Agnes took out her wallet and showed off the red sticker she had placed there. "This is what that hand was putting there. I don't know if there's any meaning to the color or if it's to better block out the light."

After staring at it for a minute, Derek asked, "Have you ever bought art?"

Agnes was going to shake her head, but then she remembered. "I once bought a painting from my aunt, of my mom. Her face was kind of twisted, a little melty. Disturbing, actually. It's in storage."

"At art galleries that's a sold sticker placed next to art."

Her gaze flicked back to the screen, and she stared at the odd blockage on the camera image. "Who brings gloves with them in July?"

Derek leaned in. "I didn't know what that was, but now that I've seen this"—he indicated the red sticker—"that looks like an art-handling glove to me."

The only fact she could add to Derek's wonderful deduction was that it had to be someone with enough height to reach the camera—and not just reach it but reach it with the accuracy to place the sticker where it needed to be: that narrowed the list. There was a slight perimeter of light, as if the whole lens hadn't been obscured, only most of it.

Someone could have even taken the gloves from one of Charlotte's rooms that night. They might be her own gloves. Agnes wondered if Emmanuel would know. *How detailed was his plan for her death? Did he come up with every step, every plot beat, or would someone else have filled in and polished it into a better draft? A ghostwriter, so to speak.*

Chapter Sixteen

If Hugo fancied himself an artist, maybe he also had gallery gloves for his work? Yet to Agnes, starting with him felt . . . naive. Especially if everything was pointing to Chase.

Too much, actually. Maybe the killer left breadcrumbs from the gallery world to lead suspicion away from them?

Back upstairs in her place, Agnes looked online to see if his work was still on display at Charlotte's gallery. She was surprised to see they had an event that night. *Why wasn't it canceled following her death?* But she supposed it was a business and the artist had been booked months in advance. His bio indicated that he was from California, so no doubt there were already wheels in motion: shipping of the artwork, and travel. Did that mean that Chase's work had come down?

Agnes fed Hulot and dashed her fingers through her hair, and then she was on the subway, en route to La Musa to speak to Matias or Tabitha, or whoever she might find there, when her phone bleated. It was a slightly different ring than her messages. She was on the L line. The train had just stopped at First Avenue, and now the doors were closing as they zoomed west toward Union Square. She thought it might be Ethan, as she'd left him a voicemail all about the video footage and her discovery of the gloves. But when she dug the phone out of her bag, she saw the only reply from Ethan had been a tapped heart on the Alfa Romeo photo. The tone was due to a WhatsApp message from an unknown number.

There was no message, just a PDF. Before she could decide whether to open it, two more files appeared from the same number. They looked like screenshots. This was no spam Bitcoin offer—she instinctively knew. She tried to click on them, but her phone wouldn't load them until the train pulled into the next station.

The first was a screenshot of anonymous users:

@ArnoldSchwarzenegger
@BruceWillis
@SylvesterStallone
@CarlWeathers
@DolphLundgren
@StevenSeagal

The other screenshot featured a snippet from a conversation that had been posted on a board. Growing up in a small town with nothing to do, she'd seen plenty of action movies on DVD late at night with her brothers or with high school friends. But some of these names were beyond her, especially after nearly two decades in New York City, where celebrity city councillors and Broadway actors who used her bodega ATM had taken their places in her brain.

@BruceWillis: This is too important. We need transparency.

@CarlWeathers: I disagree—it leaves us all at risk.

@ArnoldSchwarzenegger: These things could easily be unrelated.

@DolphLundgren: Coincidence is a cop-out in storytelling. In life, too. And people already know.

@ArnoldSchwarzenegger: That is a ridiculous point. Who knows?

@SylvesterStallone: If the police were informed they dismissed this.

@DolphLundgren: You already chose to leave @ SylvesterStallone. So don't weigh in if you aren't in this group, please!

It went on, but zooming in with her fingers on a moving train was too difficult. The text was too small to make out more without digging out her glasses. *A literal boys club,* Agnes thought with astonishment. Complete with deeply internet-style humor—muscular avatar names from 1980s action flicks and the occasional GIF of George C. Scott yelling "Turn it off!"

Whoever was Bruce Willis obviously saw himself as the good guy. She didn't know who Dolph Lundgren was, but the reference to story-telling made her suspect Emmanuel. But that meant he was still playing host with the Perfect Murder Society.

Does "people already know" refer to me?

Agnes drew a breath and clicked open the PDF.

The Perfect Murder of Chase Manhattan

The proposed victim is a) greedy b) susceptible to flattery c) not so bright and d) a non-driver.

The location is a) hipster hell and b) impossibly remote.

The plan will require some backstopping: VPN servers, IG accounts, a fake website and Wiki entry. Maybe work for one of our junior members!

A fraudulent invite for a short-term, well-paid artist residency in Marfa, TX will be sent to Chase Manhattan. It will be for something irresistibly obnoxious, like designing a new sneaker in a collaboration between Louis Vuitton and the (utterly fake) Marfa Arts Alliance.

He'll be picked up alone at the El Paso airport.

Of course you think: Wait! How will you know he'll be alone? Wouldn't he bring a friend or a girlfriend?

The invitation will come from a young female curator who will also friend him on IG, sending sly and flirtatious messages about being "excited to finally meet him."

At the airport a black car will pick him up and begin the three-hour drive into deep West Texas. Halfway, the car will turn north instead of south, and the victim will be none the wiser. After an hour drive into nowhere, close to a pre-dug hole, "car trouble" will cause them to stop and get out. From there the murder is mob-hit simple. I like a gun for this—clean, way less chance of DNA and, you know, when in Texas . . .

Meanwhile, the murder team will drive into Mexico and fly from Ciudad Juárez to Mexico City to

Los Angeles to wash their tracks. Digitally, all references to Marfa Arts Alliance will be scrubbed and since friends expect him to be away, Chase won't be assumed missing for weeks. The concerned will quickly put together that he flew to Texas but from there the trail will be cold because it doesn't exist.

If the body is found—and let's be honest, sometimes a ranch dog gets lucky out there—his body will be planted with a substantial amount of cocaine to tilt the narrative towards troubled young artist who ran afoul as part of a deal. And that one old dumb Vice article he wrote about scoring drugs while traveling? That's the chef's kiss.

Agnes felt nausea grip her. She got up and stumbled toward the subway doors, grateful when they opened. It was only when she felt the platform solid beneath her that she saw an edit balloon attributed to @BruceWillis.

@BruceWillis: A very elegant plan. Big Cormac McCarthy vibes. But the airport pickup worries me. Cameras. Cameras. Cameras. What if Chase arrives at the airport and he gets a text? "Sorry, your ride got stuck behind an accident. Can you take a cab to . . ." and an address of some closed landscaping office on the outskirts of town. After he's dropped off there, then he's picked up by us.

But it was the edit note after, by @DolphLundgren, that stopped her.

@DolphLundgren: Nice add-on. But it has to be one of us he's never met! TBH, my best friend is currently sleeping with him. (She's in a dirtbag phase.)

Without a doubt @DolphLundgren was Emmanuel. Also: Chase was not a member of the Perfect Murder Society, unless they had started to turn against each other. Whatever thoughts she'd had that he could've hurt Charlotte were gone. If Emmanuel's *best friend* was Charlotte, that also dated this post to a month or two ago, back when she'd been first infatuated with Chase's work—probably just as it was going up in the gallery.

Even if the plan was old, the killer could have found their confidence with Charlotte's death, and Chase might easily be the next victim. Chase Manhattan wasn't his legal name, of course. Ethan had prepared a file that first night she'd pulled him into the situation. Chase had some social media presence—twenty thousand followers on IG—but didn't seem very active lately. She could DM him—or she could search his legal name, which was Curtis Cooper, and try to phone and warn him. There were thirty-two Curtis Coopers in New York, though. It was possible Chase himself would be at the art opening, and if he wasn't, someone at La Musa would definitely have his number.

Agnes dodged around a group of NYU students who had decided they were fine with walking four abreast. She nearly bumped into a mom with a stroller coming out of the Old Navy on Sixth Avenue. Agnes turned and bolted down Twenty-Second Street toward Seventh Avenue, as fire engines streamed past, sirens warbling.

"Oh shit." Agnes paused her running after only a few blocks. "Shin splints." She leaned against a building, stretching her leg. She'd done some jogging during the pandemic, like everyone, but it had been a long time since her high school track-and-field team. She started again, dodging around a Citi Bike stand, which was as dangerous as a stampede—the blue bikes became unholstered weapons, wielded by clumsy tourists and dazed hipsters alike.

Agnes hopped from the curb down into the street, where the screech of brakes and the angry blurt of a horn alerted her to the fact she'd narrowly missed becoming crushed as a white utility van veered out without signaling. She rounded the corner onto Seventh, where the sidewalks were wider, but now there were restaurants and patios—waiters to dodge. A blue-haired canvasser—in an orange ASPCA vest and holding an iPad—tried to stop her with a fervent "Excuse me," hoping to recruit future dog rescuers. "I can't handle another dog!" Agnes yelled, rushing through the intersection before the girl could say any more.

On the other side, Agnes paused a moment and checked her phone. *Damn, it's on Ninth!* Panic had made her forget. She took a second and texted the screenshots and the files to Ethan. Then she was off again. Immediately, she heard a response ding in her pocket but didn't pull it out again to answer.

Up ahead, a small crowd for the opening was milling on the sidewalk near the address of La Musa. Agnes pulled a hand through her hair, twisting her curls into a more fashionable shape. She'd sweated through what she was wearing, but at least she had on real pants and a blouse. She took a deep breath and attempted to summon up enough saliva and air that she could walk up and say a simple hello if she needed to.

Outside the gallery, she spotted Tabitha in conversation with Nic. They were both dressed in basic black, the older woman more expensively in a silk cami and black skirt, and Nic in the rock version—a black tank top and black jeans with frayed seams.

Before she could decide on her best approach in this highly bizarre situation, Agnes's phone began to ring, and she fished it out of her pocket.

"Who sent these?" Ethan burst out. "Emmanuel?"

Agnes sighed. "I don't think so. Emmanuel isn't responding. I keep getting 'Notifications silenced' for him. I ran all the way to La Musa hoping Chase might be here."

"Yeah, he should be warned unless . . . unless he did this. Maybe it's a red herring—writing *his own* murder. It would be very conceptual."

"He's not that good of an artist," Agnes pointed out.

"I was wondering something."

"What?" Agnes practically yelled at him, wanting to get into the gallery.

"Did Evie ask about me?"

She hadn't told Ethan about the subway kisses yet—there had been so much more to discuss. As she walked up to the small throng outside the glassy storefront, she noticed her pulse had returned to normal, and she'd stopped sweating. Agnes thought about how Ethan was helping her out and thought of a quick lie. "She thought you were nice."

As Agnes clicked off, she knew she was about to *go ham*. She had googled Evie's phrase earlier that day. It was the soft way of saying *Go hard as an MF*, without the *F* of course. Agnes wove through the crowd and strode up to the gallery.

Chapter Seventeen

"I need to find someone," Agnes blurted out, but Tabitha had already started to greet Agnes warmly, hugging her one armed, a baby held in a stylish black sling across her chest, so close to her it blended into her fashion.

Another one? Agnes thought as the baby practically bumped against her. "They're so . . . new," she said, her voice rising in surprise.

"Three months," Tabitha said. "It was a beautiful birth. I was stocking carrots at the Park Slope Coop when she started to crown. So that's her name—Carrot."

"But her middle name is, like, Marianne, right? Just in case?"

"No. Just Carrot. Because she came out of me like a carrot comes out of the ground."

Agnes breathed deeply and thought, *Brooklyn kills me.* She cut straight to the point. "Is Chase here?"

Tabitha's expression changed. She glanced at Nic, as if they'd already been talking about it. Agnes remembered that Lewis had thought Charlotte had an assistant—maybe that person was Nic. She remembered how Jessica and Nic had been talking about her boss at the memorial after-party. For some reason, she hadn't realized Nic was working for Charlotte. It made sense: Nic had seemed to know everything about Charlotte's apartment and personal connections at the salon that first night. She recalled something Nic had said: "The guest list is always changing." She hadn't been at the party as a guest.

Musicians always need money. Pickup work.

"Come with me," Tabitha said.

They moved through the other attendees into the overly cool air of the gallery, and then Tabitha took her up a staircase. There was a gallery room overlooking the street, hung with many small commercial illustrations in frames; then Tabitha headed into the empty offices and beyond—a back room with a rough concrete floor and utility sink. A large portion of the room was stacked with paintings. With only a glance Agnes recognized the style as Chase's. One of the paintings contained a torn image of crossed gunslinger pistols, McDonald's arches, and chunky bloodred blobs. The words of the piece, SLIPPERY WHEN WEST, were etched into the thick paint.

"Matias told him to come get his work," Tabitha said. "But he hasn't shown up, and no one can find him. Not unusual, but definitely annoying." She sat down in an office chair with a sigh. She lifted up her shiny black top and began feeding. The tiny baby kneaded at her breast like a cat pawing a blanket into the right shape. Agnes forced her eyes away after looking for that split second too long.

Tabitha went on to say she'd told Chase at the memorial that all he had to do was give her an address and she could have the unsold work packaged and shipped to him. Charlotte had agreed to hold some in case of sale, but they couldn't keep all of it. While the baby fed, she went on: "I had to deal with calls from Veronica all morning too. She wanted to return the art I sent her. Can you believe it?" Tabitha shook her head in disbelief.

"The art *you* sent her," Agnes repeated.

Tabitha looked down at her child and baby talked. "You should never mix friends and business. No, you shouldn't, Baby Carrot. Not ever." Agnes audibly sighed, and Tabitha spoke normally again. "Sorry. Charlotte would tell people what they want to hear. They get angry when reality hits them."

A people pleaser, Agnes thought. *It fits.* "I get that," Agnes said. She thought of the lie she'd told Ethan just to make him feel better. "There's a reason Charlotte and I clicked."

"And Chase? She tried so long with him."

This was a new view of Charlotte. Tabitha wasn't judgmental. She had been the one to notice Agnes's fogginess at the party. She liked to take people under her wing, Agnes realized, almost as much as Charlotte did.

"Give me his number, and I'll talk to him," Agnes said, laying on soothing tones that surprised her. *What am I trying to do, mother the mother?* she wondered.

Tabitha stood and put her baby into burping position. She bounced toward the computer screen. A few taps, and she'd pulled up Chase's info. She had an email and phone number, but no address. "I thought you knew him?" she asked as Agnes wrote it down on a sticky note.

Agnes was already keying him into the contact list on her iPhone. "Yes, and . . ." she answered absently. Then as she started to descend the staircase, she stopped the lie and turned back. If the ripples were getting wider, maybe she shouldn't pretend. She looked at the squirming shape of the gray-and-black sling and thought, too, of the little girls she'd seen Tabitha with at the memorial. For a brief moment, she felt compelled to disclose. "Tabitha, be careful."

Agnes dialed Chase's number as she exited onto the street. Each ring felt interminably long. There were four—and then voicemail. It wasn't even his voice, just an automated "The customer you're trying to reach is unavailable." Before Agnes could decide whether to leave a message, Nic the black-clad musician, was grabbing her arm, intent on talking to her.

Agnes noticed again the faded bicycle tattoo on Nic's gym-defined shoulder. She was thin but muscled, her grace reminding Agnes of a copperhead snake. Could she have killed Charlotte and then bicycled home right after, leaving no trace of her path? Very Brooklyn. A bicycle was untraceable, unlike an Uber app, subway cameras, or the toll bills acquired by vehicles. These thoughts were beginning to strike Agnes as almost comical—cartoonish—and she was starting to have sympathy for Emmanuel. When one thought of it as an exercise, it stopped being real.

After they'd walked a few paces from the art gallery, Nic cocked her auburn head to one side and spoke softly. "Some people are talking about you, Agnes."

Agnes deadpanned, "I don't know why."

Charlotte had bragged about her DIY Detective article to everyone at the party. If the anonymous Perfect Murder Society screenshots were from someone other than Emmanuel, it must be because of that.

She was beginning to think that Charlotte emphasizing that didn't have to do with status anxiety. If she followed Tabitha's opinion of Charlotte, it was maybe a maternal urge. She liked to champion people. She'd slept with Chase, but she also wanted to nurture him, even down to shielding him from his own failures. Perhaps that's why Agnes had responded to her so much. Who wouldn't want someone to brag about them? Agnes's parents almost never bragged.

She fixed Nic with a stare and waited. It was true: people couldn't wait to talk if you made the space for silence. She needed Nic to spit it out and let her get on her way—she had to leave that message for Chase; it was just a matter of choosing her words.

Nic shrugged. "Journalists love words, and Lewis talks a lot when he's drunk. He said you were 'looking into things.'"

"Maybe," Agnes conceded.

"Well then you should know that no one can find Emmanuel. Chase is a fuckup. Going offline is normal for him. For Emmanuel, it isn't. He has his moments but never misses a call. He was supposed to meet me earlier today at the bank for the funds Charlotte had allocated for the production to get transferred. We talked about that at the memorial. She'd already signed off on that. He said he'd be there." Nic bit her lip.

Agnes had a hunch she knew what Nic would say next. "But . . . ?"

"He didn't show. And he's not picking up. Everyone in the cast is having a breakdown."

Agnes thought of the silenced notifications. She'd hoped it was Emmanuel who'd sent the screenshots, but of course, she had Emmanuel's number, and WhatsApp would have synced it.

Nic's mouth flatlined into a nonexpression, on the cusp of saying something more.

"It's okay. You don't have to tell me," Agnes said, hoping it might relax Nic.

"Whitney told me yesterday she was the one who called 911 the night Charlotte, you know . . ."

"Whitney?"

Nic hesitated, watched a pair of pedestrians passing by who were headed toward the stairs to the High Line. She shook her hair again. "Look, I don't know if it means anything. But she must've stayed at Hugo's that night. And I don't know if Charlotte knew."

Fifth floor. Agnes thought of the man at the window that night. It had to have been Hugo who had looked out. Whitney hadn't. So she hadn't seen Charlotte's body crumpled below but had made the phone call. The onyx *was* from Hugo. He had given the same stone to both women.

Agnes remembered Charlotte's tone, how warm it had been, speaking about her summer love. Later in the night, when Charlotte had phoned Agnes, her voice was drastically different. Maybe she'd found out about the two of them by then. *Definitely a possibility.*

Agnes wanted to get away and figure out what to do about Chase, and the missing Emmanuel, but Nic was too good a source to walk away from. She pushed for another piece of information. "Was Charlotte close with anyone else, do you think?"

"Close?" Nic said, with a raised eyebrow that said, *Nice euphemism, Mom.*

"Okay. Boning."

Nic leaned back on one heel, considering. Even with her height, she was wearing strappy black platform sandals. "She's always been close with Jamie. But not, like, sexual vibes."

Not sexual. What does that mean, for a woman whom everyone is reporting as being hypersexual?

"And he organized the memorial." Agnes tried it as a statement rather than a question, to see if Nic would disagree. She didn't.

"They may have been together at one time, but it's more a brother-sister energy with them," Nic said.

Immutable. Agnes remembered Jamie had written as the last word of his tribute. *What does immutable mean? Is there a slightly negative connotation to it? Does it have anything to do with muting?* Agnes tried to remember, but this was no time to go searching for the *Merriam-Webster* definition.

"What do I do about Emmanuel?" she asked Nic plainly.

The musician shook her head. She'd unburdened herself, and now she was removing herself. "You sound like you think you're responsible?"

"At a certain point, I am."

Agnes had just walked away when her phone dinged. Glancing down, she saw a message from Evie. It said: **How's things?** It was followed by a second text in close succession: **Hang again soon? Maybe something more chill?**

It gave Agnes a surprising thrill to know her date had reached out to her first. She hated to admit that made her feel valued, but it did.

Two more people may be dead, Agnes thought with a shiver. *But my dating life is going well finally.*

She tapped a thumbs-up on the message. Normally she wouldn't send just a symbol, but someone's life was on the line.

Agnes studied Emmanuel's home address on her phone. *Forty minutes by subway.* The theater was an easier first stop. Ethan had mapped most of them out, and the spread was impressive. Emmanuel (Park Slope); Alexander (Greenpoint); Whitney (Astoria); Jamie (Greenpoint and Park Slope); Jessica (Woodside, Queens); Agnes, Hugo, Derek, and Jonathan (all in the Williamsburg condo); Cody (Long Island City);

Nic (Bushwick); and Lewis (Bedford-Stuyvesant). And then Veronica and Anthony, the true Manhattanites, separate from the bridge-and-tunnel people.

Agnes realized that New York could hide most of its crimes just with its size and all the distances within it.

Chapter Eighteen

Along the way to the Garland, Agnes paused, out of breath, at Cooper Triangle to phone Chase again. As his voicemail picked up and Agnes was about to say *I have to know if you're okay*, she was interrupted by a terrifying sound from a monster. "Mom! Where is my deposit?"

Agnes swung her head around, and on the park bench behind her was an art student from Cooper Union, maybe a sophomore, yelling into his phone. "Are you a fucking idiot? Of course I need it right now. My laundry wasn't delivered. Everyone else is going to Ireland's estate in the Berkshires. She'll break up with me if I don't go. I don't know why you're being such a bitch about this! I get five thousand a week. A week!"

Reaching her New York limit, Agnes stalked around to the other side of the bench and jabbed a finger into the student's bony chest. "One: I'm trying to make a call, too, and maybe the world is bigger than your problems. Two: you apologize to your mother, right now."

She jabbed again for emphasis as the student muttered "Sorry" into his phone.

After walking away, she turned back. The sulky brat had already picked up his portfolio case and moved on. That's when she texted Ethan: Find Chase's mom. If we find her, we'll find him.

Agnes realized Charlotte was just a stand-in mother in Chase's life; maybe without her, he'd gone back to the original source.

To make up for lost time, Agnes took an Uber, but no call came from Ethan.

As the car worked its way across the avenues and then down through Alphabet City, she studied her list based on height. *Who has big murder energy among them?* Alexander, Whitney, Hugo, and Jonathan were all possible suspects for placing the camera sticker. Nic was tall enough, but Agnes felt it was unlikely given their interaction at the gallery. She wasn't sure, but Derek and Cody were both possibly too short. Anthony and Lewis were average. Emmanuel had been caught on camera leaving before the sticker was placed, so even though he was tall, it couldn't be him. The positioning of the camera right by Charlotte's door made it unlikely someone could return without their image being picked up. Veronica might be tall enough, especially in heels, and had cause. But her determination to unload the paintings after the fact drew attention to her. Her brawling also drew attention to her. And Agnes doubted there were women in the murder society.

The bartender was tall enough and had needed to go out for ice—but that was earlier, before Agnes went into the bedroom, wasn't it? The sticker wasn't placed until after Agnes left. What about Cody and Jessica together? Then there was Jamie. From Ethan's research, she knew Jamie had two addresses listed, one in Park Slope, which was probably where he lived full time, and another near his election office on Manhattan Avenue, not that far from the Kentwood. Agnes tried to remember how tall the politician was and couldn't conjure it. She'd been wearing her black heels, which took her from five-three up to five-five, and he'd been taller than her by at least five inches. Average, then, most likely. Five-ten or five-eleven.

How many of these people could be in the Perfect Murder Society?

The driver sounded his horn and muttered the expletive Agnes had been thinking. She took off her glasses and put them away. They were only a couple of blocks away, but traffic was still thick. In the few minutes it had taken to move from west to east across the island, evening had settled in, with a perfume of gasoline and anxiety. The pedestrians were no longer office drones waiting for buses and crawling home but girlfriends dressed for dinner out and packs of men creeping up from the subways, ready to hunt excitement. Shops were closing and bars becoming fuller, a sexuality of darkly lit windows.

Emmanuel had said *men*, but how did he know that if the submissions were anonymous? Perhaps based on whom he'd invited or had assumed others asked into the society. She really needed to find him and talk to him. She wanted to ask him about the files she'd gotten by WhatsApp and see if he would show her the original murder plan for Charlotte. If Nic knew she was investigating—officially or unofficially—others would as well. In which case, anyone with Agnes's number could have sent them.

Before she could get to the theater, she googled Dolph Lundgren: a ripped shirtless blond Adonis. He'd been in everything from *Rocky IV* to *The Expendables* to *Aquaman*. He was six-five and had even played He-Man. He was everything Emmanuel wanted to be.

And Lewis is Stallone. The one who left the club. He told her he'd never been in but had been invited—he might've stuck around just long enough to dislike the others. That seemed very Lewis.

Agnes's phone lit up in her lap, and she jumped. Looking down at the screen, she saw a number with a 313 area code—Detroit. That only meant home. Agnes swiped the screen and said a tentative hello.

"Hey," came a flat male response. It was her brother Paul. "I'm calling you from a pay phone." His voice was strained. Good thing she'd taken the call. Paul almost never phoned, much less on a pay phone. Usually he texted things to her like Love to come see you but where the hell would I park my Ford Raptor in New York? Or Just checking in. Fox News said Monkey Pox is making gay people explode. You alright?

"Is there something wrong?" she asked, hearing the scrape in her voice that happened only when she was on edge.

"Mom."

"Oh God, is she . . . ?"

"She's, um, in the hospital. It's—"

Paul had a tendency to mutter at the best of times, and the driver chose that moment to sound his horn loudly again, which was followed by a call-and-response from all the other cars that weren't moving. *Damn.* Agnes undid her seat belt. Whatever strategy she'd been coming up with was suddenly wiped from her mind. Her goal now was just to make sure her mom was all right. "I'll get out here," she told the Uber driver—she already had the door open.

"Say that again," she told her older brother as she dodged around the cars and toward the sidewalk.

"Katie was there, visiting, when Mom collapsed. They're just giving her fluids, and they're going to do some tests."

"Katie?" Agnes said. Her fingers went so numb she almost dropped her phone.

"Cousin Katie."

"Yeah, no, I remember. It's been, what, twenty years?"

"I don't know. I guess Mom talked to her on Facebook or something. Dad was in Florida with his sister—he's flying back tonight."

Agnes walked toward the theater, dismissing the cousin conversation and trying to get all the facts about their mother's condition from a Michigan man who was more comfortable around deer than people. Patricia Nielsen was sixty-eight, and although Agnes didn't think of her mother as old, she hadn't been young for some time either. Her retirement had been sedate, and she'd painted all the spare rooms she could paint and then sat down to watch TV and let her hair go ashy. She had begun to shrink from arthritis and had been warned to watch her diet to avoid prediabetes. If Agnes asked her about either of those things, her mother would chastise with Midwestern stoicism, "Oh, stop it—I'm fine. Everyone dies of something, you know." The only place they aligned was on books and politics. Agnes mailed her mom new books almost monthly, and her mom emailed her news articles. For this civil exchange, Agnes was grateful. She knew many of her friends had less in common.

Agnes stood on the street corner, feeling like there was a stone in her stomach. She hated to think of her mom in a hospital gown, afraid or uncertain. But their dad would be with her soon, she told herself. "It's, um, really not a good time for me to hop on a plane," she told her brother, "but I will. You just have to tell me."

"I'll call you if it gets serious," Paul assured her.

Shaking, Agnes tucked her phone into her pocket. *What is Katie doing there?* That was like saying an actual ghost was visiting your mother, flipping through photos and exclaiming *Cedar Point, 1995! That's Agnes with braces and the Alanis Morissette shirt she won.*

Life at the end of your thirties was full of these moments. *When is it serious? When do you fly home? Can you ever trust your parents to tell you the truth?* Dealing with suspicious playwrights sounded safer, and she found herself heading down the narrow leafy street.

At dusk, the theater reminded her of a sleeping face. Its marquee was unlit, and its bustling feeling the other morning had all come from the inside, she realized. With its brown brick facade and lack of windows, now it was impossible to tell it was an active space. So many buildings had gone vacant during the pandemic and still were waiting to be repurposed. A vinyl banner above the doors was the one indication a show might indeed be staged there. **COMING SOON! A NEW PLAY: DECOHERENCE BY EMMANUEL HAIGHT, PULITZER PRIZE WINNER.** Through the small panes in the red wooden door, she could see the alcove was dark. She supposed when they didn't have a show, there was no reason for staff to be there, even on a Friday night. There were no posted hours, but when she tugged the door, it opened without an argument. Unlocked doors in New York would never cease to amaze her.

Agnes stepped inside. She felt apprehensive but told herself she was just rattled by the news about her mom. She didn't hear anyone. Someone had left the light on behind the desk in the ticket booth. She glanced in. No one there. It felt too bold to walk back to the practice space, though if anyone was here, working, that was likely where they'd be. She went instead toward the door of the stage space. Someone had put two buckets upside down and a strand of green painter's tape between them, blocking the most convenient set of double doors. Hand-lettered on a piece of paper in black Sharpie were the words **WEST PAINT**.

As she got closer, she saw the *S* was crossed out, but to her it looked like a dollar sign. She paused, assessing. "Hello!" she called out, in neither one direction nor another. Someone must be there, working. The question was where. She didn't want to startle them.

Maybe that was why Emmanuel's phone was on silent mode. He'd thrown himself into a revision like a neurotic writer—she certainly had experience with them. Agnes recalled reading on his website that the previous year he'd received a Playwright in Residence Award from the Garland. Maybe they still let him keep an office or come and go from the space more casually than others. Agnes pivoted and peered down the hall toward the workroom, but it seemed very dark. She heard nothing.

She came back to the buckets. Carefully, she stepped over the green tape and opened one of the doors, her hand on the handle, not touching the door itself in case that's what had been painted. She sniffed. She didn't smell paint. The place smelled a little like Clorox and wood soap.

Peeking in, Agnes saw the theater was empty and dim. Long dark rows of seats, like teeth among red gums. The balcony seemed to smile. Dim, but not dark, she recognized. It meant someone was here.

She recalled that Jacob Kroll, private eye to the stars, had said in his YouTube class, "Investigation begins with opening up your point of view. Ask yourself how you would act in a similar situation. Then ask how someone else would." Where would Agnes want to write? She wouldn't work on a stage, or a large, gaping room, but in one of the cozy, private dressing rooms behind it. They would have good lighting. It would be easy to suspend one's doubts there and be moved by imagination, begin to make words whirl like music. As she headed down the aisle toward the stage, she saw a portable music stand that an actor might use for their script. It had been left at the lip of the stage on a taped X. As she came to the edge, she saw a sheaf of white pages there.

Curiosity compelled her, and she scrambled up onto the stage and picked up the top sheet. After lifting it, she could see the papers below were blank. An artifice or trick, implying more had been written than actually was. Her heartbeat sped up, and she felt her breath grow shaky. The paper shook between her fingers. It was typewritten, faintly, by a machine that needed a new ribbon. She grabbed her glasses out of her bag and read:

DEATH OF A PLAYWRIGHT
SCENE 1

AGNES enters the theater. It's empty but full of old feelings, as theaters often are during the daytime. She makes her way to downstage center. It's the natural magnetic pull of the space. Once there she finds a printed script on the lip of the stage.

AGNES
(picking up pages)

What the?

To Emmanuel's credit, if he was the writer of the page in her hands, that was what she now said out loud before she continued reading.

Agnes, smart but not clever, is confused by the playwright's confession. She has misread Emmanuel Haight from the beginning. All his career striving and obsession with his body masked deep feelings of inadequacy and self destruction. The Perfect Murder Society was a place for him to safely explore those feelings but it became too much and he needed to make things real. Charlotte had made him, and never turned down an opportunity to remark exactly that. We all resent our makers don't we? Our parents? God? Agnes had seen him leaning out Charlotte's window. It was a dry run, almost a measuring of her casket, and a part of him wished, "Why didn't she stop me right there!" But now she will become the audience for Emmanuel's most dramatic exit.

Agnes drops the papers and looks up. EMMANUEL enters from above.

"Above?" Agnes couldn't help but do what the script said. With only the ghost light illuminating the stage, the rafters were dark. All she could see was the end of a rope that swayed back and forth in the air. Knowing from high school plays that untied ropes were dangerous, she reached up, then gently began to walk the end over toward a rope tie.

As she stepped, she heard a deep groan of metal. She took cover toward the wing but looked up in time to watch the aluminum catwalk fall to the stage with an earsplitting *clank*.

She looked up to see what had made it fall. Tangled in the rafters was Emmanuel's body. It bounced and swayed at the other end of the rope she still held in her hand. She swallowed and watched his Doc Martens–clad feet as they twisted, then untwisted, then swung back and forth, silently. His face looked pinched and tired and swollen like a balloon.

Agnes dropped the rope and dashed from the theater, hurtled the painter's tape, and was out and into the night, attempting to disappear.

She spun around, confused in the streets, feeling their sudden loudness. Then the hot scents of the city rushed at her. The dark-green aroma of pot smoke, a twist of laughter that seemed as harsh as thunder. Competing blaring television screens and music from various restaurants and venues, the screech of car brakes, and thump of bass. Friends yelling to friends, or enemies uttering obscenities and threats. Even side streets swelled with noise, weighed against the empty, tomb-like theater. She sprinted through Tompkins Square Park, a place she normally associated with stoned pigeons and vague menace, which she now welcomed for its people. Its witnesses. Later, she found herself in a cramped East Village bar with a drink she didn't recall ordering. She was standing among a crowd of wild soccer fans in jerseys, who cheered and shouted at a flat-screen, where the players circled on the green field. England was playing Spain. The fans jumped up and down as if in slow motion.

Looking down, she saw she still clutched Emmanuel's page. She didn't believe it was anything Emmanuel had authored himself. There was a perfection to it that could come only with fiction—a lie. She didn't know how all the mechanics at the theater had worked, but she knew his hanging body didn't necessarily mean suicide. The threatening tone of the letter seemed off. She realized Emmanuel had started a game, only to have someone invited in who had become the master of it.

Yes, the murderer wanted to frame Emmanuel, but why include her as a character in this script except to terrify her? *Open up your POV,* Agnes remembered again. *Whoever killed Emmanuel wants me to go to the cops. Hand them the confession that ends any investigation.*

Agnes looked down at the one-page play in her hand. She crumpled it up and shoved it deep into the bottom of her purse.

Chapter Nineteen

Hulot licked her awake. The dog's warm tongue pushed across her face, and Agnes groaned and felt for his head. She ruffled his ears and then got up and walked blindly to the bathroom, where she washed her face. Her hair was disheveled, and she was wearing clothes from the night before. She sniffed at her armpits, then ran an antiperspirant over them before shoving on sandals and grabbing the dog's leash. When she'd gotten back to her neighborhood the night before, she'd bought a burner phone from a vape shop on Bedford. She'd waited until midnight to call 911 and make sure Emmanuel would be found but late enough that any news coverage would be pushed to the next day. Instinctively she'd known she needed a little more time.

Now, as she crossed the street and made the short jaunt to the park, she looked down at herself.

Clothes. From the night before.

Emmanuel's shoes.

He'd been wearing the Doc Martens at the memorial. He had to have gone directly to the theater after telling her about the Perfect Murder Society. When had he replied on the thread to the PMS posters? When had he parted ways with Wyatt? To know, she would need to talk to Wyatt. But doing so meant lying about having seen what she had seen.

As the dog pulled on the leash, her phone rang. It was Ethan.

"I have Chase's family's phone number," he said.

"Good work, Ethan."

"I have today off, and I want to use that list of addresses. I think we should—"

"You know, there's stuff happening with my family, so I'm kind of taking me time today." Agnes was lying. Small lies were within her skill set; big ones were less so. She felt guilty to use her mom's illness, though.

She could hear his surprise when Ethan said, "Oh. Of course." *Is it surprise or hurt?* She had reached out to him for help, and they'd become friends again quickly. She knew he was sensitive and often felt the sting of rejection deeper than others, sometimes dwelling on some little thing someone had said or the tone of a voice for days.

With Emmanuel dead, and the killer very much aware of Agnes, she also guessed he was aware of Ethan. *Or they . . . or she . . . though, statistically speaking,* Agnes thought, *he/him is a good placeholder.* She absolutely couldn't risk Ethan getting hurt. From here she'd have to do this alone and, she realized, do nothing. Refusing to play the game would frustrate Charlotte's killer more than anything else. He'd come to Agnes eventually.

"Listen, Ethan. I'm sending you some money through Zelle."

"You don't have to do that. You kind of saved me with the apartment sublet already. If not for this place, I'd be paying twenty-five hundred a month, or even three thousand."

Like a family, we deflect our emotions, retreat into facts, Agnes thought.

"Take it. Payment for the work. And if you don't hear from me in a couple of days, call Derek Anand at my building." She clicked off before he could protest—and before she could change her mind and draw him back in.

She took the dog down to an off-leash area beside the soccer fields at Bushwick Inlet. Hulot seized upon a tennis ball that someone had left behind. She clucked, and the dog brought it over and relinquished it to her. She threw. He flew. A flawless game of fetch. She watched as he hopped over rocks and spun about the small garden area in chase. His eyes wild with the hunt. She threw a fake ball, and he started, then came back, unfooled. He cocked his head. She lobbed the ball, and off he went. His hind feet and front feet practically overlapping with his speed, nimble as a deer. He was obsessive about the ball in a way that only a Lab–border collie could be.

Obsessions don't require logic.

Agnes sat down on a boulder, still halfheartedly tossing the ball each time the dog returned it. *Thump. Thump.*

Who among the group is obsessive? she wondered. *Or fixated on winning?*

She stopped playing. It was important to call Charles and Sheri Cooper in Nyack. She dialed the number. A woman answered, and Agnes started right in, asking if she was related to Chase.

"Curtis is here," the woman said uncertainly, calling him by his given name. "Are you . . . a friend?"

"I am," Agnes confirmed. She was relieved he was still alive. She still wanted to give some kind of warning to Chase—yet didn't know how to open up the topic of the Perfect Murder Society with someone's mom. Agnes also hadn't decided if, after the murder of Emmanuel, Chase was at risk of being framed (the gloves and art sticker pointed so directly at him). Sheri Cooper sounded like a suburban mom, though Agnes noticed she didn't seem in a hurry to get Chase or put him on the phone. Agnes began, "I'm really worried about him."

"We are, too, dear. But we've been through this before."

"Oh, you have?"

Chase's mom sighed. "He's here but can't talk. Not until we can get him some help."

"Did someone get to him?!" Agnes's voice rose.

"We confiscated his phone so his dealers can't call him. He's able to enter the rehab facility in a couple more days. Leave me your number if you'd like an update, but we have to keep him safe for now."

"Please do," Agnes said, then clicked off.

Before Hulot could protest, Agnes pushed the tennis ball into her purse and snapped the leash back on him. Her phone began beeping with notifications as the dog tried to leap up to tug at the purse with his teeth, still wanting the beat-up ball. It was Ethan texting.

HOLY SHIT!

BODY FOUND AT THEATER!

NO NAMES YET!

What do you think happened?

Four more texts followed. She looked only at the preview of Ethan's texts and left the rest unread for the moment. The killer would have to adjust his plan now. He'd left a false confession for Agnes to find and to call the police about. Agnes hadn't gone to the police. Had he watched her run from the theater? Probably. Did Agnes relish the idea of him waiting nearby for police to show up at the theater, then having to give up, then panicking? She'd save that feeling for a rainy day. Agnes was confident he'd send her an invitation to a new dance soon enough.

She closed her eyes and tried to remember everything she'd seen at the Garland. The paint sign was definitely suspicious. The spelling mistake was done on purpose, she now realized.

We$t Paint, it said. Was it meant to frame Chase, like the art stickers and the gloves?

Agnes scrolled to her messages and opened Evie's number. Evie picked up on the third ring.

"Hello?"

"Hi. It's Agnes, from the date?"

"Did you think I would forget about that in two days?"

Agnes laughed. "I guess that's good. Listen, I have a question about theater."

There was a long pause. She knew Evie was probably wondering whether Agnes had no boundaries. She knew she ought to have started with pleasantries. It was before nine in the morning, and she'd called out of the blue.

"Yeah, I've done some theater." Evie didn't sound angry, just confused. "It was in Canada, so it was seminude and weird."

Agnes had done some stagehand work in high school, but it was more an excuse to paint backdrops with the art teacher, Ms. Spencer, whom she'd had a crush on. The high school gym was no comparison to a working Manhattan theater. "Who has access to a theater? Are keys usually floating around?" Agnes asked.

"Usually that's the theater manager's job. It might be different if it's a bigger production."

"If it was someone like Emmanuel?"

"Oh, Emmanuel Haight? Yeah, well, he's famous."

"And fame opens doors."

"Most times."

"How famous are you . . . if I wind up needing to get some doors opened?"

"Uh . . ." Evie laughed. "I'm not *un*famous?"

Agnes laughed too. "I really didn't know you were famous when I asked you out—I'm sorry."

"Yeah, well, you didn't even mean to ask me out. But that's okay. It was kind of cute," Evie said on the other end. Agnes felt something inside flutter when Evie said the word *cute*. Then . . . "Do you usually just phone without texting first? 'Cause you know, normally I wouldn't pick up. I'm not into U-Hauling, just so we're clear."

Agnes and her ex, Lise, had fallen into that pattern—it had begun with a spark and shared excitement as Agnes had wound up becoming a local celebrity for a minute, but within a few weeks they'd been like an old couple, Agnes texting **What's for dinner?** to her caterer girlfriend to find out the leftover menu items she might look forward to. Tech bro party short ribs? Mafia wedding Chicken Marsala? Book launch cupcakes? At the same time, Lise had stopped just short of *I love you*. The closest she'd gotten when Agnes had said it to her was an "I care about you too," and that was when Agnes had really felt the sand wash out from under her. So going slow wasn't a bad thing. And she liked that Evie stated her needs up front.

"Of course," Agnes conceded. "I'll text ahead from now on. By the way, how's your nose?"

Evie said it was healing and that some of Leonardo's people had reached out to her for her reel.

"As long as it's not his dog walker."

"I guarantee you it's not." Evie had a lovely tone to her voice; it conjured up a warm feeling in Agnes. What Charlotte had said about a butterfly releasing, Agnes understood that better now.

"So what you're saying is I have some competition?" Agnes asked.

"DiCaprio? I'd say you do." Evie's smile carried through a phone line.

"Do you like cars?"

"Actually, I kind of miss having a car in New York."

"I have access, just for a little while, to a 1965 sports car, if you want to go for a ride?" It felt like the right moment for a brag, and when she told Evie the make of the vehicle, Evie said an interested *Ohhh* into the phone. "All right then, I'll get back to work and figure this thing out. And when I do . . ." But she had no idea where she would take Evie after how they'd begun. It was okay. Evie filled the space with her laugh, and they said their goodbyes.

Agnes opened her purse to throw her phone in. She hadn't meant to spend so much time on the call, but it was better than letting a good thing drop just because she was busy.

Hulot looked up and barked at her hand in her purse, believing she was going to pull out the tennis ball again. Agnes zipped the bag quickly. They left the park, and she allowed the dog to jog back to the

Kentwood. Hulot's tongue became a pink flag as they ran, and she noticed they were almost keeping pace with a familiar figure. A tall muscular man in green running shorts and a white workout shirt was jogging in the bike lane just ahead of them. It was Hugo. Agnes could slow down and observe him, or she could let the dog's enthusiasm pull them up apace. She decided on the latter. Hugo hadn't been at the after-party. Did that mean he might have been taking care of Emmanuel?

He glanced over. "Oh . . . hello." He was slightly out of breath and slowed his gait. They were only another block from the Kentwood.

Agnes brought Hulot to her side with a low whispered "Heel," surprised he did what she wanted. "Don't let us stop you," she said. She felt suddenly apprehensive—she knew too much about him but also hadn't thought enough about how to approach him.

"No, I really need to cool down." Hugo took a bandanna out of his running belt and mopped his forehead.

"Why? Are you angry?" She hadn't meant it as a joke, but he took it that way.

He smiled. "Should I be?" He was in his midforties, she guessed, by the number of wrinkles that creased his forehead. But he was in excellent shape.

"I like to run," Agnes said, trying to determine how to draw Hugo out. She thought about the photo of Charlotte in his garbage. There was more she needed to know about Hugo.

He bent, and the dog tentatively sniffed his hand. "I run from here to Transmitter Park and back. Most days. It's not that far. Where do you run?"

"Uh . . . the city sometimes." She *had* run in the city yesterday—twice, actually.

"Over the bridge? That's a long one." He was impressed by her exaggeration. But she was younger than he was, so maybe it was believable.

"I love the bridge. Have you painted it?"

"Bit of a cliché. As far as subjects go. But how do you know I paint?"

"Charlotte told me."

Now she was outright lying, and she hoped it didn't sound cagey. She stared into Hugo's broad, friendly face and tried to imagine him as the type of man who was cheating on his girlfriend with Whitney, the type of man who threw away a photograph of Charlotte the week she died. The type who was in a murder club.

He smiled. "I do portraits. It's my stress release. And I like learning about people that way. Without talking. It's the opposite of my practice. So quiet."

Agnes nodded and bent to give Hulot a treat so her voice and eyes wouldn't betray her.

"I didn't know you were fast friends with Charlotte," Hugo said, mopping his forehead again as they walked up to the Kentwood together. Where he'd been friendly upon spotting her, there was something flat now in his voice. He surprised her when he said, "If you're interested in what I paint, why don't you come by later? Maybe even sit for me?"

Agnes resisted texting Ethan her updates. I found Chase. He's safe and going to rehab. I've been invited to lunch with Hugo—he's so weird and tightly wound I'm bumping him to #1. She typed it, then backspaced.

Three wavering dots appeared on their text chain. He was thinking of texting her too.

As she went through her mail, she found an envelope with no return address, only hers in block lettering. When she flipped it around, she saw the phrase We$t Paint. She dropped it on the floor and instinctively ran to shut her curtains before returning to it.

After feeling the envelope's weight again and bending it slightly, she determined it was too thin to be anything dangerous. It could contain anthrax, she thought, then immediately reconsidered. That doesn't fit the pattern. Strangling, and blunt force trauma. Charlotte and Emmanuel were both killed in ways that are simple and personal. She opened the envelope.

Victimology

A single woman in New York with viral fame and a day job, still needing a moonlight gig to get by. A.k.a.: She's a frenetic, walking disaster. Then there's the messy dating life. She's dating a woman too young for her, and her best bro is looking to swoop in. But really her most solid relationship is with her dog and that's what this plan exploits.

Crime Scene

The East River. New York's flume ride for the dead. A classic. But before the river, there's sprawling and empty Bushwick Inlet Park, where the victim walks her dog late at night without fail. Poor dog! Give him some variety. Take him over to Bedford Ave. to find some tail!

The Means

Making this look like an accident is easy enough. Wrapped around her hand will be her dog's leash and at the end of that . . . well, her dog. This isn't called the Perfect Pet Society. Obviously, Agnes went in after her dog jumped in the water, and not knowing the force of the river—which is really an estuary of the ocean—both have succumbed to the currents. On the evening news: *Sad story today.* However, we need water in those lungs! It will be mean and ugly, but we've all seen the TV shows. Fake drowning is an easy one to mess up. She'll be drowned alive near the rocks, where it's pitch black.

There'll be some thrashing. Then blissful silence. And after? Release the body. Just let it go, like an insignificant problem. The midnight low tide will take them as far as Staten Island before last call.

The Mistake

Like we say in our meetings: *every murder has one.* The mistake is the victim is getting smarter. Too smart, especially about things that don't involve her. She should think about a long happy life with her dog.

As Agnes finished reading a precise description of her and Monsieur Hulot's murders, which cruelly exploited their love of routine, she thought: *Hugo. Of course. It's simplest. He runs the same route every day, so he's obviously seen me there before.*

Charlotte loved him. He was also with Whitney—and that would have been a problem for Charlotte, knowing her. She was smoking by the window, alone and drunk, when he came back after blocking the cameras. With the cool air coming in, it must have looked like everything was going to plan for him. The broken necklace said she fought. Maybe she decided to confront him about Whitney. He maybe tried to calm her down, tried to be overly logical at the moment when an angry woman just wants to be heard. Maybe he took her by the shoulder. Then she pushed him. That was his moment. He pushed her back toward the window. She didn't go out cleanly. Her jewelry fell before she did. She held on.

Twenty floors below, Agnes had heard, "No! No! No!"

Did Hugo have time to make the 911 call? He didn't have to. Whitney made it for him—his accomplice, whether she intended to be or not. Agnes now saw the dog-noise complaint as part of an alibi setup if he needed one. The figure hadn't come to the window immediately.

He would have had time to get back down there but could say he was always in his condo. *I'm trying to sleep, but that goddamn dog.*

Or . . . maybe he wouldn't have had time for that. *The elevators could be sluggish,* Agnes thought. Maybe it had happened at Hugo's. The Death from Another Floor theory. It was hard to know.

But the fact that Agnes's rescue dog was included in the murder pitch, floating beside her in the East River—it was all of a piece. A conceptual touch worthy of a murderous psychiatrist. Or maybe Agnes had seen too many Hannibal Lecter films.

Hugo was in the same building right now, taking a shower, then cleaning his brushes, checking his oil tubes, maybe putting a knife underneath the palette. Waiting for Agnes.

Her phone rang, and she had to run quickly through the signs of a heart attack to the other side of the room. She breathed—it was the concierge. She picked up.

"Your brother is here to see you, Ms. Nielsen?"

She had just talked to Paul yesterday—there was no way he was in her lobby, especially with their mom sick. While she had two brothers, both lived six hundred miles away in Michigan. No way either of them would do a casual Brooklyn pop-in.

She could play it safe and make him wait, but if she did that, he would have the advantage, because then she wouldn't know when the confrontation was coming. Her quick decision came from her parents and decades of *Don't put off tomorrow what you can do today* thinking.

"Send him right up," Agnes said as she scanned Lise's abandoned tools.

She grabbed a claw hammer from the toolbox and held it behind her back as she put her head out the door, watching the hall. No one was there yet. In her weeks at the Kentwood, she'd already noticed that she could hear the heavy downstairs stairwell door when it swung open or shut. She didn't hear that, so she ran toward the elevator and took up a protected position off to the side. After a long moment of silence, she heard the rasp of the elevator rising.

As the doors opened with a ding, Agnes raised the hammer.

Ethan stepped out, carrying his backpack. He looked at her for a confused second as she stopped her hammer strike midair.

"You bonehead!" she screamed at him.

"You're the bonehead! Anyone could get in with that trick if you let them."

They argued like brother and sister there in the hallway until Agnes heard Monsieur Hulot barking once at them from her unit. She lowered the hammer and ran down the hall, afraid for him after the morning's threat.

The place was as she'd left it, and the dog was fine. Just in case, she went to the patio door and made sure it was locked. Hulot jumped up and began to lick Ethan's hands and kneecaps.

"You're wasting your time with Hugo," Ethan said after she'd told him of her plan to go up there. He was still angry she'd tried to cut him out, and that made him obstinate. She had explained she was trying to protect him after discovering Emmanuel, but he didn't want to hear her. Ethan was sitting on the one IKEA kitchen chair she'd managed to put together. The other was still in a box leaning against the wall.

"Hugo's strong enough, tall enough, definitely lives in close proximity. The 911 call came from his unit. And there's this—" She extended the written murder plan she'd received that morning.

"But he has no motive—for either Charlotte or Emmanuel." And yet, Ethan's face went white as he looked down at the *We$t Paint* mail and his eyes scanned the contents. He took his horn-rimmed glasses off and began to clean them using his shirttail. When he looked up, he had changed his tune. He was fervent. "I can't let you go to someone's apartment alone, if there's even a slight possibility they may have killed someone."

"At least it's the middle of the day," she deflected. She moved across her space and put on her shoes.

Ethan stood up. He snapped, "Even you can't be that stupid!"

Agnes was about to make a retort, but she realized that his concern was genuine even if he expressed it badly. *Fuck. I can't bring Lise's hammer and still be conspicuous.* Her master class had not contained anything on dangerous meetings—probably because Jacob Kroll didn't want to be sued by relatives when bodies were later found in the East River.

"Don't think I need a man to save me," Agnes said, in spite of knowing Ethan was on her side.

He raised an eyebrow. "You know me better than that. But what are you looking for?" He slapped the back of one hand into the other, like a coach demanding plays. "And don't say the jewelry connection—it's a bullshit coincidence."

"Nic confirmed that Hugo was sleeping with Whitney."

"Nic . . . which one is he again?"

"*She.* The musician—and Charlotte's assistant, it turns out. Come here." Agnes brought him to the bathroom door and pointed to the photograph of Charlotte she'd garbage-picked. She had tucked it into the mirror frame of her medicine cabinet. The cabinet was the one thing she'd done to the condo so far that she could be proud of: midcentury, wooden. It had small shelves on one side (holding the washcloths, perfumes, and Q-tips) along with a mirrored panel that opened. She'd hung it herself the first week, using her ex's power drill.

Ethan stared at it, the old photo at odds with the new mirror.

"Hugo threw this picture out," she told him. "This week."

She could see Ethan was impressed. "You went through his trash?"

"I went through his trash."

"Still not motive."

"Not nothing either."

They agreed that Ethan would be ready if need be—he would text her, innocuous things in case Hugo saw, and all she had to do was thumbs-up emoji if she was okay and thumbs-down if she wanted backup or for him to phone the police.

Ethan said, "Tell Hugo about Emmanuel and gauge his reaction."

"That was the plan," she said, because although they'd patched things over, she wasn't about to let him get one up on her.

Chapter Twenty

Agnes had barely entered Hugo's space when she saw the photograph of Charlotte she'd found, replicated exactly in oil paint, enlarged, nearly three feet across, perched on an easel. Charlotte seemed to smile and invite her in. Her large eyes, her long neck. Head slightly cocked.

Agnes felt even more apprehensive. *How can he look at that every day, given what he's done?*

Hugo had changed into a pale-blue collared shirt with black pants. He gestured her into the room. She hung her purse on a chrome hatstand but kept her cell phone in her pocket. As Agnes stepped closer to the painting, she realized Charlotte's hair had a whirled quality—although Hugo was good, he had not quite perfected his technique. *We'll talk about Charlotte,* Agnes realized. It was direct but the easiest way to begin.

"It looks like her," Agnes said, standing in front of her oversize face. Remaining close to the painting also kept her within sprinting distance of the door, she realized. An advantage in case everything turned.

She could see he'd done the background of the painting in a deep indigo—that was what had left the blue paint on the photo. It must have been clipped there, on the easel, or even at the corner of the painting before he'd finished it.

Hugo smiled, as if relieved at the reception, but there was something edgy about him. "It's from a photo—I have it here somewhere." He turned and began rummaging through some items on a shelf, as though the image would be there. DVD cases and books. From across the room, she noticed a few books about empathy stacked alongside a copy of *Rocky IV* and a box set of *Arrested Development*.

He doesn't know it went into the garbage? Or has he been watching me? Does he know I have the photo?

Agnes saw there were other, smaller paintings on the walls that he'd done—he favored dark backgrounds for all: bergamot, chocolate, jet black. Women's hair and eyes peeped from the rough canvases—he hadn't framed these. From where she stood, she saw they were almost all women. *What a dog.* She could see he'd made the mistake of rushing some of them; there weren't enough layers and had a flatness like the paintings she often saw in cafés. Not that she should judge. Her knowledge of art and technique were limited to visiting MoMA once every three or four years. One canvas was of a small dark-eyed child with coiled buns and red ribbons, but the rest were Edward Hopper–influenced women with unrealistically reddened lips. He'd done a much better job on Charlotte's than these. Agnes's gaze came to rest on a round chrome-and-glass table, where a takeout bag sat.

Agnes's stomach roiled. It smelled too much like the containers from the garbage bag she'd dug through, and she was already too nervous to eat. The conversation with Ethan had made her more wary. Between it and the search for the missing photo, she felt like he really *must* know somehow. She tried to recall if there had been a camera in the garbage room. If Hugo was the one to place the art stickers, he obviously was highly aware of all the cameras in the building.

A laptop lay on the table, too, and a ring light had been set up, though it was switched off. "Is this where you Zoom with your patients?" she asked, gesturing to that corner.

"Sure, painting is only a hobby." Hugo seemed nervous about having her in the space. He moved in a slightly jerky manner as he picked up the computer, unplugged it, and moved it onto a shelf. "I took some art classes in college, but my parents wanted me to be a doctor. I started painting again during the pandemic."

He offered her coffee and said he had taken the liberty of ordering lunch for them. He would go get some plates. He went into the kitchen, and she could hear him opening cupboards. His kitchen was more separate than hers or Charlotte's. She went over and saw that the receipt said mango salad and fried rice. Ordinarily, it wouldn't be unappealing—it was just the association, and her edginess. She didn't even know if she could take more than a swallow of coffee. She hadn't thought about this. She had been drugged at the party; what if he did that now? Even if she hadn't spoken to him, maybe he'd known who she was and wanted her out of the way that night.

Her phone dinged, and she visibly jumped. She was glad Hugo was in the other room. She looked at Ethan's absurd "innocuous" text: Is this papaya still good?

Agnes had never bought a papaya in her life, and she doubted Ethan had either. She clicked a quick thumbs-up.

The layout of the space was different from hers—different from Charlotte's too. Hugo's unit was a two-bedroom, but the bedrooms were at either end of the condo—she could see there was a door beyond the kitchen, and the other room was toward the front. *If he paints all over the living area, what does he use the other bedroom for?* She suddenly wondered if someone else lived there, too, but she didn't sense anyone else in the apartment. Everything was quiet. The front room must have been where he and Whitney had been. She felt almost magnetically drawn to it—she had to go in that direction, as if there might be something of Charlotte's there that would reveal itself.

She could hear Hugo whistling and opening the cupboards again. *Is this easygoing thing a ruse, and at any moment he'll pop out with a gun instead of two forks?*

But she willed herself to calm down. That wouldn't happen when she hadn't confronted him at all yet. *A peek won't hurt.* The door was already ajar. Agnes crept toward it, pushed it slightly, and was surprised at what she saw. The room was as messy as a teenage boy's—the bedding tangled, half on the floor. A basketball lay in one corner.

Hugo seemed a bit old for it. But then she thought, *He jogs—maybe he still plays sports?* He'd left an ironing board set up. In spite of that, there was a haphazardly used laundry hamper, more akin to a clothing volcano. Men's socks and underwear surrounded it. Shirts hung off it, off the board, and off chairs. The air was heavy with cologne. And there, the window.

Agnes stared. It wasn't as big as Charlotte's, she realized. *You couldn't throw someone out of that.* As she retreated, she realized with dismay that she felt let down at the thought. *Did I really like my theory of Death from Another Floor so much?*

She turned and hurried back to the table, reaching it as Hugo returned with a tray of cups and plates, which he distributed in a businesslike fashion. She watched as he loaded her plate in spite of her protests of "just a little."

"There's a reason I asked you up," Hugo said, moving his fork through a small hill of rice.

What if he comes right out and confesses? Agnes felt her brow wrinkle. She pushed her food around on the plate like a child, unable to bring herself to eat. Her phone dinged again. She pressed a thumbs-up, barely looking at Ethan's message. In good news, it meant she'd been there ten minutes already. How much longer would she risk this?

"Sorry, my brother is visiting. He doesn't know where anything is in my place. Hopefully he won't bother us every two minutes."

Hugo commented that they looked alike; he'd seen Ethan at the memorial.

Agnes froze. He had been watching her. She coughed, then took a gulp of coffee, even though she hadn't meant to touch a thing. She changed the subject by staring at the painting of Charlotte. "It's so lifelike. Like she's looking at us."

He turned and looked over his shoulder at the portrait. He swallowed. "I feel that way too. Like she's watching my every move."

Agnes got a terrible feeling, creeping up her forearms, a chill. Ethan was right—she shouldn't have been alone with Hugo. Her eyes moved to the bookshelf again: a copy of *Predator*. No doubt about it, he was in the club. She'd left her purse on the other side of the room. No room for a hammer there, but it turned out it did fit a screwdriver from her ex's toolbox. And now, it was far out of reach.

When Agnes was going off to college, her mom had insisted she carry a nail file in her purse for self-defense. In true Midwestern fashion, her mom had told her to smile and say hello if someone in the park or on the street seemed to pose a threat. "It shows confidence," Patricia Nielsen had said, "and tells the would-be attacker that you've seen him and can identify him." *Him—it was always a him.* "I can't identify him if he kills me," a teenage Agnes had retorted. At that time, she'd doubted that there were men waiting in every shadow to rob her or assault her, which maybe was the healthier way to go through life. New York had definitely been bigger and pushier than she'd imagined, though. "Another thing to do is throw sand in his eyes," her mom had said, though how she'd have access to sand close to NYU, Agnes couldn't imagine.

Although she'd never employed her mother's methods of self-defense, the nail file her mom had given her had become a secret running joke with Agnes and friends; every time she switched over between a purse or backpack, it would be moved into some side pocket of the next one. Having brothers meant she knew how to tackle someone or throw a punch, but she honestly hadn't done so since childhood.

Just before coming up to Hugo's, she'd swapped the nail file for the tool. *A nail file is too ladylike to get a job done,* she thought.

"I can't stop thinking about Charlotte," Hugo said now, his voice sounding raw.

Agnes decided to take her mother's advice a little: look him right in the eyes and speak to him. *Show him you're smart, a fighter.* Agnes made her voice hard. In these circumstances, it wasn't difficult. "You said earlier that you feel like Charlotte's watching you? Tell me about that."

"Lately, I feel like I can't get away." Hugo laid his fork down on his napkin, sounding like a guilty man.

For God's sake, why doesn't Ethan text me now? she thought. Agnes glanced about—she had hot coffee. It could be a weapon. She wrapped her hand around the mug and reeled it in, just in case.

Agnes tried for something neutral. "You're having a lot of feelings, it sounds like."

Hugo pulled his cup toward himself, too, mirroring her body language. "Healer, heal thyself." He snickered, but it sounded bitter. This was not a man about to confess. This was someone who was about to play with her, she thought. He went on: "I actually think hers is the best one I've done, but I can't keep it."

Don't ask why not. "Why not?"

"It's causing a lot of tension. The green-eyed monster." He reached to the shelf behind him and snagged something—a Polaroid photograph.

Now the text from Ethan: Do you ever clean your place?

"Monster?" she asked.

She hesitated a moment, then tapped at the phone, a thumbs-up, in spite of her reservations. *Let's see where it goes.* Between Hugo's fingers, she saw the Polaroid was a shot of Whitney.

Hugo pushed it across the surface. "Whitney would like me to do another painting—of *her* this time. I spent a lot of time on Charlotte's because she was paying me. My first commission. Pressure's on. 'I better do a good job,' I said to myself."

"Charlotte was paying you . . ." That made sense. She liked to sponsor people.

"Maybe I did too good a job."

Agnes stared at the painting behind him. *He'd done too good a job. Ergo, Whitney was jealous. Ergo, Whitney had thrown out the photograph of Charlotte. What else might Whitney have done? She can't have pushed*

Charlotte out of his window, but maybe from Charlotte's own. Whitney's also tall enough to place the sticker on the camera, Agnes remembered. *And Whitney brought me one of my drinks!* Agnes took an overzealous sip of the coffee, burning the roof of her mouth.

Hugo noticed and extended a small pitcher of cream toward her. For a man with such a messy bedroom, he had everything else in order, even down to a useful little porcelain vessel. *The bedroom doesn't fit,* she thought.

"I thought maybe, if you were good friends with Charlotte, you might want it?" he said. "Can you take it?"

Agnes stopped considering the pitcher and added the cream. "Me? What?"

"The portrait of her, of course." Hugo nodded. "She paid me several thousand dollars for it. I don't feel right keeping it." He crumpled his napkin and left it on his plate, then stood up and took his coffee with him as he moved across the room to the easel and stared at it contemplatively.

Charlotte owed everyone money, and meanwhile here she was plying Hugo. And paying him up front.

She bought people's love because she was insecure, Agnes thought. The idea was shocking: someone as interesting and beautiful as Charlotte didn't truly have the confidence she projected. Agnes felt a twinge of sadness at the idea.

"Whitney felt it was inappropriate for me to take the commission. But I was flattered. Someone in the art world coming to *me*." He stared into the painted face. "I know she had a crush on me, but I didn't want to think it was about that."

"A crush. But I thought . . ."

Her phone dinged again, and she tapped a thumbs-up without looking this time. When she glanced down, she saw the message wasn't from Ethan. It was Jamie, asking for that date they'd talked about. *Oops, don't need that right now.* Too late—the thumbs-up was agreement.

Hugo fixed her with a long stare. She couldn't tell if he was angry. "Why in the hell does everyone seem to think that? That chef she hangs around implied that too."

Agnes tried not to let her mouth fall open. She shook her head. "Energy."

He shook his head slowly, again mirroring her movements. *It's odd. Is it a tactic?*

"Charlotte said some things that night," Agnes pressed, hoping to draw something out of him. Hugo had to have been dating both women and didn't want to admit it: from *ménage à trois* to a *ménage à* tumble, whether he or Whitney had instigated it.

Hugo shook his head again. "In psychology it's called *transference*. She developed a warm feeling about me because I was trying to help her. I wasn't her therapist, but I am one. I can't help that the manner comes through. I suggested she stop using so much medication. We had a few long talks about it. What we had was . . . a friendship. That's all it was."

It was Cody who'd said that Hugo was a party boy. But Hugo had taken meds *away* from Charlotte, and Cody had misinterpreted. The evidence of that was in the green garbage bags.

"Whitney is your *girlfriend*," Agnes said as it clicked. They had to have been seeing each other awhile, even if it wasn't official. Charlotte had not been involved with him at all. The summer romance she'd described was just that—a romance, a fantasy. In her mind Agnes tried to replay what Charlotte had said at the party. She'd hoped. But it hadn't been real. Not yet.

"Yes, two months now," he confirmed, and as he thought of Whitney, his expression seemed softer. Then his smile flickered, and he added, "My son lives with me part time, too, so it's complicated. Nineteen, just got into Columbia University."

Suddenly, Agnes was watching Hugo turn into a regular person in front of her, and maybe not the threat she'd thought when she had entered his space. But then again, he could still be in the society—so not as normal as he seemed. An intellectual game seemed right for him. All the men who had been in the club so far were the ones who'd enjoyed showing off their intellect at the party. Agnes decided to roll the dice.

"Columbia," she echoed as she stalled. A nineteen-year-old explained the front bedroom. It hadn't been Hugo at the window that night. It had to have been his son. "You must be so proud."

Hugo hadn't looked proud when he'd announced it, though; even now he looked worried. *Worried about finances?*

He went on to say that he was happy for him but that it was a juggle to date when one had a child at home. Hugo returned to the table and set down his empty cup. "So you'll take the painting," he asked, though his tone made it more of a statement than a question.

Agnes could see his gaze had turned intense. For him, the lunch had been about this—finding a home for things that were no longer wanted. She had been asked there only for this purpose: to bring harmony back to Hugo's relationship.

"Maybe," she hedged. "Who was it meant for?" She knew Charlotte couldn't have wanted a portrait of herself.

He began clearing the plates and repacking the leftovers. He didn't seem fazed that she hadn't eaten. "Her father. Vernon Bosch turns ninety next week. He's not in great health, so she made amends with him recently. She had decided to go to the party—but her cousin was trying to dissuade her. He said she would stir things up and cause even more family fallout. That her penchant for drama could kill her already-weak father."

Agnes dropped her spoon on the floor with a clatter. *Charlotte wasn't estranged from the Bosches.* Agnes felt crushed twice over. Charlotte had lied to her about being in a new love, and she'd lied to everyone about breaking away from one of the most-hated families in America. Or had she been going back to them because she needed the one thing they had—cash? If the patriarch was getting ready to pass, there had to be a trust. Even if Charlotte wasn't hard up, she had habits, and spending money was one of them. Her money went far, but her family's money could buy a lot more plays, a lot more artists, a lot more up-and-coming restaurants. *It fits.*

Hugo must have seen her expression, because he bent and picked up the spoon for her. "Even people who hate their parents want to please their parents." He placed the spoon on the pile of used things. "Trust me. Every other session I do is about that conflict. Both feelings are valid too."

Agnes neither hated nor worried about pleasing her parents, but she did feel a sense of duty, and it was at odds with where she was now. But she needed to put that out of her mind. She stared at Hugo's face. *He's too calm,* Agnes thought. "Who do you hate, Hugo?"

Hugo laughed. "What?! I don't hate anyone." He took the plates and left the room.

Is your Wifi network Sapphocalifragilisticexpialidocious? Ethan texted.

Agnes didn't press a thumb on it. Not yet.

"You added to it, didn't you?" she called across the space, moving toward the door and lifting her purse from the rack.

"Excuse me?" Hugo came and stood between the rooms, wiping his hands on a towel. His glance flicked toward the painting, confused perhaps that she was getting ready to go but wasn't taking it.

"Not the painting." She heard her voice turn tough. "The murder plan. Emmanuel wrote it, but you polished it with your understanding of human psychology. Or maybe you got just close enough to her to add a few winning details. How much do you guys play for? There must be money involved."

This group of men—their silence, their complicity—frustrated her. How nice they acted in person. Emmanuel, Anthony, Lewis, Hugo. No matter how involved each had been, none had spoken up. Not enough.

"I don't know what you mean," Hugo replied, but his expression said something else. A false indignation. Columbia was the most expensive school in New York, and she'd guessed it. He was in PMS, and they were playing for a large prize. Agnes could see him sway slightly, as though the air had gone out of the room for him.

"Emmanuel's dead. They found him at the theater." Agnes was surprised by how coldly she could deliver the information.

Chapter Twenty-One

There was a firm knock on the door behind her. She opened it before Hugo could say anything more. Ethan was there, looking nervous. She stilled him with a look that said *I've got this*.

"What are you talking about?" Hugo glanced between the two of them. "What happened to Emmanuel?"

"I was just telling Hugo here about the 'suicide,'" she said. Ethan came in and shut the door behind him.

"Suicide?" Hugo echoed. It was hard to say if he was distressed by it.

"Well, Carl Weathers, we think that Emmanuel had a bit of help," she said. She nodded to the shelf of DVDs on the other side of Hugo's place.

At the sound of his handle name, Hugo looked like he might bolt from the room. Then something flickered in his expression, like a curtain falling away, and he glared at the painting of Charlotte. "I didn't hate her," he said, but his voice betrayed conflicted emotions.

"Silence has a price," Agnes said through gritted teeth.

He sat down, not answering for a long minute. Agnes stared at him until finally Hugo's head dropped in shame. "Ten thousand."

"For the winner?" she asked.

He nodded. "But there were bonuses for those extra special touches."

"You needed more players. That's why Anthony asked Lewis in. To up the ante." Agnes didn't play poker but assumed it was similar.

"Anthony is part of it?" Hugo looked confused.

"*Transparency*," Ethan said, quoting the screenshot post. He came farther into the room, standing beside Agnes. "That is a lawyer word. Bruce Willis. Of course."

"Lawyers protect themselves," Agnes said, realizing at that moment that the screenshots had been sent to her by Anthony. He wasn't guilty of anything except being in the club, but he also didn't want the involvement traced back. He'd asked for her number at the after-party.

"One person invites you in, similar to a chain letter," Hugo said.

Agnes had no idea what a chain letter was. She gazed at the portrait of Charlotte. She was so beautiful—and what they'd done to her while she'd invited them all into her home . . . Agnes glanced at Hugo and saw he was looking at the painting too. She decided to use silence and see if he'd cave.

"Arnold Schwarzenegger invited me. But I won't say who he is."

Agnes pulled a hard breath in through her nostrils. She turned and swept the easel with a quick, swift kick. The painting toppled, and the easel fell over with a crash. "Did you care about Charlotte at all?" Agnes rasped, glaring at Hugo.

Ethan jumped, startled by her anger.

Some protector.

The way Agnes saw it, Hugo was strong enough to have climbed into the rafters with Emmanuel's body. Whitney wasn't. He was more hypocrite than killer but could easily be someone else's enabler, which made him very dangerous. *Danger is what you can live with. The slow slip of your morals,* she thought.

"Charlotte was a friend, but she wasn't always kind." Hugo's voice turned icy. "She used people and kicked them away. These patterns of behavior are tiring."

"So you thought it didn't matter if *you* used *her?*" Agnes looked down at the painting. From the floor, Charlotte's smile seemed obscene suddenly. Not her smile itself, but the fact that he'd used it for his own gain. He'd charmed her on purpose.

"It's a thought exercise. If it doesn't hurt someone, why not? I wanted the best for my son."

Hugo stood up, and Agnes moved out of his way, frightened now that he'd revealed his calculating side.

"And Whitney had nothing to do with it?" she asked.

Hugo turned to Ethan. "Who would you invite into a club like this, a girlfriend you still wanted to impress or a guy friend?"

"You gifted the onyx as an apology," Agnes said, drawing a shaky breath. "To both women. But only Whitney knew what you were apologizing for. She told me there was a personal story—but she didn't say what. Your guilt," Agnes declared.

"Why don't you let me be the therapist in the room?" Hugo sighed. But then he surprised her. He moved with purpose to the shelves, opened a cupboard below, and located a bright-green folder among some other books and files. He handed it to Agnes.

She let the folder fall open. They were proposals. "You printed them all out?"

"I distrust technology. I keep thorough records. That goes for my patients, my billings, and . . . my hobbies."

"John Duffy, owner of the New York Knicks?" Agnes read out the murder proposal on the top of the pile. She glanced at Ethan. He knew more about the team than she did. From her perspective, sports could be fun to do but were dull to watch, especially on television. Fandom in particular confused her—it was so infused with group dynamics, a code of togetherness, the flip side of which she saw as exclusion.

Hugo turned and looked at Ethan. "You follow basketball?"

"Sure." Ethan was gangly, but at five-eleven he could throw a few baskets. In their younger days, Agnes had seen it.

Hugo spoke directly to him now, as though Agnes weren't there. "So you can tell her: John Duffy's still alive, right?"

Ethan nodded. "Yeah. Still alive."

"We did five imaginary assassinations during my time in the society. Why would this one be any different? That's what I mean when I say a thought exercise doesn't usually hurt someone. Curiosity. Simple problem-solving."

According to Hugo, contributions to the plans were rated one to ten on the following attributes:

a) Feasibility
b) Aesthetics (rated from brute to elegant)
c) Originality
d) Deflection of MMO (motive, means, opportunity)

Hugo said that the last name drawn before Charlotte's was this one: John Duffy, owner of the New York Knicks. Among the men of the club, his villainy was deemed to be profound, as he was ruining their beloved team with bad trades, mistreatment of coaches, and a personal lack of savoir faire. A best friend of Donald Trump, Duffy had been married at Mar-a-Lago. Fancying himself a serious DJ, he'd also "spun" at the event. By any metric, John Duffy simply deserved to die.

With publicly aired grievances and dozens of active lawsuits, it would be easy for police to find suspects with a grudge, thus deflecting attention away from the society. However, Duffy's limited intellect and lifestyle presented a challenge of opportunity to the society. He didn't travel, and he didn't work. His only outing was his courtside seat at the Knicks—a sniper at a packed stadium? Bold but suicidal, never mind the impossible security. He was otherwise ensconced full time at his Oyster Bay estate on the North Shore of Long Island.

While researching, Hugo had caught a small but useful detail in an otherwise anodyne profile in *Architectural Digest*. Duffy's third wife, Bohdana, fancied herself a wellness influencer and said she was determined to wean her husband off his lethal Shake Shack and Marlboro diet. To assist that, he was banned from smoking inside their renovated estate. A cheeky portrait showed a smoking, grumpy Duffy in an Adirondack chair near a firepit.

From there, Hugo opened Google Maps and compared the shots to satellite images. This smoking spot would be visible from the waters of Long Island Sound, leading him to the best possible plan: nautical incursion.

He calculated likely nights Duffy would be at home (nongame nights), time frames that smokers inevitably step outside (after dinner mostly, as he didn't care to contemplate when "after sex" would happen). He also looked at weather charts for maximum night visibility and calmer tides. That was how the dates and times were settled: any non-playoff night in late April, to be precise. "And let's be honest, the Knicks would never make the playoffs," Hugo declared. The society would lease a fishing boat across the sound in Connecticut. (A cross-border challenge sneaked in there for lazy Long Island cops? *Très bien!*)

Agnes noticed that Hugo was getting animated as he detailed how he'd come to his plan. His eyes lit up, and the self-contained, organized man she'd seen up until now appeared to be a passionate, organized killer serving up the head of his victim. She and Ethan both stared in silence.

"At dusk," Hugo said, a hand held aloft, palm open, as though plunged back into a scene he could visualize easily, "we sail the boat ten miles across the sound toward Oyster Bay. As night falls, I anchor with lights off only a hundred yards from Duffy's estate. With a stabilizing mount on the rifle, in case of waves, we wait for Duffy to take his spot at the firepit, the spark of his lighter . . ." Hugo paused for effect. "A burning white bull's-eye on the nightscope."

"Do you know about guns?" Agnes asked.

Hugo shook his head. "In a fantasy, we're good at everything. We're all sharpshooters."

"How would you get away, though?" Ethan came over and sat down on a leather footstool.

Hugo leaned forward. "Figure it would be twenty minutes to an hour before Duffy's discovered. Probably another hour before detectives figure out that the shot could only have come from the water and not the surrounding estate. By then my rifle, gloves, and job clothing have sunk to the bottom of the sound, and the boat's docked again in another state. An hour after that, everyone's at home, and the Knicks—and New York's basketball fans—are all free of their tyrant. It's for the good of the team."

What terrified Agnes was watching the two men unpack it all. Standing behind him, she saw how easily Ethan was drawn into the game. Hugo looked incredibly smug—pleased with himself.

"What's the only clue the police would have?" Hugo pressed Ethan.

Ethan was quick. "They have the bullet."

"A common rifle bullet used by thousands of hunters. Even if a record check of boat owners in Connecticut—and how many of those are there?—connects any Perfect Murder Society member, all they find is a person with no record, no ties to the victim, the mob, or big business."

"Damn, it's brilliant. Elegant, even."

"I liked to think it had the frisson of a salty sea adventure. Like guessing a Wordle in two attempts. And this one was a tough one for the society to top. We didn't pick any in May. Nothing seemed good enough." Hugo's smile flickered. "That's most of the reason we decided to up the theoretical risks and start planning murders of people we knew."

"The murder of Chase Manhattan," Ethan said.

"That was Stallone's. He wrote it in May, but it got discarded—too easy. And yet people liked the idea."

She'd been right: Lewis was Stallone. He had pettily written that— Charlotte stopped sleeping with him to sleep with Chase, and his art show had run throughout the spring.

"And that led to Charlotte's?" Agnes asked, and the men looked up.

"I hadn't thought of it that way, but yes. Everything leads to another," Hugo said. "One foot in front of the other. That's how it goes."

He was smart, but his casualness was appalling. Agnes remembered on the screenshot, Anthony (a.k.a. Bruce Willis) asking for transparency, and Hugo (Carl Weathers) protesting. As flattered as he'd been by Charlotte's attention, it didn't stop him from being cruel.

"Who's Schwarzenegger?" Agnes demanded again, raising her voice this time.

Hugo and Ethan both turned to her, and she could tell they were surprised by how angry she appeared. Coming over to stand above Hugo, she growled, "Either Schwarzenegger invited you or he didn't. Earlier, you said he did. So you know *his* identity at least."

She could tell that her standing while he was sitting shifted the dynamics in a way that made Hugo uncomfortable. In his profession, he was used to asking the questions. He sat there a moment, saying nothing. Then he gestured to the file folder sitting now on an end table.

"I could never *say* who is who—that would break my word. But if you happened to take something while here for lunch, who could blame me?"

Always the strategist, she thought with disgust.

Then she realized: he was afraid of the others in the club. She picked up the folder and leafed back through printed-out discussions. In some, @StevenSeagal, @Jean-ClaudeVanDamme, and @SylvesterStallone appeared more active than in the screenshot she'd been sent. On the page she was looking at, they were commenting on the murder of the basketball-team owner.

> @Jean-ClaudeVanDamme: Perfect murder in Russia is simple: pay off cop. If person is very important, pay off government. Bing-boom, dead.

> @ArnoldSchwarzenegger: Makes for a short movie.

Agnes recognized instantly that the first entry was Alexander and that he wouldn't last long in the club. He was like the student in the creative-writing workshop who couldn't imagine the creative part. This made Seagal and Schwarzenegger the only unknowns.

"And when they're not active anymore, are they still in it?" she asked.

Hugo shrugged. "It's not a union. We don't revoke your card. Three players didn't pony up in June. They're not *out* per se, but they ran out of funds or lost interest in it."

"Could they see the new proposals, even if they weren't playing?" Agnes asked.

"Probably."

"Jonathan? Derek?" She guessed at the remaining members. She glanced at Ethan, hoping he could attach an actor to each player based on his understanding of the action genre, but he hadn't met everyone, and she could see he was playing catch-up in his mind.

Hugo cocked his head and ticked a finger in her direction. "I'll ask *you* a question, and then I have a two o'clock and will have to ask you both to go. Do you think Derek would play a game of this sort with people Anand Holdings collects mortgage payments from?"

Everything about Derek said that he played not completely but mostly by the rules. Even the pet warning he'd given her had been stated.

"Van Damme is Alexander. Seagal, Jonathan," she announced. "And Schwarzenegger . . . Jamie."

If she recalled right, Schwarzenegger had argued for coincidence in a story; he had more presence in the group post—and both of those things seemed like the position that would be taken by a politician who was always spinning.

There was a long silence.

Hugo confirmed by not correcting her. He got up and went to the door, clearly showing it to them and closing the conversation.

Chapter Twenty-Two

"We'll know when we know," Agnes's mom said, holding the phone far away from herself. She was only partly in frame. Agnes's mom could text but wasn't used to video chats. The inexpert phone framing made her suddenly seem twice as old and helpless. Agnes noticed her mother's voice was thin and quiet—it was hard to hear her. That was unusual. But she was glad to see her mom sitting up, not in a hospital gown. She wasn't wearing makeup, but her hair was combed. Patricia Nielsen looked petite, smaller than Agnes remembered from last Christmas. Her mom had lost weight. That might have been the diet they'd warned her to follow, or it might have been this new illness, whatever it might be. They'd done blood tests and scans but were still waiting. Agnes had that terrible sunken feeling in her stomach again.

"Dad's here," Patricia said distractedly, attempting to pass the phone and cut short any interrogation by her daughter.

Agnes had the feeling that her father would be the one to give her the bad news, but it didn't come. He held the phone more adeptly and angled it to put them both in the chat window, then sat down on the edge of the bed.

"Hey, kiddo," he said, his tone declaring nothing more serious than the Tigers' new draft picks would be discussed on this call. She could feel a buildup in her throat.

A long, difficult night awaited her, and she had no idea how to convey to them what she'd signed herself up for. Her father, Lars, had coached her soccer team one year in middle school, and his tactic was to put everyone into the game who had shown up earlier that week to practice, whether they were the best players or not. The other parents crowed a lot about it, especially when the team sank to the bottom of the roster, but he taught her to choose fair over winning, and this was probably the reason Agnes didn't feel at home in her new building.

"Is she okay?" Agnes asked her father, hoping that with his sense of integrity, he would tell her more if directly asked.

"Okay as every day," Lars said cheerfully.

It was on the tip of Agnes's tongue to tell them. Something could go wrong tonight in Brooklyn, and her parents would never know what happened. "I love you," Agnes said suddenly at the end of the call.

It burst out of her as if it had come from someplace deep, even though she knew her father was from a generation that couldn't say it back easily. Instead he replied with a trembling, "You betcha."

The murderer was dancing. When Agnes arrived at the bike lane dedication under the expressway, she saw him, crouched over, stepping back and forth with a little girl in butterfly wings to Chumbawamba's "Tubthumping."

Jamie looked up at Agnes and smiled, acknowledging she was there. He raised his dance partner's small hand above her head, and she did a pirouette to finish. Some in the crowd clapped while a woman who looked like she worked for the city fussed with a small speaker and tapped a microphone with her hand.

He was different now—Jamie had ditched his tight sports coat and skinny slacks from the party for young-politician wear: jeans and a hoodie with the sleeves rolled up in things-will-get-done determination.

When Agnes had texted back earlier that she would see him, Jamie said he had an event first and she should meet him there. It was a bigger gathering than she'd expected. Thirty or forty people, mostly families with their bikes and one news crew. As Jamie took the microphone from the woman, Agnes wondered how much of his performance was now going to be for her. She was certain Jamie—worth millions, if not more—didn't really care about bike lanes or local traffic flow. They were just a way to court favor in the neighborhood. He cared about power, and this was the dukedom he was stuck with until his coronation.

"This bike lane is not everything we wanted, but we're in first gear now, and we won't stop." Agnes stopped her eyes from rolling at the speech copy, but the crowd applauded Jamie as he pointed down at the freshly painted lane. It curved from the street to underneath the Brooklyn-Queens Expressway and then out the other side into what she knew could be a mass-murder amount of truck traffic. Like all bike lanes in Brooklyn, this one seemed to be mapped by a child throwing pickup sticks on the ground.

"It's just a beginning. If I'm elected," Jamie said, turning the event into a full-on campaign stop, "I will *not* settle for less than we deserve." He looked right at Agnes. "I will fight for everything."

After the speeches, she watched him charming the news crew. He was taller than she'd remembered, but that wouldn't have been enough to take Emmanuel. He had to have been unsuspecting. *Hit from behind? Drugged, maybe, like she had been?* She felt queasy as she watched Jamie nodding and smiling, playing an earnest role. He finished his spiel while Agnes leaned against an orange plastic divider.

It was getting dark, and the expressway overhead meant the area was dank and deserted; was this a safe place to begin their date? What if he'd chosen it purposely? The families and cyclists were dispersing now, although a McDonald's across the street looked busy enough. Agnes had resolved to keep it short. She should stay only as long as she felt safe and could draw out information. *Be okay,* she told herself. *You just have to be okay.*

"Hey," Jamie said warmly, coming over. "You want to grab a drink at the Water Tower?"

It was a boutique hotel bar in Williamsburg—on a rooftop at that.

"How about something more low key?" she suggested. "Pete's Candy Store?"

The oldster bar was a little closer—below McCarren Park and always crowded. It was as likely to be hosting a rock singer's daughter's bat mitzvah as it was a poetry reading.

"Pete's, huh?" he drew out with a raised eyebrow. His expression said it all—to him, it was a dive. The tables and chairs were mismatched, and the drinks were still cheap. He shrugged, and they crossed to walk along Meeker Avenue. Like all politicians, he was uncomfortable hanging out where his potential constituents did.

With the tangerine sky glowing over Manhattan in the distance, she glanced at Jamie every now and then. She nervously smiled and finally realized why her friends who dated men seemed so stressed out by the endless possibilities: *Is he going to push me into the traffic? Knife me in the park? Make me go see a fourth film in a Marvel series?* She had no idea what he was thinking.

"I like your necklace," Jamie said, his gaze lingering on her neck. His eyes had a dead shine.

Agnes felt cold for the first time ever during a Brooklyn July. Her hand crept up, and she touched the silver chain—it was one she'd had for years, a small medallion with the name Boblo, an amusement park from her childhood. Irony was always easier than beauty for her.

"Places are important to you?" Jamie asked, his date-like banter more unnerving than if they'd gotten right to confronting each other.

"The old places, sure," she answered automatically, truthfully. "But Brooklyn is home." He had to think she was clueless. That meant he was underestimating her—and she was getting very good at using that.

It was dark by the time they made it to the bar on the edge of the park. As they entered, she saw there was a table for two left empty. Agnes sat down, and Jamie said he'd grab their drinks at the bar.

"I'll help you!" Agnes quickly said, running to catch up with him.

When they sat back down with their matching gin and tonics, she was able to look at Jamie and was close enough to smell him. He wore a morning-old spray of Chanel Bleu, a lawyer's cologne that didn't match with his Brooklyn fighter image. She scanned his face for any resemblance to Charlotte; then she saw it in the cheekbones.

"I was thinking about you right before you texted me," Agnes said.

"Is that so?"

"Charlotte's circle was artists and writers and then the money people. But you. You're so . . . earnest. I guess that intrigued me." Agnes tried to draw him out.

Jamie was silent for a moment, and she didn't know if he was angered by her observation. Then he smiled slowly. "I did want to go into creative writing, but my father, he was pretty adamant that it be law school or an MBA. Politics is an art form, though. It's like storytelling. I'm finding that, anyway."

Agnes suspected the writer of the perfect murder scenarios sent her way was a frustrated author. Some talent but a little showy yet.

"How'd you meet Charlotte? Door-to-door donations?" she asked.

"Further back."

"Your family is close to her family? Vacations together at the Vineyard?"

"You're a little aggressive. That's not a bad thing. But I'm wondering what you're getting at?"

"I've seen your Instagram. You took a private jet to Burning Man," Agnes said.

"It belonged to Grimes. A friend of mine is her manager."

"And tonight, your community group was christening a bike lane. Don't you think your voters will start to see the contradictions?"

"Not in my zip code." He had a few fine lines around his eyes, and his irises were a pale gray blue, like pencil lead.

From the far back room, she could hear an acoustic set beginning. A guy who sounded like he'd never smoked a cigarette or worn torn jeans was doing a version of Nirvana's "Where Did You Sleep Last Night?"

Agnes took a drink. Jamie wasn't giving her much. *He knows it isn't a real date,* she deduced. But if that was the case, she figured she might as well push some buttons. "It takes money to get elected, right?"

Now he leaned back, and that cocky smirk she'd seen the night of the party came out. She'd found the topic that mattered most to him. "A *lot.* And I say that being from money. I've always been up front about that."

She raised an eyebrow. "The same money as Charlotte?"

Jamie leaned back and let out a long sigh. "You're good."

"Everyone googles before a date now," Agnes said. She cocked her head and let one hand climb up to play with her hair, imitating stereotypical behavior she didn't usually engage in. "We're all CIA agents meeting in Budapest over lunch. Like, 'I've seen your dossier. Would you split fries and a salad?'"

He laughed at her joke. "You're right. And you probably might know that Charlotte and I, we were a little bit related."

"How related?"

"Not close. My mother was her father's sister."

Agnes didn't miss a beat. "That's first cousins." Hugo had mentioned a cousin. She felt a thrill that she'd gotten it right but didn't let it show on her face. As Nic had said, they were close, but not *close* close.

"It's a habit. With that family name, her real name, you have to be careful in how connected you say you are. But I lost my mother a couple of years ago. Charlotte was there for me. You start to put aside all the petty things when you realize people aren't around forever, are they? One moment you're alive. The next, you're gone."

A spin and a threat delivered with a wink and three-day stubble. Jamie couldn't help but radiate his belief that he was the smartest in the room. *Chilling, really.* Agnes rose. "I'll be right back."

As she got up, Agnes took her drink with her. She set it at the bar. She didn't want to leave it alone with him. When she arrived in the back room where the restrooms were, she tried the first door. It was open. She closed it again and looked toward the front room. Jamie was gazing out the window. Agnes moved on to the next door. It was locked. She quickly tapped out a rhythmic knock. Ethan opened the door.

She pushed in past him and switched the lock closed. The room wasn't much bigger than a closet.

"Jesus," Ethan said. "Do you know how many people have tried the door? What took you so long? You said you'd be here at eight."

"He admitted he's related to Charlotte. First cousins. His mother must have been the co-owner of Bosch with Charlotte's dad. Margaret Bosch: I remember that name from the archives. The marriage must have come later. That means the entire family trust would be controlled by Jamie and Charlotte—once her father passes. Imagine . . . he's spent years thinking it would be all his because Charlotte was estranged. He even said, 'I won't settle for less than we deserve.'"

"He confessed to you?"

"No. He was being passionate about bike lanes—but it was so obviously a hand tip."

Ethan gave her a dubious look. "The royal *we*?"

"He wants to brag almost. I think we can get him."

"How?" Ethan asked.

Agnes was genuinely at a loss. "Stay in here for a few minutes."

"I already smell like toilet freshener."

"Just a couple of minutes and I'll be gone. I'll text you when we leave. He's still playing this date like a game, so I'll take it back to my place. But you'll be there first, and we'll confront him."

"Gather in the parlor and run down his entire murder plot in front of him while he politely listens? He's not British."

"He's rich. Maybe he'll act like a gentleman?"

When Agnes returned to the table, Jamie had bought two fresh drinks. She looked at the tumbler and could see the condensation drip off the glass. For a moment she thought she saw a white wisp of powder on top of the clear liquid.

She froze, her fingertips resting on the table's edge: the glass seemed to glow as she stared at it, trying to wrap her head around how she could avoid touching it. Then she smiled for Jamie. "We could drink those here, or we could drink at my place?"

He looked up at her. "Sounds fun."

The game was beginning.

As Agnes and Jamie walked through the streets of Williamsburg, which could alternate between unlit industrial voids and sudden bursts of drunk bar girls, storefronts, and pubs, she wondered what route Ethan would take with his bike and if he would make it back ahead of them.

It was hard to keep up her end of the small talk. *Why are all dates about finding out how many siblings someone has or what their first concert was?* Jamie's first concert was U2, and he had no siblings—which fit Agnes's theory. If Vernon Bosch died this year and Charlotte was already gone, he could inherit the money to the tune of "One." In fact, it was almost a guarantee that he would have the money before his campaign finished. But now Agnes was stuck talking about her family—she could make her brothers bigger and more protective of her than they were. But Jamie wouldn't be intimidated. This wasn't high school. *Dates should be about finding out whether someone enjoys the idea of murdering you,* she thought. *What questions do women ask to figure that out?*

"What's the craziest place you've ever done it?" she asked.

"Helicopter. You?"

"Uh . . . restaurant bathroom. But a nice one, the Algonquin Hotel."

This was pointless. What she really needed was to confirm means, motive, opportunity. But she already knew. Means: this remained elusive. He was in good shape but carried no weapons that Agnes knew of. Motive: the entire Bosch empire hung in delicate balance. Opportunity: he was close to Charlotte. He smoked. They'd smoked together that night in her room. Maybe he'd stayed late to hear her sad tale of how the man she was infatuated with was dating Whitney.

They passed by the inlet park along the river. Agnes paused at the entry to look in at the night soccer games, hoping to give Ethan more time to arrive ahead of them. She fixed her stare right on Jamie and needled him. "This is where I walk my dog."

"You have a dog?" he asked in a way that lurked between question and statement.

"Is that a problem for you?"

"I love dogs." Jamie turned to move on. "Can't wait to meet him."

Him. Even if he remembered that she had a dog from small talk at Charlotte's salon, he shouldn't know her dog was a boy.

"Wait," Agnes said, and he stopped. She looked at his cheekbones and brought up the image of Charlotte by the window. Agnes leaned in and kissed him while thinking of her. At first, it was tentative, but she knew she had to stall for time—she put her arms around his neck. She'd bring him back to meet her dog, but instead there would be Ethan in the apartment.

She let it go on just a little longer, letting her hands hover over Jamie's pockets, checking for weapons. Only what felt like a wallet. But she couldn't continue it indefinitely—there was a hardness even to the kiss, like kissing a wall. And she could smell his cologne again; her mind trick was over. She broke it off and looked at him.

He was suddenly weak, his lips hanging open slightly. She could have pushed him over with a pinkie right then. He had not been expecting that. Agnes felt power return to her side.

Chapter Twenty-Three

As they approached the Kentwood, she tried to think about where and how she and Ethan would question him—in their preplanning they'd been all bravado, but could either of them really pull off the bad cop? What would they do if Jamie cut and ran or turned violent? After the kiss, they'd been walking close, their arms occasionally grazing one another's as if they actually liked each other. She was suddenly aware of how, under his bland politician wear, he was fit—likely the result of a well-paid personal trainer. But unlike a person on a real date, Agnes didn't find it attractive or impressive but disturbing. He'd been able to overpower Emmanuel, or maybe surprise him from behind. Agnes tried not to think about it.

Get him inside, and there are two of us. Tell him what we already know. He's already been admitting to everything. It was a simple plan, like something out of an old noir movie.

Agnes searched for Ethan's retro green Electra Loft bicycle as they walked in, but it didn't appear to be locked in the rack out front. That didn't mean he wasn't there—he may have come from around back and found another place to lock it. She was so intent on spotting it she almost missed Jamie's glance. Then there it was, just a few moments before they headed under the Anand Holdings sign. He looked up. It was more than a peek up at her patio, though—he tipped his head quickly and scanned the rooftop. And without a word spoken, that was when Agnes knew: Charlotte hadn't fallen from her window. They'd been up there. *It's his tell.* Her different-floor theory wasn't wrong.

"I didn't even ask what you have to drink at your place?" Jamie politely inquired, smiling, as they crossed the lobby. They were still going through the motions of a man meeting a woman in a bar and then getting his pencil sharpened on the first date.

She didn't know what the condo contained—probably half a kombucha and a bottle of white wine. She wasn't planning on entertaining. "Scotch," she said, thinking that's what he wanted to hear.

Agnes heard a ding from her pocket. "My brother," she said. "My mom hasn't been well." She pulled out the phone, paused, and scanned the text, which of course was from Ethan. I'm here—I've got help with me, it said. She couldn't imagine who Ethan would bring for backup. *A film blogger? A game designer?* Still, it couldn't hurt. He was there. She sent a thumbs-up, relieved she could bring Jamie up.

They walked into the elevator, Jamie on the side closest to the panel.

"Floor two," Agnes said.

He pushed the button for "Doors Closed" and then hit "R"—roof.

"That's not my floor," she said. Her voice was rough, panicked. In her relief that Ethan was there, she'd assumed everything would be fine, and in that moment she'd made a mistake.

"Nice night." Jamie smiled, but it was crooked, like he knew she could see through him and didn't care. "Maybe we could see some stars."

Are we still playing the romance game? Maybe he actually liked that kiss I laid on him.

Agnes looked up, but the elevator camera where she'd found the red sticker was now completely gone—there was just a wire hanging. It had been torn down.

"You see that? Funny thing," Jamie said, his voice warm and sonorous, like a man who wanted to show off to his date. "All you have to do is call the CCTV company and say you're Derek and you want new cameras put in. The old ones get pulled down, but the new one's not installed till next week. Nothing runs to schedule in New York. That's one thing you can rely on."

Agnes lunged at the control panel, swatting at the next floor's button, hoping to hit it and jump off. But Jamie blocked her. The next thing she knew, his hand wrapped her wrist tightly. She was stunned that no matter how she tried to pull away, she couldn't break his grip.

"Let go," she demanded. She could tell he was leaving bruises, but that was the least of her worries.

He smiled and held her firm, like it was nothing. "When you go to Phillips Exeter, you train with former Olympians."

"Well, I went to Huron High in Ann Arbor. Our mascot is the river rat." Agnes stomped on his foot, and he let go of her. She retreated to the corner as he yelped. "Don't do this, Jamie. I just wanted to talk to you," Agnes said. She knew she could talk him down—she was smart and knew she could find the logical argument that would shake him from whatever he had planned.

"I want to talk too. That's all this is. Let's see if our interests can intersect in some way."

The elevator opened on the final floor—and Jamie tugged her out into the hall. Through the long glass windows, she could see she wasn't lucky. No one was lounging in the rooftop garden area. *Fuck.* Jamie banged open the door and yanked her out onto the patio. To her relief, he released her. Instinctively, she ran across the space. But that was pointless—there was only one way onto the roof, and moving away from it put her closer to every edge.

Jamie wasn't following her anyway but turning and looking around, checking for anyone who might have come up to have a vape, a phone fight, or some fresh air. He slowly walked over and sat down on one of the outdoor sectionals. Patting the seat cushion beside himself, he said, "Sorry about the elevator. All I want to know is what you want."

Agnes didn't need anything from Jamie other than the truth. But she saw immediately that he was looking to make a deal—and that was preferable to where they'd been only a minute before. Cautiously, she went over to the seating but remained standing a few feet away. In her hand she now clutched her phone. He looked at it and rolled his head on his neck. There was such a cold, casual way about him now.

"You brought Charlotte up here that night, didn't you?" Agnes asked.

"No, she brought me up here. She doesn't like to smoke in her place, you know."

"But if you closed out the party, who placed the sticker?"

"Seems like we'll be here all night while you process things. Scotch would have been nice," Jamie mused.

"Let me go downstairs, and I'll get some," she suggested.

Jamie laughed. He was perfectly relaxed in a way that terrified her. But she knew she couldn't show it. Agnes had to wrestle back control.

"You left and came back," she said, feeling her chin lift. *You could come back without being detected,* she thought, *if you placed the sticker on first exit.*

"Never heard of someone doing that at a party." His voice oozed sarcasm. Then he said, "Come on, now—I'll be nice." He twitched his head toward the rattan sofa beside him.

"You're talking about a deal. Why should I trust you? You haven't offered anything," Agnes said, but she came a little closer.

"The nylons in the bedroom—I didn't use those."

Agnes stared. No one could know they'd been lying out except the last person to be in her place. Jamie wasn't trustworthy, but he was giving her something. She sat down in the large patio chair across from him. "Why not?"

Jamie made a breathy sound in his throat like a candle sputtering. "That was in Emmanuel's original plan, but I thought it was cliché. Stealing nylons? Too much . . ." He cocked his head. "Anyway, I didn't really plan to *go through* with his proposal."

"You were going to talk her out of attending her father's party," Agnes stated. Although her heartbeat was still elevated, she thought she might be able to tease out more from him. *Facts. Stick to facts,* she told herself.

He sighed. "Didn't matter. She was already back in his good graces. Vernon Bosch added her to the trust after a single lunch. So yes, there's the evidence of her charm—she did have some. In case you were starting to think she was the monster some of her exes make her out to be."

"After years of being the last heir, that must have made you . . . feel something." Agnes leaned forward, the phone still in her lap but her hands between her knees like she was running a basketball play with him. "Angry enough to push her . . ."

"Oh no. If anything happened, it wasn't in anger."

She waited. It was the best move. Jamie did what she wanted. He provided a better explanation. "I liked Charlotte, but we've never really seen eye to eye. She believes in people, and I know better—you should never trust anyone, because they will only disappoint you. You know, you work hard, and then one day . . ." Jamie made a gesture like things were going up in smoke.

He didn't like that Charlotte could waltz back in, Agnes saw. He felt rejected by his uncle. It wasn't just that half wasn't enough. The inheritance was a justification. *Money becomes meaningless once you have that much,* she thought. *What's the emotional difference between four billion and two billion? But a shifting alliance and warm paternal eyes turning back to his little girl come home? That must be a special kind of heartbreak.*

Agnes's gaze went to the roof edge: the sky so black and all of Manhattan bright in the distance. He and Charlotte would have simply strolled over to smoke and look. *It was why I heard her—because they weren't inside her apartment when she screamed.* They had been outdoors, standing in the Brooklyn sky.

Emmanuel's plan might have given Jamie the idea, or he might have simply seen an opportunity—fools he could frame for what he'd already wanted to do.

Probably Charlotte hadn't even wanted to talk about family. She'd had other things on her mind—Hugo and Whitney, the fight with

Veronica. She would have already been feeling drained when Jamie broached the issue of the family trust. Jamie didn't take no for an answer, and Charlotte was used to people who looked up to her, those whose loyalty had been won by her charm and tenacity. She wouldn't have been used to an argument, Agnes thought.

"She was drunk, angry with me—if anything, she pushed me. The recoil from that. That was what made her fall," he said, his glance skimming over to the edge of the roof, the skyline.

Agnes nodded. "I can see it." *Absolutely it did not happen that way,* she thought. Jamie could argue it was a crime of passion, but he'd already put a whole plan in place, starting with the stickers and gloves. Embarrassingly premeditated. But she wanted to pull it out of him if she could, then get herself to safety.

"She did fight with Veronica earlier that night. We all saw how physical she could be," Agnes supplied.

"You're very analytical," Jamie said. "You ever do any political work? Speech writing? I could use someone like you. Excellent pay."

There it is. Did he think people were so easily bought? A murder— two—and he could make it go away with a public sector job?

"How much do you inherit now?" Agnes asked flatly.

Jamie just smiled.

"What about Emmanuel?" she asked. "You lured him out with . . . a promise of money—"

"No, it was flattery. That was the easy way in with him."

"Flattery as in . . . ?"

"Flattery as in flattery," Jamie said, unbudging. "He came to my place very easily that night."

"You're both in Park Slope."

"Everyone had been talking—" Jamie said.

"On the message board," Agnes supplied.

He nodded. "I said I'd changed my mind. That we needed to sort it out, report it all. Together."

Agnes went for it. "And then you drugged him. Like you did to me the night of the party. Because he was talking to me."

Jamie admitted nothing but didn't deny it. So he'd been concerned about Agnes from the start, that she would short-circuit his plans. He'd handed the drink to Whitney to bring through the condo—it had been so simple. A sleeping pill, or Xanax. Not a roofie, because he hadn't planned that part. He hadn't known there would be a detective—even an amateur one—at the salon.

She found herself staring at him and had to will herself to stay neutral, not get angry before she had all she needed. Before she could think what to say, he spoke.

"Give me a number," Jamie said, raising an eyebrow. He was asking her price but without saying it directly. There were lights near all the shrubs, and the long shadows cast a dark patch on his face, though she could see his expression had hardened now.

She had to be careful. "My number is Charlotte and Emmanuel. Was it worth it?"

"What pamphlet did you read as a kid that said everyone acts right?" Jamie practically yelled at her. He stood up.

Agnes shook her head and waited, as she'd learned to do.

Jamie sighed. He moved away from her, over to the railing, framed by the bridge and the Empire State Building. To his left the **DOMINO SUGAR** sign flashed.

"Charlotte was figuring things out. That's why she called me. She wanted to hire me," Agnes said. "That means you had already said something to her, earlier, at the party."

"My family is smart," he replied, glancing back at her.

Agnes stood, her phone gripped tightly in her hand. She glanced down to check that it was still recording. She'd started it before going over to sit with him. But he was farther away now. Would the audio of his bribe come through? The evening was warm, but a breeze had picked up, and she expected that could affect the sound too. If she were to leave and hand her phone over to the police right now, she supposed what she'd already recorded might be enough. But she had to be sure.

Although Saturday-night Brooklyn stretched below them, full of laughter and music, Agnes felt like her heart was beating so hard she couldn't hear anything else. If she wanted the recording to be usable, she had to go over there. She took a few steps across the roof. He watched her come, his gray eyes wolflike.

She reached the railing and grasped it with her other hand. Agnes needed to understand. "Didn't you feel anything for her?"

"Business is like a story. When you start it, you have to finish it. You have to accept that it's not personal. I mean, the Bosch company has killed thousands of people. My father didn't go to jail. He died in his sleep in Palm Springs."

Not personal, he'd said. She stared at Jamie and didn't say anything. Unconsciously she glanced down at her phone, just for a second. *I got it,* she thought.

"It's a story," he said, his lips twisting up at the corners smugly. "Here's another story. 'After a night of drinking, Agnes, obviously in love with Charlotte and all broken up about it, copies her death.'"

Agnes reacted quickly, stepping away from the railing. Jamie grabbed at her wrist, and her cell phone dropped from her hand. She stared as it bounced on the boards of the rooftop deck and fell between them, face up. Its screen awakened, and she could see the voice-memo app and its ticking time, showing how long she'd been recording: 6:26 and continuing to count. He saw it too.

They both lunged for it. Agnes's hand grazed it, and the recording stopped, but Jamie was stronger than her. He pushed her hand aside, grabbed the phone, swiftly strode to the edge, and tossed it over.

"Of course you were recording," he said, his voice cold now. "What's your plan now, Nancy Drew?"

"iCloud," she said. "I finally figured out how to sync it."

Jamie scoffed cruelly. "You wish. Just you and me now."

Agnes backed away slowly. But further reasoning was futile. *He'll kill me no matter what I say or do. After all, he tore out the camera—no, wait, the rich boy had someone do it for him. It's been his plan from the beginning.* She turned to run.

She'd almost made it to the egress—the safety of the hall and elevator—when Jamie caught her from behind. He grabbed her hair, and she was jerked back with a force she didn't know possible. Her hands immediately went to her scalp, trying to lessen the hot pressure. She took several steps backward with him, submitting to lessen the pain in her head. A voice inside her mind urged her, *Scream. You heard Charlotte scream, didn't you?*

So Agnes screamed. As loud as she could.

Jamie let go of her hair immediately, and she took a dazed step away. Suddenly her voice cut—she felt the chain of her necklace tighten around her throat. She tried to kick backward. No connection. Agnes could feel Jamie's breath on the back of her neck. He was grunting slightly. She could feel his body, hot with effort as he pulled, holding her close to him, the thin chain piercing as he clutched it mercilessly. He walked her backward a few steps, strangling her with her own necklace. Her fingers raked upward at the silver chain, but there was no way she could halt its journey into her throat—he already had it tight.

Jamie bent over with her. She was now staring at the deck boards, her eyes watering.

He was enjoying her pain. *Seconds,* she realized. That was all she had. She couldn't breathe. She flailed. Her purse flapped below as she tried to push past the other useless objects that collect in a bag. But then she had it in her hand, the screwdriver she'd put there earlier in the day, its yellow handle and Phillips tip. She felt the chain on her windpipe like a hot wire and tried to lean back against Jamie, hoping to show she'd given up fighting. She tried to get the word *please* out, but it was only a gasp with no sound to it.

She felt him straighten with her slightly, his body relax a little, just for an instant, and then she struck. She took her best swing, straight behind, the screwdriver from her purse embedding in his gut.

Jamie let go. Agnes fell forward. She turned and saw him gasping, against the railing. He'd dragged her much closer to it than she'd realized. He was looking down in shock. There was blood quickly seeping onto his T-shirt and sweatshirt. He wiped his hand across the word **BROOKLYN** on his chest, leaving a red streak. His face had turned pale and sweaty, but there was still a cold resolve in his eyes. "A screwdriver?" he muttered.

Seeing she was about to escape, he grabbed at her—but she was already crouched, and Agnes twisted low. If she let him lock arms with her, he'd toss her over the edge in a heartbeat. She knew that from his grip in the elevator, and if she ran—well, she knew that one too. He had a grip on her shirt when the door burst open on the egress and Ethan ran out, yelling, "Let her go!"

Lewis Grant was behind him. Jamie glanced—but didn't let go, his fist still clutching the white fabric of her shirt. If anything, he smiled at them.

She came back up as hard as she could, planted her shoulder into Jamie's hip—and he shot upward. For a moment, she felt triumphant at besting him. And then, she watched him fall as if in slow motion—and felt a gaping pit in her stomach. She watched his perfectly cuffed jeans and the soles of his shoes disappearing over the edge. Five long seconds, and there was a loud metallic *thud* below, but she couldn't look. She already knew what that sight could be.

Chapter Twenty-Four

Agnes sank to the deck, coughing, still trying to regain her breath. She heard Ethan's footsteps as he ran over.

"Where . . . were you?" she gasped.

"Right here. Are you okay?"

She nodded, but that hurt. Ethan was crouched beside her, but Lewis dashed to the edge to peer over. She wouldn't have guessed the journalist could move that fast. "Whoa." He flinched back. "He landed on the cop car."

"When I realized you weren't coming back to your place, I looked everywhere," Ethan said.

"And him?" Agnes whispered. She hadn't completely lost her voice, but every time she breathed, it ached. She sat up and wiped her face with the back of her sleeve. Lewis could hear her, but for some reason Agnes didn't trust his showing up there.

"You're shaking. It's the adrenaline," Ethan assured her and helped her stand.

"I was outside the building when Ethan got here," Lewis said, coming back toward them. "I wanted to warn you. I figured out it was Jamie. We called the police." Lewis gestured between himself and Ethan.

"Guess you got the story when I did," Agnes admitted, somewhat reluctantly.

"Lewis was the one to notice the cameras were gone," Ethan said. He held his arm around her, and although she was perfectly capable of walking on her own, Agnes let him. There had been more than a moment where she'd thought she might be finished, and it felt secure beside a friend.

"I'd like to go inside now," Agnes said.

Agnes spent half the night in the hospital and the other half at the police station—she'd been both treated and questioned. Ethan made a good witness. He and Lewis were both on her side, professionals with no record, like her. When the story hit the eleven o'clock news, Anthony texted to say he could help if she needed a lawyer—but Agnes knew that was more ass covering. The police didn't charge her immediately, but it was clear they weren't done with her. There would be things kicked up with a case involving this many big names: a pharmaceutical family, a well-known art dealer, an ambitious politician, a Pulitzer-winning playwright. But thankfully the roof recording had saved to her iCloud, and by 9:00 a.m. they were making a search of Jamie's home and office.

"Apparently there were lots more mistakes than the Perfect Murder Society members could conceive of," Agnes told Derek when they met in his office two days later.

"I'm just glad the club never met at the building." Derek looked somber. His building wasn't getting publicity for being a place you wanted to live. But he raised an eyebrow and let her have her moment. "Okay, tell me. What did the society not think of?"

"Namely you shouldn't keep the laptop of a person you murdered. That's one." Emmanuel's computer had been found at Jamie's home. "Two, his political office had a typewriter that could easily have been used to write the fake play/suicide note as well as the note that was mailed to me." The detective had taken the threat Jamie had mailed for fingerprinting. She moved around on the swivel chair and wished Derek had offered her a manager's chair like the one on his side of the desk. She hurt in weird places and would probably never wear a necklace again. She raised a third finger, counting the errors. "And three, Jamie had Charlotte's phone in his car glove compartment. Which is really cocky. He just didn't expect to get caught."

"I thought he was one of these green guys," Derek said. "He's not a cyclist?"

"Jeep Grand Cherokee."

"Ah, politicians are all the same—doesn't matter which side." Derek glowered.

Fixed on the wall beside him was a new plaque. Under a sepia-colored photo of the Brooklyn Bridge were the words BROOKLYN: LIKE NO OTHER PLACE IN THE WORLD. On the desk between them, Derek's phone lit up with messages, even though he had it silenced. He tapped his lips with his fist like he was deep in thought. "You know, maybe I will become a producer after all. I have been thinking this would make a great movie."

"Yeah?" Agnes smiled. It was the first time she'd done that in twenty-four hours.

"You know any famous actors?" Derek asked.

"I . . ." Evie's lovely face popped into her mind. "Actually kind of do."

"Famous?"

"Getting there," she bragged.

Derek mentioned that his older brother was taking over building safety now—and meeting with someone to see about sixty-inch guards—eighteen inches higher than the required railing. Derek clapped and dusted his hands off as if he was done with it. "And yet, this part is his job now, not mine. What about you—your job? You want to continue?"

She'd been surprisingly happy chasing around the city for information but hadn't thought beyond next week. Most days she hadn't thought beyond that minute. "What do you mean?"

"You've proven it—this is your . . . métier. Also, I have another gig for you."

Agnes protested with a slight groan. She couldn't imagine doing anything this dangerous again. Not right away anyway. Her scalp still burned from Jamie's hands dragging her by her hair. She needed time to recover—not just from what he'd done, but from what she had too.

Her phone dinged—the new one she'd bought. She'd had it only a few hours. When she leaned over, she saw the message read: It's Evie. Ethan filled me in. Just putting my number in your new phone. Agnes smiled, then flipped the phone face down on the desk and asked Derek what the job was.

His youngest brother was going through a difficult divorce—he needed someone to find out what his wife had been up to, whether she was cheating, hiding money in secret accounts, things like that. Derek gave Agnes a few intimate details she hadn't asked for, then pressed: "This divorce will cost the family. Do you think she's being unfaithful?"

There it is again, Agnes thought. *Money like a serpent, rearing its green head.*

"Quick answer: probably she is. Or maybe they both are." She felt that the topic of divorce was beyond her—the unhappiness of couples hard to measure.

When Agnes had agreed to take a look around Charlotte's apartment and ask some questions ten days before, she hadn't expected to kill someone—even if it was in self-defense. She had never realized she could be capable of it, even unexpectedly in a moment. It gave her pause about how she was going to choose her future situations. Agnes had a flash of herself joining a CrossFit class to befriend a sexually unsatisfied woman. She hedged and suggested, "Maybe we just shake hands on this one first?"

Slowly Derek nodded, though she could see his disappointment. He located his checkbook. It was underneath a newspaper that had been unfolded and sloppily refolded on the filing cabinet beside the desk. She hadn't expected payment, but he said, "My lawyer insists I pay you. No arguments, please."

As she heard the crinkle of the check being passed over, Agnes asked, "Any chance I could borrow that newspaper?"

Derek gathered the newspaper and handed it to her as she stood.

When she glanced down, she saw the amount on the check was a no-questions amount.

"Don't let it change you, Agnes." Derek smiled, but there was a seriousness in his eyes.

They shook hands, and she left the Anand offices to walk out in front of the building. Joggers and traffic were slowly pouring down Kent Avenue. The July heat had broken. It was a pleasantly overcast day, the smell of morning rain in the air, though no doubt it would warm up later.

One of the front-page headlines read: Bosch Patriarch Passes.

The article reported that Vernon Bosch had succumbed to a heart attack following news of the death of his nephew, James Metzger, who had been implicated in the murder of Bosch's only daughter, Charlotte Bond.

Agnes supposed if heartbreak was still possible even for the most hardened, it ought to give her hope for humanity. She wondered who inherited the Bosch fortune now before realizing it wasn't her task to sort out the various wills of the deceased—Charlotte's or Jamie's. It was a constellation she couldn't decipher. One mystery she could understand was that there were two journalists named on the article, and neither name was Lewis's.

She unlocked her phone screen and read Evie's messages again. The second was: Damn, you went hard. If you want to go soft sometime, let me know.

The idea of tea on a sofa was incredibly appealing. But Agnes had some calls to make, so she typed one word, Yes, and pressed a simple red heart.

Agnes went back up to her place, where she stopped and took a minute to empty out the cardboard box that contained her shoes. She carefully tucked them into the Container Store bins she'd bought when she'd moved into the condo. Monsieur Hulot looked up curiously from his bed as she packed up Lise's tools and snapped the case shut. The Phillips was unrecoverable, but she supposed being down only one tool was better than not returning them at all. She took cleaning spray and tidied up all surfaces. As she dusted her bedside table, she picked up a small saucer where she sometimes put her earrings. She paused over the rectangular onyx necklace that was there too—the one she had picked up that night on the deck.

The police had not cared to notice those first clues Charlotte had left behind. Holding her onyx necklace now, Agnes felt her throat grow hot. She knew it had another meaning. It had broken when Jamie had grabbed her.

She gathered it in her palm again and put it in her pocket.

"Walkies?" she said to Monsieur Hulot, and the dog jumped to his feet and raced toward the hook where his leash hung.

As she was taking the dog out, she got the call she'd been waiting for.

He was sitting on the back patio, the same café where they'd met before, his laptop open and his phone lying casually on the table. With a single glance at the face-down phone, all her plans about Lewis had changed.

Easy, keep it easy, she told herself. She carried a seltzer and let the leash hang loose so that Hulot led the way. Lewis visibly shrank even though the dog dropped and sat on command. It was one o'clock, but the gray sky meant the patio was mostly empty. A few customers were inside the café. Out here only a man in a fedora and a vintage MIAMI VICE T-shirt sat nearby, his bored face constantly bent toward his phone as he scrolled. Agnes tried not to roll her eyes; she thought fashion was finished with irony, but apparently no one in Brooklyn had gotten the message. Across the patio, a woman in shorts and a tank top was writing in a journal.

Lewis stood and gave Agnes an awkward hug where they barely touched. "Hey, how are you feeling?"

She nodded. "I'm all right. How about you?"

Lewis drew a breath and nodded. They sat down. He left the phone lying screen down between them as he packed his laptop into his satchel. He looked around the patio and sniffed back, like a young boy without a tissue.

"You seem a bit lost without your notebook," she remarked.

"You too. What will you do now that you don't have to interview anyone anymore?" Lewis went for a laugh.

"I was surprised you didn't have the lead article today." Agnes tried to give him room to open up about it.

"I . . . uh, didn't make the deadline." He nervously tapped the side of his paper cup with his thumb. "They'll run my piece later."

"Sure. What's in it? What did you learn about her?"

Lewis made a face like he was thinking, pushing his tongue over his teeth beneath his closed lips. "The same things you did, pretty much. That Jamie was her first cousin . . ."

That was from the article that had run. When he didn't say any more, Agnes led him. It was the simplest way to go. "And the campaign donations. The restaurant. Did you know about her involvement there?" she supplied.

"The restaurant, right!" His face lit up. "And the art . . . that she hadn't sold Chase's work. And she reunited with her family just before she died."

These were things Agnes had given him or that had appeared in the article he didn't author that day. He didn't have any new facts.

"I brought you this." Agnes retrieved the necklace from her pocket. She laid it on the table between them and spread the chain out gently with her fingertips. She watched as Lewis eyed it.

He looked sad and agitated. "Is that Charlotte's?"

Agnes nodded. "Did you know she and Hugo weren't dating?"

"What are you talking about?" Lewis shook his head.

"Nope, she wasn't with him. Friends only. And Chase, I don't think she was with him, either, except once or twice at the beginning. You dated quite a while, didn't you?"

Lewis reached out and tentatively poked at the pendant. She could see he was thinking about it, something that had been hers, had been close to her skin. "Off and on. We hit it off at that first salon."

Agnes went for it while he was off guard, while he was thinking about Charlotte. "What made you come to my place instead of phoning? The last time we met up, you just phoned me—out of the blue. You could have called or texted to warn me."

Now I have his attention.

Lewis sat up straighter. "My battery ran down. I was close by, so I just went to your place."

Agnes pursed her lips and fixed him with a solid stare. "Why did you know about the cameras being removed, Lewis? You told Ethan that."

"I have an eye for detail, just like you." Lewis folded his arms across his chest.

She put her hand down close to the table as if to pick the necklace up and put it back in her pocket. But then she let it sit. *Keep a piece of her where he has to look at it,* she thought. "Did you know I heard Charlotte yell that night? Did you hear her?"

"What are you talking about?"

"Weren't you there? On the roof?"

"I was on the roof with you and Ethan the other night." He peered at her now. "You seem mixed up. Are you all right, Agnes?"

"She said, 'No, No.' She yelled it twice. As if she was waiting for someone to intervene."

"That's awful. You must be so traumatized still." Lewis ran a hand up through his hair.

He did that at the memorial, she recalled. *He's flustered.* Agnes felt a chill creep up her arms. She pressed on. "I just want to know if you were on the roof or only at the theater. I know you've been let go from the paper. I called this morning, and they confirmed you haven't been employed there for two months. So you haven't been doing any investigative journalism for *them*."

Lewis placed his hands on the table and began to stand. "What are you accusing me of? Jamie's your guy. He tried to kill you, so obviously you solved this already. Congratulations."

At Lewis's tone, Agnes felt Hulot's leash move. The dog had edged out from under the table and sat up, on guard. She'd never heard him growl before. But he did now.

"Take it easy," Agnes said to both of them. She made a clicking sound with her mouth.

Lewis was trying to explain himself now. He mentioned something about a family photo he'd seen of Charlotte and Jamie in an article. Lewis named a publication that Agnes knew.

Possible, but unlikely. Keep him talking, she thought.

"And I knew you'd be in danger after Emmanuel," Lewis explained. "He was talking too much. If Jamie killed him, obviously you'd be next."

Seeing her chance, she said, "So you knew it was Jamie who killed Emmanuel?"

"Yes, because—" Lewis started, then glared at her. He'd backed himself into a corner.

"Did you go to the theater with him?" she shot back.

"No!"

Make it easy for him now. She softened her voice. "I know you didn't do it—I know you were just Jamie's cleanup crew."

Lewis was silent. He stared at her.

Is he shocked that I'm accusing him or shocked that I put it all together? Agnes wondered.

"A crime like that needs an accomplice," she said. "Charlotte, on his own, Jamie could do that. But Park Slope all the way to the Village? Rigging it up in the rafters. He was strong, but not that strong. Or clever. That takes two people. You needed money. He bribed you just like he tried to bribe me."

"I bet he did try to bribe you. What number did he give you?" Lewis asked.

"Not enough. What number did he give you?" She knew they had to have settled on a number. You didn't do what Lewis had without firm enticement. "One million? Two?"

"I loved Charlotte more than two million dollars," Lewis said.

When she looked at him, she could see his face had turned red. His gaze was downcast, on the necklace. He was talking about Charlotte, not Emmanuel. *There it is.*

"Two million is an interesting number," Agnes said gently, as if they really were just friends having a conversation over coffee.

"Why?" Lewis raised his head to look at her.

"It's point zero five percent of the family's four-billion-dollar worth. A lot less than the fifty percent Charlotte would have gotten."

"I didn't kill her—or Emmanuel," Lewis said, his teeth gritted.

"But you didn't report it."

"No. But I would never hurt her." Lewis sighed. "Charlotte had told me Jamie was her cousin. So I held that piece right away."

"You *held* that piece. And what did you do with it?"

Lewis corrected himself. "*Had*, not *held*. I said *had*!"

You didn't. Agnes fixed him with a hard look and went all in: "Jamie glanced up at the roof right before we walked into the Kentwood. Almost unconsciously. You were supposed to be up there already, weren't you? Ethan got to the building first, and he intercepted you. Change of plans."

She could tell by Lewis's expression she had nailed it. And it also meant that she ought to be dead. *If things went as they intended.* He and Jamie both would have thrown her off the roof.

"What makes you so sure these wild theories are true?" Lewis asked, trying to wriggle out from under the house of cards that was falling all around him.

Agnes reached across the table and flipped his phone over. "This. Only you had an issue with Chase. Jamie didn't." Over the camera eye there was a circular red art sticker. It was stuck there so intentionally it looked like part of the case design. That was why she'd missed it the other time she'd met with him. He must have tested it on his own camera before he and Jamie placed them. But he drank too much at the party and forgot to remove it. The evidence had been there, carried around, flashed in public, for a week. Agnes had caught it just now when she'd approached the table. She'd had a hunch and told the police she thought there was an accomplice, but now she knew for sure. And so would everyone.

Panicked at the sight of the art sticker, Lewis shot up and looked around, seeming to take in his surroundings for the first time since she'd arrived. He didn't even try to grab his phone back as he realized it was a sting—he was leaving too quickly.

The man in the fedora and the woman with the journal were already on their feet. She was pulling her badge. The undercover cops, who had seemed so obvious to Agnes, had blended in for Lewis. With luck, this time there would also be a clean recording. She'd worn a loose shirt so the mic an officer had taped there for her wouldn't show.

Before they could arrest him, Lewis started to run, but then he fell, crashing face first onto the cement. Hulot barked, and Agnes realized the dog had bolted at Lewis's sudden movement. His leash had tripped Lewis and stopped him from making a clean getaway.

The detective closest to them grabbed Lewis's hands behind his back. "You're under arrest as an accomplice in two murders. You have the right to remain silent . . ."

The only other witness to Lewis's shame was Monsieur Hulot. As the two plainclothes detectives pulled Lewis back up, Agnes scooped the onyx necklace from the table and put it back in her pocket. Maybe it would protect her from evil intentions after all.

"Why?" Lewis spat at her. His eyes were already shining with tears.

"Three very prominent dead people. They were eager to arrest someone—anyone, really," she told him. "Thankfully it's not me."

Lewis went without a fight. Unlike Jamie, he knew what he'd done was horrible. He almost looked resolved as he slouched between the arresting officers. Picking up Hulot and carrying the small dog against her, Agnes followed them carefully through the business, past a couple of shocked customers inside, and then out onto the sidewalks of Williamsburg to a waiting cruiser.

Emmanuel was right, she realized. *Even a perfect murder has a mistake—therein lies the art.*

Epilogue

Agnes was already sweating as she climbed the subway stairs and emerged from the G train. There was a reason everyone who could afford to flee New York in August did so for places like Fire Island, Montauk, Provincetown, or even upstate. But Agnes had always loved being in Brooklyn when it was emptier—it reminded her of when she'd first come to New York for school, all those years ago. Back when Mrs. Nielsen had handed her daughter a nail file for her purse. Turned out her mom hadn't given such bad advice after all.

As Agnes walked over to Fort Greene Park, she wondered if she would tell Mia about Katie. She wondered if she had ever even told Mia about her cousin over the years, hidden, as it was, in the Midwestern vault of all things you didn't chitchat about. At one time, when Agnes and Mia had lived close to here in their shared apartment, they'd known every tree and hollow, the flattest place to spread a blanket, light a joint, and open a ten-dollar bottle of wine. They had also known which restaurants would let them use the bathroom without buying anything—an essential hunting skill if you were going to live in a city like this. Summer cutoff shorts always seemed to help.

Agnes had seen Evie several times in the last few weeks. They weren't quite "girlfriendly" yet, but they were letting something grow between them, and slow brunches had started following sleepovers. Something in Mia's voice when she'd phoned made Agnes think that she had news or things to disclose. Had she and Victor broken up? Agnes would keep her good relationship news in her pocket until she knew for sure.

Mia was standing by the forked tree when Agnes spotted her. In a prominent place at the bottom of the park, the great bur oak split three ways and seemed to grow straight out in all directions. Long ago they'd taken a photo of themselves with it. Agnes should have known that was where she'd pick to meet.

Mia was wearing a white skirt and green tank top, mint-colored pointy flats, a large pair of black sunglasses. She had always loved fashion and eased into any climate scenario. She'd bronzed while living in California and looked like a movie star herself. She turned her head and looked Agnes's way. Then, in contrast to her composure, she yanked the sunglasses off and waved as if Agnes were someone she hadn't seen in decades, even though it had been only several months. "I'm a little angry at you," Mia said, even as she pressed Agnes closer. She smelled like Earl Grey and jasmine.

Agnes realized for the first time that her best friend's perfume was similar to Charlotte's. She let her hold on an extra moment, then broke away.

"What for?" Agnes shook her head.

She was smiling, though Mia had stopped. In fact, pulling back, she saw that Mia's eyes were glazed and teary.

"All Ethan is talking about is doing investigations with you. He's fragile still. And he's a sort of filmmaker. Not a sort of detective. You have to be careful." Suddenly Mia sounded like someone's mom, though Agnes supposed she'd always been a little overprotective of Ethan.

"He's a good person," Agnes said. "I owe him a lot now."

Mia's lips turned up slightly. "True . . . but you need to know my relatives were phoning me. Everyone read about it—everyone saw it on the news."

What Agnes was hearing was that it was *Mia* who was still fragile. Still putting things back together after the attempt on her life a year before by Ethan's ex, Zoey. Agnes reminded herself to be patient. Already Mia had begun walking into the park, climbing the hill to find a place to sit—hopefully in a bit of shade. "Everyone was like, 'Your friend Agnes . . .'"

"Don't worry—*your friend Agnes* is retired."

Mia looked around the park. "You shouldn't. You're good at it."

Agnes pointed out a vacant area beside a towering green umbrella of another oak tree. There was a grassy bit of space there between couples, friends, and picnickers. They sat down side by side. Agnes started, "Did I ever tell you about my cousin Katie? Katie Harp? The one who went missing?"

"Yes."

"I did? And you remember it?" Agnes asked.

Mia leaned to one side, propping herself up on her hand. "Hard to forget. Junior year after finals. You drank too much ouzo, told all of us, and cried before you—"

A sense memory of anise made Agnes shudder. "Okay. Yes."

"Why? Is there news about her?"

"She's back."

"She's back? That's big! Kind of makes my news seem selfish," Mia said.

Agnes recognized there was something more serious happening behind the conversation than a catch-up. When old friends reunited, it could be a bit awkward; one always expected that. But they were the oldest and best of friends, and Agnes could see this was not simple disconnect creeping in due to the time that had passed.

"I want to do this one right, Agnes. And there is kind of a job I need you for," Mia said, blushing. "I honestly don't think I can find anyone else for it . . . I need a bridesmaid."

"Bridesmaid . . . like, me in a dress?!" Agnes exclaimed. Her gaze flew to the left hand of her friend. A perfect white diamond on a delicate gold band wrapped her finger. Mia and Victor were engaged.

"You wear whatever you want to wear," Mia answered seriously.

"You didn't tell me?" Agnes couldn't believe it.

Now Mia smiled, a grin that left no doubt she wasn't really angry at Agnes. "You were busy and answering all my texts with thumbs-ups. I'm telling you now. And honestly, it's come together quickly. A fall wedding. Here in New York. We're still picking a venue."

A blast of music came from a group on the blanket near them, and they exchanged looks and stood up. Intuitively, Agnes could tell she'd rather walk and talk.

"Wow, congratulations!" Agnes hugged her, laughing. "Did he get down on one knee?"

As they walked, Mia leaned toward her and whispered, "That's not us. I proposed to *him*. We picked the rings out after."

Agnes loved Victor, and she knew he was better suited for Mia than her first husband, so why did she experience a sudden wave of possessiveness? They'd known each other long enough that she'd seen how Mia could be impulsive and race toward the thing that made her happy, only to decide a few months later that it didn't at all. Her first husband had hidden many of his problems and activities.

Mia played with the ring. "I was thinking of the second Saturday in October. Will that work for you?"

Agnes thought, *Bridesmaid? I've never been one before.* The women rounded a path, and the lighthouse monument rose into view like sudden news. Agnes stared at it and then at her friend. Then there was that Mia look she knew well. Open mouthed, about to speak but pausing. The one that announced the stinger was on its way. A part of Agnes expected her to say *It will be kind of a second reception*, but instead Mia said there might be a second job for her.

"Wow. Can we just start with bridesmaid?"

"It's security. Zoey will be out of jail by then. I didn't think it would be that fast, and I don't know who she is anymore, or what she'll do . . ." Mia's voice trailed off into the quiet of genuine fear.

Agnes could only say yes. She thought of all she'd done for Charlotte, a person she'd known for a shimmering blink of time. After all, without friends, Agnes had no idea where she'd be.

ACKNOWLEDGMENTS

Thank you to my agent, Chris Bucci, for your expertise and guidance, and everyone at Aevitas Creative Management. I'm grateful to my editor, Jessica Tribble-Wells, for guiding Agnes into her own book series. I'm indebted to Sarah Horgan for the novel's stunning design. Thank you to my publishing team: Tara Rayers, Katie Kurtzman, Ellie Schaffer, and everyone at Thomas & Mercer.

For support and inspiration I'm thankful to: Aerhart, Ariel Brogno, Tobias Carroll, Roberta Colindrez, Cecilia Corrigan, Brian Gresko, Faye Guenther, Jim Hanas, Rob Hart, Alice Kaltman, Dawn Lewis, Jenny Grace Makholm, Rebecca McClellan, Kristine Musademba, Athalie Paynting, Michael Seidlinger, Sarah Seltzer, and Ben Tanzer.

Thank you to my girlfriend, Hannah Meyer; my partner, Brian J. Davis; and my son, Henry. You inspire me to do better.

ABOUT THE AUTHOR

Photo © 2024 Heroic Collective

Emily Schultz is the author of *Sleeping with Friends* and *Brooklyn Kills Me*, both from Thomas & Mercer. She is the cofounder of *Joyland Magazine*. Her novel *Little Threats* was named an Apple Books Best of 2020 pick. Her novel *The Blondes* was named a Best Book of 2015 by NPR and *Kirkus Reviews*. *The Blondes* was produced as a scripted podcast and translated into French, German, and Spanish with over one million listeners worldwide.

Her writing has appeared in *Elle*, *Slate*, *Evergreen Review*, Literary Hub, CrimeReads, *Vice*, *Today's Parent*, *Electric Literature*, and the *Hopkins Review*. Schultz lives in Brooklyn.

For more about the author and her work, visit her website at www.emilyschultz.com.